OWEN'S DAY

Helen Yeomans

GUARDS PUBLISHING

Published by Guards Publishing, an imprint of Yeomans Associates Ltd.

www.helenyeomans.com

This book is a work of fiction. Names, characters, places and incidents either are the product of the author's imagination or are used fictitiously. Any resemblance to actual persons living or dead, events or locales is entirely coincidental.

Library and Archives Canada Cataloguing in Publication

Yeomans, Helen, 1949-

Owen's day / Helen Yeomans.

Issued also in electronic format.

ISBN 978-0-9693219-1-0

I. Title.

PS8647.E65O94 2011   C813'.6   C2011-902879-4

Cover design by Elizabeth Mackey

Printed in the United States of America

For my sister, Janet,
who liked it from the first

1

"He was off side!"

"Was not!"

The boys milled around on the ice in front of the net.

"The goal doesn't count!"

"Does too!"

Nine- and ten-year-old voices rose clear and shrill in the night air. A man glanced down at the floodlit ice as he walked past on the sidewalk above and disappeared into the darkness.

They were skating on a small tributary of the river. No one could recall when the river itself had last frozen but the stream froze every winter, and the top end was always roped off for skating.

"It's three-one for us, so there!"

"Is not! It's two-one, you cheaters." Randy Casilio wound up and slapped the puck sideways. It sped across the ice, under a sign, "No Skating Beyond this Point" suspended from the rope barrier, and into the darkness.

Stunned silence gave way to furious outcry. Neither brought the puck back. The boys skated to the barrier and stopped, squinting into the darkness. They could just make it out: a black blemish on the white surface.

"You have to get it, Randy."

"I'm not getting it. You get it," said Randy.

"No way! If I go 'cross this line my dad'll kill me."

They stared out at the puck. It seemed to stare back, taunting them.

"Bet I can get it." Tom Newton stepped over the rope barrier and skated toward the bank, then started for the mouth of the stream. The others watched in silence, their breath rising white in the night air.

He began a shallow arc toward the center, and they saw that he meant to come within stick's length of the puck and then curve back into the opposite bank. They could hear the rhythmic swish, swish of his skates and make out the white pompom on his wool hat.

Now he was approaching the puck. He bent his knees, still with the same measured rhythm, and extended the stick. The puck was five yards from the end of it . . . a yard.

Tom seemed to stumble and his legs disappeared. A crackling sound carried crisply back to the other boys.

*   *   *

The man dug his hands deeper into his overcoat pockets and lengthened his stride along the sidewalk. For a mile he had had the river on his left, the road on his right. Then the river had veered away and he passed a small park and playground and the frozen stream. The wind was light on his cheek and he lifted his gaze to the night sky, to the stars remote and benign. He was glad he'd decided to walk.

He'd heard the boys arguing, their shrill voices carrying over the occasional passing cars. Now they were behind him and the river was back at his left elbow, broad and dark and still. The city lights twinkled beyond the far bank.

Ragged yells then a shriek pierced the night. He turned abruptly. Clearly visible under the lights, the boys were milling round in panic. Two cut away from the rest, streaking toward the benches below the sidewalk. His eyes followed them, then swept back, beyond the group toward the mouth of the stream. Unbroken ice—then a black hole, a splash of white.

He pulled off his gloves, running for the top of the bank, and shed his coat. He slid down a sloping concrete retaining wall and clambered across the debris and boulders, slick with frost. He heard the river as he neared the water's edge and felt a thin stab of fear: it was not still at all, but moving in powerful, oily undulations accompanied by a deep, ominous murmur.

He reached the edge and peered upriver into the darkness. The black surface was smooth and unbroken. His glance fell to the water's edge. Ice had formed in crannies along the bank. He hesitated. Another glance upriver, then he plunged in, gasping with the shock.

*   *   *

When Tom broke through the ice, the water gripped his legs and abdomen with chill tentacles. He thrashed once or twice, hampered by his skates and the shocking cold, and inhaled convulsively. His head fell forward as he coughed and the water rushed down his neck. He went down choking and the current pulled him under the ice.

The inky darkness filled him with terror and he inhaled reflexively. Before his body had even reached the river, he had mercifully lost consciousness. His skates pulled him downward and his head fell forward on his chest, but a quirk of the currents and the folds of his jacket preserved a pocket of air over his chest, keeping his body roughly upright, like a marionette with its strings cut.

The river played with him, bobbing him from the bed up to the surface and down again. Each time his head broke the surface, the white pompom gleamed against the black water.

Downriver, the man glimpsed a flash of white, fifteen or twenty feet out, heading for the middle of the river, and he dived forward in a crawl, keeping his head up, straining for another glimpse.

Down again went Tom's body into the deepening water, and the pocket of air burst. The water flooded over his chest and he folded over. His skates dragged along the riverbed as the current swept him downriver.

*   *   *

The man could feel the strength leaching out of him. He trod water, fighting the current, his arms and legs growing numb and heavy, eyes searching the surface. It must be deep here. He suddenly tasted fear, nauseated by the unknown depths beneath his legs.

He looked back at the rocky shore. How distant it was! Certainty flooded his mind, that he'd lost, that the boy had drifted past either below him or to one side.

He'd have to go back, he could hardly move, he could hardly think. He began to swim leadenly for the shore.

*   *   *

A skate blade tugged against a wire. The wire was buried in the cement of a huge slab of reinforced concrete, deposited in some past flood, half buried in the silt and canted upward like a loading ramp.

Nudged by the current, the body inched up the ramp, then stopped. The skate blade tugged again, but the wire held fast. Another tug, more insistent, and another. The skate came free, the body tumbled up the ramp and the river spat it up toward the surface.

It cannoned into the man's stomach and with a cry he went under, shoving it aside. He surfaced coughing and saw the white pompom. A face turned toward him, the body rolling, passing. He grabbed it clumsily.

He hooked an arm round the boy's chest and ploughed toward the shore. The body was dead weight, his legs were dead weight, his free arm sluggish and ineffectual. Street light. The far side of the road was lit and he fixed his eyes on a street light and labored on.

Eventually his feet touched bottom and he waded out, brain numb, the boy clasped to his chest. He stood in the shallows, shaking violently, staring at the boulders.

He needed two hands for the boulders.

He slung the sodden bundle over his shoulder, and part of his mind registered a warning cry as he began to make his way back over the boulders.

He reached the concrete retaining wall and stopped. Small boulders were set into it and he confronted them, waiting for guidance. A voice penetrated his mind and he looked up. A middle-aged woman knelt there, hand extended.

"Give me your hand. Quick!"

He translated her words and raised an arm, and she took hold of his hand.

"Come on. Quickly now, up you come." She hauled backward and he set his toes in the stones of the concrete and heaved himself upward. The boy's torso was thrown toward the woman and she let go the man's hand and took hold of it, lifting the sodden body off his shoulder and lowering it gently to the ground.

She began to talk, whether to herself or him he didn't know. He rolled up onto the top of the wall.

"Check for a pulse and check for breathing, we have to be careful not to jar him or his heart might stop. Thank God you were here, you poor man," a quick glance at him, then: "You're shivering, that's good. Get his jacket off then we'll wrap him in mine."

The man staggered away, wringing out his sweater in handfuls as it lay on him. He retrieved his coat and put it on, found his gloves and shoved them in his pockets.

"Oh! There is a pulse, he's got a pulse!"

He returned and knelt by the boy, fumbling at the zipper of his jacket. The woman had pulled off the woolen hat, and was feeling inside the mouth.

The other boys arrived in a headlong rush. They stopped, jostling each other for a view, staring at the lifeless body.

"It's Mrs. Griff."

"What's she lookin' in his mouth for?"

They inched forward. Mrs. Griff began to administer mouth-to-mouth resuscitation, while the man eased off Tom's jacket.

Randy came closer and crouched by Tom. He poked his hand. Nothing. He jabbed his side, then retreated into the group.

"He's dead," he announced.

"Is not."

"Is too. Look at him."

Tom's sweatshirt was stripped off between breaths and Mrs. Griff took off her ski jacket. The man wrapped it round the boy as she continued the mouth to mouth, never missing a beat.

A squeal of tires sounded loud in the silence, followed by a tinny thump, then a yell: "What're you, trying to get yourself killed?"

"Sorry!" A man ran into their midst, his face anguished. "Sean? Oh God, Sean?" He knelt by Tom's side.

"Hi dad," said Sean. "It's Tom."

"He's dead, Mr. Miller," said Randy.

Miller looked round at the boys, grabbed Sean, hugged him and swept off his wool hat. "Run home, son. All you kids, you get along home."

They watched silently as he snugged Sean's hat down over Tom's ears. An engine idled; a car door slammed. The driver who had nearly run down Miller joined the group.

Tom suddenly coughed weakly, his head moving from side to side. The group watched raptly, Miller involuntarily gripping Mrs. Griff's arm. No one noticed as the rescuer rose to his feet and left.

"I'll take him to the hospital if you can show me the way," said the driver.

Miller gathered the boy carefully in his arms and rose to his feet, Mrs. Griff with him. They moved to the car, idling in the road with its flashers blinking. The boys watched as the driver opened both near side doors, then ran round and climbed in the driver's side, turning the heater up. The doors slammed and the car moved off, Miller and Tom in the back, Mrs. Griff in the front.

The boys stood in a cluster, reluctant to move away.

"That old witch," said Randy, "she had her mouth all over him."

"Ugh! He'll throw up when he finds out."

"Who was that guy, anyway?"

"Betcha he's another witch."

Randy snorted. "Guys aren't witches, guys are—." He stopped. The same thought came to them all and they wheeled round. But the sidewalk was deserted. Except for themselves, they discovered when they peered into the darkness, there was no one.

For a long moment they stood motionless in a frozen huddle, then they turned and pelted headlong toward the welcoming lights of the skating area.

It was the night of November twenty-third.

2

The story appeared on November twenty-fifth in the morning tabloid, the *Star*, a brief account on page two, "Boy Saved from River by Unknown Rescuer." The sheer audacity of the act arrested the eye, for the river had claimed many victims over the years and its danger was widely known. The article also conveyed a hint of romance, provided inadvertently by Mrs. Griff. Alone of all those present, she had actually looked at Tom Newton's rescuer. Gerald Miller hadn't: his gratitude was heartfelt, but he'd been too concerned with Tom to notice the man by his side. Tom himself, of course, had seen nothing. Nor could any of the other boys add anything, except for Randy Casilio. Randy recognized the man. He'd seen him before, maybe on a poster or something. He gave it as his opinion that Tom's rescuer was a child molester whose evil designs had been thwarted only by Randy's timely arrival on the scene. The reporter, Jackson, looked up from his notes to see Randy's mother marching her son out of the living room.

Which left Mrs. Griff. Although it was dark, although he slipped her mind altogether in the rush of events, so that she didn't even think of him until several hours later, she was able to provide a description of sorts. "He was tall, dark and handsome," read Fred Griff in the *Star*. He looked up involuntarily at his wife across the breakfast table.

"Well, he was," she said defensively. "He had a—a nice face, Fred. Not Mel Gibson or anything, but nice, you know?"

She glanced out at the river. The Griffs' house sat on a rise overlooking the road and park in the subdivision called River Reach, a small community of well-kept older homes on winding cul-de-sacs. Childless herself, Mrs. Griff always watched out for the children at play in the park, and on the night of Tom's rescue, after Miller had taken a boy with a bloody nose home, she'd kept an eye on the others from her kitchen window and had seen the accident occur. The police had now closed the park to the public, and none too soon in Mrs. Griff's view.

"That poor man. He was so cold, Fred, and he never said a word." She poured herself a cup of coffee. "Definitely the strong, silent type."

Heroism, mystery, romance. Small wonder that the story struck a chord. The *Star* received 153 calls during the day, all positive. The evening news hours took up the tale, with brief clips of Mrs. Griff, Tom Newton and his mother, and the following morning the *Star* carried a plea to the rescuer, under a picture of mother and son captioned, "Come back, Shane." Speculation as to the man's identity occupied a good portion of two radio talk shows, while a third started a "Find the White Knight" contest and logged 1,500 responses in the first twenty-four hours. Every male who could be construed as tall, dark and handsome found his name put forward by wife, mother or girlfriend.

Perhaps context had something to do with the level of public interest. In an age of violence, here was an act of unalloyed good, a courageous deed by a solitary individual in an age of committees, subcommittees and special interest groups. People could relate to it, even if many were honest enough to admit they would never have done it themselves. Yet the hero refused to announce himself. Why? Admiration became tempered with puzzlement.

Belatedly, the subject of hypothermia arose.

"He could be lying dead in an alley," suggested Jackson to the editor, Hoch, on the third day. "Even if he made it home, he could be lying dead in bed." Flick Jackson was twenty-three and this was his first big story. He'd done his homework, and now he cited the case of sixteen Danish fishermen who spent an hour and a half in the North Sea after their boat sank. "They were picked up by a trawler. They climbed up on deck and walked to a cabin, each under their own steam." He glanced at the editor, who nodded, and went on, "Then they sat down and died, one by one. All sixteen of them. They sat in that cabin and died."

"Afterdrop," said Hoch briefly. The paper ran something on hypothermia every winter and he was tired of the subject.

"Right. When your core body temperature drops, you don't warm up right away. It keeps dropping and your heart gets so sluggish it can stop completely."

"Our guy was only in the water for fifteen or twenty minutes, Jackson."

"But what about after? It was fourteen degrees that night. How long was he outside? We know he didn't get a cab, so he must have walked for some length of time."

The same point was made on the evening news by an expert on hypothermia. He spoke at length of ratios of body area to mass and the relative conductivity of water over air in drawing heat from the body. The rescuer's exertions, he noted, would have accelerated the dissipation of his body heat.

"You mean, the harder he worked the colder he'd get?" the interviewer translated.

"Correct. Furthermore, if he stayed outside in his wet clothes for more than, say, an hour and a half, his physiological condition might well correspond more closely to chronic rather than acute hypothermia." He was invited to describe the symptoms. "The victim stops shivering and exhibits signs of ataxia, i.e., the inability to walk a straight line or speak coherently. Now let us suppose that at this point he was immersed in a hot bath. The shock would in all probability have killed him."

The city reeled. Here was a man who had saved a life and only now did people realize he might have paid the highest price for his deed. Bathtubs were scoured, and parks and alleys, while tall, dark, handsome men found themselves the object of searching scrutiny. Hypothermia became the hot topic round the water cooler, with opinion divided as to its significance.

"The guy just likes his privacy, for pete's sake. This whole thing's a media show."

"I'm not so sure. Did you hear about that child who froze solid? She was in a coma for months. He could be lying sick somewhere."

"He's dead. I just feel it in my bones."

"Why should he be dead? The boy's okay."

"They said last night that little kids can survive better than adults because their bodies shut down."

"My body won't shut down, not when you're around."

"Oh shut up."

Gradually two schools of thought emerged. One, which might be termed the Randy Casilio school, held that the man was a criminal of some kind who would never come forward. This argument gained credence after the *Star* published a police artist's sketch of the rescuer based on Mrs. Griff's recollections. "It doesn't really do him justice," she said.

"Good thing," observed Fred Griff. "If Tom had seen that he'd have died of fright."

The second, or Shane school of thought held that the boy had been rescued by a visitor to the city, a stranger who had done his good deed and gone on his way. These adherents remembered the picture of the boy and his widowed mother, and the wistful look on both their faces. The rescuer must surely have left town, else how could he resist that haunting appeal?

On the fifth day, City Hall added its voice to the appeals, with the announcement of a Civic Medal for the unknown hero. "Run with that tomorrow," Hoch instructed Jackson. They had exhausted most other angles on the story.

"What if he turns out to be a child molester?"

"Then we'll remind the Mayor of his offer." Hoch's teeth showed white and even in his face. The *Star* had backed the other candidate in the last civic election, and the loss still rankled.

But the days passed and no one came forward. The incident worked its way into church sermons and school projects, became part of the river folklore. Children drew pictures of the River Rescuer in art period, and teenagers were assigned essays: What kind of man is the Ice Man? (Be sure your description fits someone who both risked his life and ran away.)

November drew to a close. The clear bright days of a three-week cold snap gave way to lowering cloud cover, and the city steeled itself for the dark winter months ahead. Then, in the early hours of December third, an event occurred that drove all thought of the rescue out of people's minds. Twenty miles east of the city, a train consisting of three locomotives and thirty-eight tanker cars loaded with industrial chemicals derailed outside the farming community of Staple.

In a more primitive era, say at the beginning of the century, railroad engineers would have fixed the rails and righted the overturned cars while railroad officials recompensed the town for any damage to people, farms and livestock, both then departing as quickly as they had arrived. But as the decades passed and society grew ever more intolerant of the unexpected, the response became more and more complex. Now, as the end of the millennium approached, in the late 1990s, railroad personnel still arrived with dispatch. But so did a lot of other people.

At first light the media converged on the small town. The chemicals included sulfuric acid, propane, butane, vinyl chloride and sodium hydroxide. The accident had been caused by a split rail; there had been no loss of life, nor injury. The railroad's emergency response team was already at the site, four miles east of town, together with experts from two of the chemical companies and the District Inspector for the Bureau of Explosives.

"They've nearly completed a visual inspection," the media relations spokesman reported at a mid-morning press conference. "Now they're waiting for monitoring equipment to measure flammability and leakage."

"So some chemicals are leaking?"

"Yes, but they can't tell what. Eight cars are tangled together and it's impossible to identify the source."

"Are we safe here?" asked a resident of Staple.

"In our opinion, this community is in no danger. However, hotel rooms have been reserved downtown for any families who would prefer to leave."

At noon, photographers were taken out to the site to shoot the wreckage; by mid-afternoon, the population of Staple had doubled with the influx of representatives from the Department of Transportation, OSHA, the EPA, the National Transportation Safety Board, and the Crisis Management Office, consisting of representatives from three levels of government.

Late in the afternoon, Hoch came out of his office at the *Star*. "The CMO is calling for an evacuation," he told Jackson. "I want you out there to help Lee interview the townspeople." Jackson wound up his backgrounder on train derailments nationwide, dealt quickly with an accumulation of messages, and left for Staple.

The media needed their stories. They were prepared to give equal time to all the experts, but the only experts who counted were on site and unavailable for comment. Consequently, the evening news was dominated by statements from the various agencies and by the sobering sight of an endless stretch of tanker cars twisted and toppled by the track. People watched and listened, and wondered resentfully why dangerous chemicals had to be transported this way.

*   *   *

Sara Newton looked out at the river, oily and dark. Evil, she thought. The continuous deep murmur filled her with dread and she stepped backward involuntarily, slipping on a boulder and righting herself. She had wanted to see the exact place Tom was rescued, and here it was and it was even worse than she'd expected. A weight descended on her mind and heart.

She would never be able to thank the rescuer. She had hoped that he would contact her, had answered every phone call with the springing thought, *Maybe this is him,* had stated publicly that she didn't care if he was an ex-con or even an escaped con, had waited patiently. But in vain. Now she was trying to accept the idea that he would never call. Jackson had said they were at a dead end, and she didn't know which was worse: not being able to thank him, or not knowing whether he was alive or dead. Then she remembered Tom and knew that neither of those things mattered against the fact that Tom would never meet him. *I don't know what to do, Sam*, she thought.

Last night, after she'd tucked Janey in and turned out her light, she'd gone in to Tom as she did every night. He was lying on his side and she knelt by the bed and smiled at him, smoothing the hair from his forehead.

"Happy?"

He smiled back. She rested her chin on her wrist.

"Do you ever wonder about him, Tommy?" She saw a hint of reproof in the grey eyes. "Sorry. Tom?"

"Who?"

"The man. The man who rescued you."

He'd never referred to the man since that night and now his shoulders moved in what she took to be a shrug.

"I do," said Sara. "I bet he's shy. That's why we haven't heard from him. But I wish he'd call. I wish he would. So I could thank him for saving my Tom's life."

Tom looked at her silently then turned on his stomach and buried his face in the pillow. He only did that when he had a huge secret to impart. Sara waited with some misgiving.

"Know what, mum?" His voice was muffled in the pillow.

"What?"

One eye peered at her. She smiled encouragingly.

"He's never going to call." The eye watched her.

"How do you know, darling?"

A silence, then he turned on his side again.

"Mum. You never have to worry about us. Me and Janey. I mean, I was wrong to go over the boundary, but I knew I'd be okay, see?"

"How did you know, Tom?"

"Because dad was looking out for me. He always will, mum, that's why you don't have to worry. He's an angel, like the angel in that movie when the man jumped in the water? And he disguised himself so nobody would know who he was and gossip. That's why he won't call. But he doesn't have to, because I know it was him."

Sara said nothing, just nodded judiciously then smiled and kissed him goodnight. Later she phoned Bob.

"Sam was no angel, kiddo," he said cautiously, and she wished he would stop walking on eggshells round the subject.

"I can't let Tom out of the house if he's going to think he's immune to danger because his dad is with him."

"Is this something to do with Del?"

Sara sighed. "I suppose so." Del was Adele Newton, Sam's mother, a laughing black-eyed woman who had adored her son. After his death, Del found solace in her religion and gave

Tom and Janey such glowing descriptions of heaven that Janey could hardly wait to go there and be with daddy.

"Want me to talk to him?"

Sara considered. "Only if he brings it up," she said at last, feeling she would rather deal with it herself.

Now, standing at the water's edge, she looked out over the broad reach of the river. *What am I supposed to say to him, Sam?* He had been gone more than two years, but she still consulted him regularly.

Sam Newton died on a day in June, killed instantly when his car was crushed by a heavy-laden truck whose brakes had failed. When Sara was told, she felt nothing. She'd read somewhere that when soldiers had their legs blown off in battle they felt nothing at first, and she wondered how long it took before the pain began. Once it did, she had no idea how she would cope. Nothing in her life had prepared her for this agony of mind, for the heartsickness and the terrible loneliness.

Her family ached for her and did what they could, which was at once a great deal and nothing at all. Taken en masse, including all the uncles and aunts and cousins, the Hargreaves were a fairly close-knit family. They tended to choose professional careers—Sara's father, Bill, was a well-known civil rights lawyer, her brother Bob a pediatrician. By and large, they had never acquired the habit of divorce; their marriages, however turbulent to begin with, generally settled into solid, reasonably happy unions.

Sara's parents were a constant presence in the days following the accident and Bob was a tower of strength. Only Ronnie, his wife, knew the guilt-laced relief he felt that his own family was safe and intact.

But it was Tom who helped Sara the most; Tom, whose grief and loss were in his child's way as great as her own. When she was able to see outside herself to the silent grey waif who had become her shadow, her own recovery could begin. She tucked him in that night and then got into bed with him and they slept together, Tom's arms wrapped tight around her neck until he fell asleep.

Sara began to mend. She regained her natural equilibrium and became absorbed in the children. But she never regained her youth; that had died with Sam. Ronnie noticed this and resented it, accusing her of becoming middle-aged. Sara merely looked at her. It was about that time, a year ago, that Ronnie began to needle her. Sara paid no attention: she had discovered that Sam was with her still; she consulted him frequently and she had adapted to a life without his physical presence.

This evening, however, she sought in vain for his advice, and she turned away from the river and found her way back over the rocks. Mrs. Griff leaned down and helped her climb up the wall.

"You didn't have to wait, Ellie," said Sara.

"Of course I did. You might have fallen in. I can't think why you wanted to go down there."

They walked along the sidewalk. Sara took the older woman's arm with a smile.

"I'm blessed with good neighbors," she said.

The night of Tom's accident, she'd been in the kitchen when Beth Elwing had burst in with the news from her son Tony, who'd been skating with Tom and the other boys. Beth had whisked Janey next door, leaving Sara to drive to the hospital in a haze of terror. She found Tom seemingly little the worse for wear and held him tight against her heart. The hospital was keeping him in overnight for observation, concerned about brain damage, and later, Sara had phoned the Elwings to explain that she was staying there with him.

Six-year-old Janey refused to be comforted, bursting into wails of fear. The entire family had brought her to the hospital and Sara had taken her in to see Tom and only then had she calmed down. Later, she went home with the Elwings and got to sleep over, which was a great adventure.

Sara glanced back at the river as they waited for the light to change. "Oh Ellie! I wish we knew who he was."

"I was sure he'd come forward when he saw that sweet picture of you and Tom. I can't understand it."

Sara grimaced at the memory of the *Star*'s photo.

"Come back, Shane?" Ronnie had said that night on the phone. "Was that your idea?"

"Of course not," said Sara. "It makes me look like a sheep, putting that under it."

Ronnie repeated this, and Sara heard Bob's bellow: "No, you're beautiful!"

"He thinks you're a beautiful sheep," relayed Ronnie and asked how Janey was taking it all.

Now Sara laughed out loud, and in response to Mrs. Griff's look, explained, "Janey's planning to throw herself in the river tomorrow at ten a.m. They're doing dates and times at school so everything has to be scheduled." She sensed the other woman's incomprehension and wished she hadn't started. "She was offended at being left out of the picture. Would you like to join us? I'm inviting two of her friends. We'll light a fire and roast marshmallows."

"Are you really going to let her go in the river?"

"I won't have to. But you have to call Janey on these things, or she just digs in her heels. Do come, Ellie, you can be a witness."

They walked up the road into the subdivision, and parted at the Griff driveway. Sara continued on to her own house, mulling over the problem of Tom and how to prove to her young son that he had not been rescued by his dead father in angel form.

*   *   *

Sara would have been surprised to learn that she was not the only person who, in the wake of the train disaster, was still preoccupied with the River Rescuer. He had, for example, been a week-long bone of contention in the Watson household.

The Watsons lived in the bedroom community of Minton, an hour's drive from the city. In their eighties, their principal interests were their great-granddaughter and the godless *Star*. A week ago, Gord had come out from behind the sports section to find his wife staring motionless at the front page of the tabloid.

"What is it?"

She remained unmoving and he was about to repeat himself when she raised her head and said with satisfaction, "*Isn't* that just like Martin?"

"Martin who?" He looked at the sketch on the front page. "That?" He pulled the paper toward him. "It's nothing like Martin."

"You know what I mean."

But Gord hadn't agreed, and in that tiresome way she had, his wife had said nothing more. She merely cut out the sketch and stuck it on the fridge where it irked him every time he opened the door.

The Watsons ate an early dinner, as was their custom, and this evening, as Gord got up from the table to turn off the TV, the news having finished, he saw what she meant. Glancing at the sketch out of the corner of his eye, at a shallow angle to the fridge door, he could see the resemblance. "Son of a bitch," he remarked in quiet surprise.

"Now then," said Mrs. Watson.

Gord sat down again, and gazed at the sketch. It bothered him less now that he was in the know. He ate his dinner as he studied the picture. "Can't call the paper," he said at last. "Don't believe he'd want it."

"That's what I thought," agreed Mrs. Watson.

*　　*　　*

Sol and Ruby Jablonsky saw less of their third son, Clarence, because unlike the other boys he had chosen to forego the family business and strike out on his own. When his wife and kids were away, however, he often took the opportunity to visit to his parents. Ruby was writing Christmas cards at the kitchen table when he arrived, and he went to find his dad in the den while she took out two more pork chops and finished a card:

> ...Sol retired—finally!—last spring and Mike's in charge with Aron doing the buying and Vern handling all their legal. We're up to a baker's dozen now and more in the works. Clar has two partners, and Sol's busy with the country club. Betty and Pete had another one (boy) and that makes four and <u>no more mugs</u>, honey. Sol found out and he ranted on, you

know how he does. He rants on at Pete too, but
that's another story! They're happy and that's all
that matters. How about you? Hope business is good.
Promise you'll tell me if you get yourself married,
I'm still hoping! Love from all—Ruby

They had plenty to talk about that evening and consequently it was seven before they sat down to dinner at the
kitchen table. Sol was preoccupied with the expansion of the
family business.

"Four stores, Clar! Four! I never opened more than two
max at a time. It's too many."

Clar nodded. "You want to remember he's got Aron and
Vern to split the load with and second, it's almost like a
template for a franchise now. That makes it much easier to
open multiple stores. That's your doing, dad. Mike's just
building on what you did."

Ever the peacemaker, thought Ruby affectionately of her
middle son. And while both men bent to their plates and got
on with the business of eating, she poked through the small
pile of clippings, letters, notes and lists next to her place, and
found what she was looking for. She passed it across to
Clarence. It was the police sketch.

"Oh for crying out loud," said Sol. "She thinks that's—"

"Hush," said Ruby sharply. "Who is it, Clar?"

Clarence gazed at it, then put it down by the side of his
plate and resumed eating, still looking at it. Like Gord
Watson, he stumbled by accident across the key to the
picture: if you crept up on it from the side, so to speak, a
resemblance revealed itself. He drew his head back sharply,
stared at the sketch then raised his eyes in amazement.

"Are you kidding me?" said Sol, now quite disgusted.

After another glance at the picture, Clarence put it next to Sol's plate.

"Don't try and force it, dad," he said. "Just look at it sideways on." And while Sol squinted at the picture, Clar chewed thoughtfully. "Isn't that just like him?" he said finally, and Ruby agreed.

She watched as a quizzical look came over Clar's face, and then he stared fixedly at the salt and pepper, and at last he spoke: "It wasn't anything really," he said diffidently.

Ruby snorted with laughter.

Sol couldn't believe his ears. "He wouldn't dare say that. Not about this?" He looked from wife to son. "Tell me he wouldn't say that!"

Ruby shrugged. "I don't care if he does."

"Are you going to call the paper?" asked Clarence.

"He'd hate that," replied Ruby.

They went on with dinner. "I hope he's okay," said Sol finally.

*   *   *

It was past eight p.m. when Tug Sheppard arrived home, hungry and empty-handed. Samson, the big sheepdog, greeted him at the door, falling all over himself with delight.

Tug had gone out to Staple to bring back Liz's grandmother, and as his wife came through from the kitchen he said, "Now calm down, honey, she's fine." He hung his coat in the closet next to the washing machine, while Liz's voice rose in dismay.

"How can she be fine? Have you seen the news? They're evacuating the town, Tug, how could you—"

Over her protests, he steered her before him into the kitchen. Tug was a big, easygoing man, vice-president of his family's car dealership. Liz was the reverse: thin, with an anxious air, and generally preoccupied with doing the right thing. Right now she was only concerned about her grandmother and so she said nothing when Tug liberally buttered a piece of bread to go with the (by now rather dry) chicken pot pie she set before him. In between mouthfuls, he gave her the news: the wreck was miles outside town, everything was under control, some people had chosen to evacuate as a precaution, and there were three dozen eggs in the car.

Liz brightened. If they'd had time to pick up some eggs, the situation couldn't be as bad as it sounded. The chicken farmer outside Staple kept a few free-range hens on the side, producing eggs for a select clientele. "His wife feeds them left-over broccoli," Liz liked to say. "That must be better for the egg, don't you think?"

Much of the morning, Tug explained to his wife, had been taken up with the press conference and afterward in discussions with neighbors. The consensus seemed to be that a few days downtown at the railroad's expense was a good idea. He looked at his wife. "Wouldn't you agree?" And when Liz nodded, he went on: "Yeah, well, Bee didn't."

The old lady had not wanted a free hotel stay downtown; nor had she wanted to accompany Tug. Quite simply, she only wanted to stay in her own home, and to sleep in her own bed. She had heard nothing especially alarming, she told Tug, and she couldn't see any need to leave. He had argued with her all through lunch, to no avail. Afterward, Bee had insisted they pick up some eggs for Liz.

"When we arrived, this guy was there telling Bergamini to leave, though how you walk out on five thousand battery hens, I do not know. Anyway, your grandmother asked him—

he was a clerk in the public works office—if there'd been any change since the morning. He said no, they just felt it would be prudent to leave."

He laughed shortly. "She had some sharp words for him, and for a reporter who came by the house after we got back. She said they were wasting time and money, and scaring people for no good reason." He pushed his plate away and got up to make a cup of coffee. Samson nosed at him and he ruffled the dog's coat absently. He fell silent and Liz, chin on hand, said nothing. Samson padded over to his water bowl near the door and lapped at its contents. Waiting for the kettle to boil, Tug leaned against the counter, arms crossed, staring at the floor.

"It was creepy coming back through town."

"What do you mean?"

He looked at his wife. "There were cars double-parked all over the place, and I had to slow right down to a crawl because people kept dashing across the street. Then the lights went out in the five and dime? It wasn't even five and they just closed up, and people came streaming out the doors. And this red sky over the feedstore. It was like one of those old science fiction movies where the world's about to end, you know?"

"What are you saying, Tug? Is Gran in any danger?"

"I don't know. She doesn't think so." He poured his coffee. "I told her to call if she changes her mind." He looked at his wife, not happy. "I'll be glad to go back out and get her, hon. She only has to say the word." He glanced at his watch and reached for a remote in the center of the table. It operated the TV above the fridge, and he flipped through the channels looking for news about Staple.

"I'm going to call," said Liz and got up to use the phone on the kitchen counter. Tug drank his coffee and listened as she repeated his offer to drive out and pick up her grandmother. After a silence, "You're sure, Gran?" She chatted a few moments longer, then rang off and returned to the table. "She'll call if she wants anything."

They discussed the matter a while longer and concluded that unless Bee called there was nothing else to be done.

The Sheppards did a lot of entertaining related to Tug's job, and while waiting for his return, Liz had been planning their next dinner party, scheduled for the seventeenth in honor of the dealership's biggest lease customer.

"I've done the guest list. See what you think." She pushed a list across the table. Tug ran his eye down the list, pausing in surprise at one of the names. He glanced up to see a trace of defiance on Liz's face. "It's been four years, Tug. Do you realize? And I don't see it ending. It's fine for you—you still see him occasionally. But I don't."

"Hon—," he paused, then went on, "you know he'll bring a gift."

"I don't care. You can tell him that, I want you to invite him, Tug, not me, and tell him: I don't care if he brings a hundred gifts. I'll never say anything again. Just tell him to come, that's all."

3

Sara worked for Mike Farraday at Farraday Construction. After Sam's funeral he'd told her to call on him if she ever needed anything, and a year later, when she could no longer stand the inactivity, he'd given her a job as his secretary. Within a month she was running the small office, leaving him free to manage his numerous projects and generate new business.

She went into work on Monday having reached no clear decision on what to do about Tom. December was always a slack month and she chatted with Pam, the payroll clerk, while she dealt with the mail. Mid-morning, Farraday called her into his office. "Sit down," he said, "let's talk about next year." He was a burly man in his 40s who had built his business by hard work and hustle. He'd fallen into the habit of discussing his plans with Sara after discovering she had a business degree. The news had been unwelcome at first. "You won't be staying on here, I guess."

"Not an MBA, Mike, just a bachelor's."

"Even so. What are you doing secretarial for?"

"Because I like it."

He was unconvinced. He'd given her a job because Sam had sent a lot of work his way and because he felt sorry for her. Hearing of her background, he was convinced she'd never stay, and he stared gloomily outside, composing a want ad.

"I don't want to be married to a career," Sara went on, "working evenings and weekends and being stressed out and putting the kids in day care."

He eyed her. "Why did you go to university, then?"

"To study law." At his expression, she said wryly, "You look like my father."

Her decision to forego the law had been the cause of a serious rift between Sara and her father, one that had only disappeared with Sam's death. Bill Hargreaves was not only an ardent supporter of women's rights, he had cherished the dream that his Sara would one day sit on the Supreme Court. He had no idea, because he refused to listen, of the anxiety and the hours of thought that lay behind her decision.

Sara had watched the other girls in her classes at university, had seen the driving ambition and the passion to excel, and had envied it. She knew she was capable of such drive, but law did not inspire it. "It's not just that," she told her parents, "I want to have kids at some point." Bill's reaction had made further discussion impossible.

As the product of a happy home Sara took it for granted that she would have children. She had pictured herself as a successful lawyer and then as a mother, but when she superimposed one image on the other an unworthy thought crept into her mind: "That looks like hard work." She never voiced this heresy, but having inherited a practical streak from her mother, she decided to pursue a business degree and see what happened. Marriage to a young architect called Sam Newton was what happened, and it brought out all Sara's latent ambition and energy.

Mike Farraday had envied the ease with which Sam's practice had expanded, and after learning of Sara's background, he understood why. Since then, he'd formed the habit of consulting her about his plans. Sara tried to match his enthusiasm during these empire-building sessions, concealing her cynicism at the futility of such ambitions. On this December morning, they discussed the costs of a brochure they planned to develop and mail to the company's customers and suppliers.

The call came shortly after lunch. In the midst of evaluating a new project management software program, Sara was waiting on hold for Technical Support when Trish, the receptionist, called over to tell her the *Star* reporter was on the line. Sara's heart leaped in her breast as she disconnected. She told herself to calm down. Jackson had not called in nearly a week. Surely he wouldn't call now, would he? Unless—

She took a breath and picked up the phone, and heard at last the words she had given up waiting for: "Mrs. Newton? Good news. We've found him. Can you bring Tom and meet me at the Pointe?"

*   *   *

Several miles below River Reach the river took a wide turn westward before resuming its southbound course, and on a spit of land at the onset of the bend stood an apartment complex. The Pointe offered luxury and privacy, a lavish but discreet excess that appealed greatly to its occupants. It was also exclusive, the residential tower having only seventeen floors, each with just two apartments. Security was monitored and controlled at the front desk by guards who also provided round-the-clock concierge service.

Arnold Dexter worked the day shift, from eight to four, a man of medium height with quick eyes and an ingratiating manner. On Monday morning, he was seated at the desk behind the tall counter on one side of the lobby when a cab pulled into the sweeping circular drive and stopped at the entrance. Dexter picked up the phone and punched a number. The line was busy; he unlocked the front doors and the cab driver entered, slapping his arms.

"Man, they said it was supposed to be warmer today. That wind's brutal." He glanced round the lobby. "Where's the body?"

Dexter's demeanor conveyed disapproval. One did not speak disrespectfully of the residents. "Doctor Byrd is on the—." The phone buzzed and he held up a hand to stay the driver. "Lobby," he said into the phone.

"Dexter? My cab arrived?"

"He just pulled in, doctor. I'll send him up for your bags."

"Good man. I'll leave them outside the door. Tell him I'll be down in five or ten minutes."

"Yes sir." Dexter disconnected and relayed this information. "Fourteenth floor, apartment twenty-three," he informed the cab driver, who headed for the rear vestibule. He returned some minutes later laden with two suitcases and a golf bag, and Dexter buzzed him out to the cab.

Mrs. Ruiz-Guerra phoned down at that moment, furious that the maintenance man had overwatered her African violets while she was away. Dexter gave the security board a swift glance, took his beeper and went up to twelve to pour oil on troubled waters. He returned ten minutes later to find the cab still parked in front. He stared outside in surprise. The driver was loading another suitcase in the trunk, while

Mr. Adair climbed into the rear of the cab, with Doc Byrd behind him.

The cab pulled away and Dexter returned to the desk and took out the clipboard showing occupant status. Byrd was away for three weeks in Bermuda. No notations against the penthouse slot. Had Drummond forgotten to enter it?

Bermuda! This altered the case considerably. He stared down at the marble countertop, weighing his options. Maybe it wasn't too late after all. . . .

Dexter should have been a golfer: his favorite words were "if only." If only he'd backed this hunch or that horse, what fortunes he would have made! Adair was merely the latest case. If only he'd called the *Star* when the police sketch was first published, he'd have made a killing. The *Star* would have paid anything for news of the river rescuer. But Dexter had hesitated; and now no one cared anymore.

Adair's car had been trashed at Ellis Mall on the evening of November twenty-third. Dexter heard about it the following day when he came on duty, and mid-morning he'd considered phoning the penthouse to find out whether the dealership was sending a courtesy car. But he already knew what the answer would be.

"I don't need one, thanks Dexter," the owner would say, as he always did when the Jag went in for work. "Mine should be ready in a few days." Adair was a pushover for that kind of treatment, the kind of guy who'd decline a courtesy car for fear of putting the dealership to an inconvenience.

Dexter had thought no more about it until he saw the sketch of the river rescuer. The more he looked at it the more certain he became. Ellis Mall was just off the bridge, about two miles north of the rescue site. He had consulted Drummond, but the night guard had been no help. "You're crazy," he said when Dexter showed him the drawing. "That's him," Dexter persisted. "There's something else, too. He hasn't been out since then. He doesn't have a car and I haven't called a cab for him."

"No law says he couldn't call one for himself."

"He could be lying dead upstairs, Drummond. Doesn't that worry you?" And when Drummond made no response, "You must have seen him that night. I figure he must have been walking past—"

"For crying out loud, Dexter, why would he walk home?"

"Did he?"

Drummond was an ex-cop, with pale blue eyes in a brick-red, square, honest face. He had turned away to study the status report. "I wouldn't know."

But Dexter knew, was certain of it, should have called the paper. If only he'd called! He had no fear of Adair. What had given him pause was the fear of the management finding out. So he'd waited, held off. Then the train wreck took over, and he felt once more the grinding knowledge of yet another opportunity lost.

Now he considered his position in light of Adair's departure. Maybe it wasn't too late after all. He could at least call the *Star* and find out if there was any money in it. Adair being besieged by reporters on a Bermuda beach seemed less risky somehow. Better than having them swarming all over the Pointe, asking awkward questions. He picked up the phone. Fix a meeting somewhere downtown after work, just to be on the safe side.

*   *   *

Each year at this time, Hoch began to look for a story, an issue, a cause—anything with the legs to carry him through the news-barren Christmas season. Decembers were notoriously slow, and he was already sick of the endless features the paper would carry about single mothers and bag ladies, about the ailing and the elderly alone, about school Christmas plays and concerts.

This morning had witnessed the successful resolution of two potential sagas: a robbery and hostage taking, and a fire in a downtown apartment building. Only the train wreck still held much potential, although the evacuation had been successfully completed with only a handful of rugged individualists remaining in their homes. But yesterday had brought an EPA warning of possible contamination of the water table. Thirty-five of the thirty-eight cars had been checked and the solitary bulletin from the railroad last night had stated that the leakage came from one or more of three tankers containing sulfuric acid, sodium hydroxide and acetic anhydride. On Hoch's instructions the graphics department had recycled a splendidly detailed diagram of the city's water distribution system, created several years earlier when replacing several miles of pipe had been an issue in civic elections. Now they were adding an inset showing the threat to the water table from a leaking tanker.

Busy deploying his staff on these and other stories the editor had little time for Jackson's news of a tip on the river rescue. "Who does he think we are, the *Enquirer?* Stall him on money. If the guy turns out to be a serial killer, we might be able to arrange some kind of reward from the police." He turned away to brief another reporter and Jackson returned to his desk, disappointed at Hoch's reaction, but unsurprised. The river story had low priority now, and a meeting with the informant had little urgency if the rescuer was in Bermuda.

*   *   *

Dr. Andrew Byrd glanced at his watch as the light changed to green and wondered if he'd miss his flight. Yesterday he had sold his March bond options because he didn't want to be troubled with investments while on vacation. Now he consoled himself with the thought that if necessary he could charter a jet with his profits. Not for the first time he thought of how much he owed Adair.

Byrd was a spinal cord specialist whose divorce five years ago had hit him hard financially. He had decided it was time to take an active role in his investments and while waiting for an appointment with his bank manager, he had picked up a copy of a newsletter called "Banks & Banking." He had found it engrossing and so he subscribed. The newsletter did not deal directly with investment products, but in reading about banks and legislation and currencies and monetary policies, Byrd gained considerable insight into financial investments of every stripe.

He had been astounded and delighted to discover the publisher living practically next door. One evening they met in the lobby, and Byrd asked how much Adair charged per hour.

"I don't give investment advice."

"You should. That piece you did on interest rates was first rate." He invited the great sage in for a drink and plied him with questions. Afterward, they had an argument over the bill. Byrd lost.

"I've only given you information," Adair had said. "The world's awash in information. What you do with it is your business." He reminded the specialist that interest rates were a barometer of risk and left.

In the days and weeks following that discussion Byrd conceived a mystical reverence for interest-rate investments. He was especially drawn to high-risk interest-rate futures and options, the vehicles whose workings Adair had explained that evening.

Andrew Byrd worshipped interest-rate futures. He traded them on paper for three months, and lost a fortune. He found they made his head pound so he switched to options. With these, his risk was limited to the amount of his investment, but the potential return was still huge. He formed a passionate attachment to options.

When he felt ready, he took $12,000 of his savings and invested half in options on T-Bonds, Japanese yen, Swiss francs and just for fun, gold, putting an equal amount into each commodity. Options have a short shelf life, generally from three to nine months. Byrd used the other half of his savings to renew the options that expired without making a move. Within six months of taking the plunge, he'd cashed out on two of his four investments. Within a year he had made nearly $40,000, and within three, $250,000. And he'd had a lot of fun doing it. He thought of his investment technique as prudent buccaneering, and it made him feel the hell of a fellow.

He never forgot Adair's part in all this, but had not been able to find a way to repay him. Until this morning. The publisher phoned as he was about to leave.

"I think I'm coming down with something, doctor. Can you recommend anyone I could see?"

Byrd had left his gear for the cab driver, grabbed a thermometer out of the bathroom cabinet and wasted a minute trying to find his old stethoscope, which eventually turned up wrapped in a sock in an overnight case in the bottom of the hall closet. He ran up the four flights to the penthouse to find Adair feverish and breathing with difficulty.

He wasted little time in diagnosis. The best cardio-pulmonary man in the city was Henry Spence and Byrd phoned and fixed an appointment with him for later that morning. He packed an overnight bag for Adair "in case they want to keep you in," helped him into his overcoat and took him down to the waiting cab.

The publisher seemed concerned about the trouble he was causing. "Nonsense," said Byrd. "In any case, I owe you big time." And during the drive he distracted his companion by describing his investment progress since their chat. "I think I'm just as reckless as many of my patients," he concluded. "And I probably have as much fun as they did prior to their accidents. But in my case nothing gets broken. It's only money."

He found Spence, the specialist, contemplating a series of x-rays, and filled him in briefly on Adair's condition. "Take good care of him, and send me the bill."

He wished Adair well, and dashed off to the cab, feeling all in all that he had done everything he could under the circumstances. Now they were well out of the city traffic and—he glanced at his watch—in time for his flight. He sat back and relaxed. Roll on Bermuda.

*   *   *

Nurse Jensen pressed the Ground floor button. As the elevator descended, she responded to the orderly's sallies with one part of her mind while covertly studying the patient in the wheelchair. As though sensing her scrutiny, he drew his overcoat more tightly around him and kept his eyes on the control panel.

He was thirty-seven, she knew that from his file, and lived alone, which was why Dr. Spence had instructed her to arrange for a private nurse to attend him at home. He had black hair over a tanned, strong-featured face, and a wide mouth. He looked older than his years: a sick pallor underlay his tan, his lips were tightly closed and the faint lines around his mouth hinted at furrows of bitterness in another ten years. But earlier, Nurse Jensen had entered the consulting room in time to hear Spence say, "—also known as walking pneumonia," and she'd seen his face lighten with wry amusement. He'd sensed her eyes on him and looked away, but that reaction had been all the confirmation Nurse Jensen needed. He was the river rescuer, she was sure of it, and she wondered why he'd hidden himself away and wished she were a private nurse instead of working for a dry old stick like Henry Spence.

The doors opened and she picked up his suitcase and followed orderly and patient along the wide corridor to the hospital's side entrance. She collected the prescription from the pharmacy and returned to see the cab she'd ordered pull up outside. The orderly took the suitcase out. Nurse Jensen touched her patient on the shoulder and put the small paper bag in his lap.

"You take care, Mr. Adair." He looked so annoyed at this expression of concern that she had to suppress a smile. "You're a very special patient."

The orderly returned and she stepped aside, watching as he pushed the wheelchair out to the open rear door of the cab. Cold air gusted through the wide glass doors and she shivered, then the orderly was hurrying back inside with the chair as the cab pulled away. She glanced at her watch: it was nearly lunchtime.

*   *   *

That morning, Jackson had been assigned to do an article on the water supply ("A city at risk?"), to accompany the water distribution diagram. It had seemed to him that the ground must surely be too frozen to permit leaching of dangerous chemicals into the water table but when he said as much to the editor he received a pithy lecture on the social value of accidents in forcing the public to confront and avert potential disaster.

Now Hoch leaned over his shoulder and scanned his computer screen. "Get on to the water department," he instructed. "Find out what protection the public has against drinking sulfuric acid." He turned away to scrutinize the screen of another reporter writing about the costs of the evacuation. "I don't care about the hotel rooms, dammit. Tell me what it'll cost the community in lost wages and revenues and livestock."

Jackson decided to call the water department after lunch and went out for a Big Mac and fries, pulling up the collar of his coat as he jogged down the street. The wind heralded the arrival of a warm front and snow was expected by evening.

An hour later, back at his desk, he took a call.

"Are you the one who wrote about the river rescuer?"

"That's right."

"I'm a pharmacist at St. Mike's. I filled a prescription for erythromycin for a guy called Owen Adair. I think he's the man you're looking for."

The reporter reached for a pen and pad. "What's your name, sir? And where are you calling from?" He noted the details. "What did he look like? This man?"

"I didn't see him. He's one of Doctor Spence's patients. He acted like he had something to hide and Spence's nurse got suspicious. We treated the kid he pulled out of the river, so there's a sketch of the guy on one of the bulletin boards."

Jackson noted the names of the doctor and nurse as the caller went on:

"We had lunch together. She wasn't going to tell anyone because the guy seemed like he didn't want the publicity. But I figure, hey—it's news, right?"

Adair had left the hospital an hour ago, Jackson learned. "The prescription. Erytho—"

"Erythromycin. He's got pneumonia. Oh—one other thing. He lives at the Pointe."

Jackson rang off and checked the phone book, finding several entries for Adair, O., including one on South River Road. He dialed the number but it rang without answer.

He turned to his screen and searched the paper's data banks for "Owen Adair." One reference, three years ago. He brought it up: a mention in an article on a banking conference. The keynote speaker had vigorously denied that his bank's liquidity was threatened by excessive real estate lending. The questioner had persisted, citing comments in the newsletter "Banks & Banking" by Owen Adair.

Could this be their guy? He consulted someone in the research department and leaned back in his chair a little later, considering his notes. "Banks & Banking" was published in Brand's Mill by Custom House Publishing; circulation 30,000; price $200 annually. Jackson tapped the desk with his pencil. Brand's Mill was a suburb on the west side, about ten miles south of the Pointe. He looked up the company and dialed the number, and shortly thereafter was connected with the managing editor, Wendy MacIntyre.

"I'm doing a survey of local publishing companies, Ms. MacIntyre," he said after introducing himself. "I understand you publish a newsletter on banking?"

"That's correct. Plus several books and reports."

"And the publisher is a Mr. Owen Adair?"

"Founder and publisher. I'm the minority partner." She sounded competent.

Jackson learned that their audience was both North American and international, that the newsletter was launched eleven years ago and the company eight, and that they had twelve employees. He heard a short rundown of the owner's credentials. "Any chance of an interview with Mr. Adair?" he said finally, "I could come out this afternoon."

"You'd have a long wait," she sounded amused. "When he's not traveling he works from home."

"Would that be the Pointe?"

"Correct."

All right! he thought while she explained that they were behind schedule on their January issue and Adair would be tied up for another week.

"I guess I've been misinformed. I heard he was in Bermuda."

"Bermuda?" The editor sounded surprised. "He's only just returned from Singapore. I can't believe—just a moment." She put him on hold briefly, then came back on: "He's scheduled to leave for Grand Cayman on the seventeenth. Nothing 'til then."

Jackson was beset by doubts. Could this be the local hero, this publisher? Had he even been in town on the twenty-third? "Um—how would you describe Mr. Adair?"

"Describe him?" Amusement and affection. "We think he's brilliant in this office, but we're biased."

"No, I meant, physically." He plunged ahead in the silence. "I heard he was short, with horn-rimmed glasses. Would that be correct?"

"Indeed, yes." Her voice was brisk. "And jug ears and a strawberry birthmark, don't forget."

"Oh now—"

But she launched into an acid commentary on the media preoccupation with appearance over substance. Jackson saw Hoch hovering nearby and hunched over his phone. "Stupid question, Ms. MacIntyre, really dumb," he said when he could get a word in edgewise. "I was just trying to picture Mr. Adair, that's all—look, thanks for your help." He rang off and looked round, relieved to find the editor standing a little way off, in a cluster of reporters.

The newsroom had a subdued air. He looked a question at his neighbor.

"Wasserman called in from Staple," she said gravely. "The leaking tanker held acetic anhydride."

"What's that?"

"Vinegar."

Jackson's laugh sounded loud in the hush and Hoch gave him a sour look.

"I've got a lead on the river rescue," said Jackson and added as the editor came over, "He's not a serial killer, just a journalist."

Hoch had already composed an editorial slamming both regulators and railroad for needless delay, stress and lost income, charging the railroad with carelessness and under-manning, and questioning the wisdom of shipping dangerous chemicals through populated areas. Vinegar! He could taste it. He considered Jackson's news. So the rescuer was a journalist. He thought of the *Star*'s afternoon rival.

"With the *Dispatch?*"

Jackson shook his head. "He worked on some commodities paper in New York and then in London for the *Financial Times*. That was about twelve years ago. Now he publishes a newsletter on banking." The editor seemed uninterested. "He lives at the Pointe."

Hoch glanced across the newsroom, reflecting. Tall, dark and handsome. Rich. It had possibilities. "Talked to him?"

"No. The thing is, he's got pneumonia."

Hoch's interest sharpened. "Is he in hospital?"

"No—" Jackson was conscious of losing ground. "They released him just before noon. His name's Owen Adair, looks like he's pretty successful—"

"Monica!" A stylish blonde woman in her late 40s was walking past. "Owen Adair. Ring a bell?"

Monica Stephanopoulos, the "Around Town" editor, thought briefly and shook her head.

"I'm late, Timmy—" she continued toward the door.

"Lives at the Pointe."

She stopped. "Owen Adair? Never heard of him. What's he do?"

Jackson's information meant nothing to her. Hoch came to a decision.

"Take a photographer and get over to the Pointe. Call the Newton woman and have her meet you there with the boy. You," he looked at Monica, "go with him."

He overrode their joint objections. If anyone could get Jackson into the Pointe, Monica would.

4

Wendy MacIntyre disliked trial subscribers. They were expensive, fickle and a damned nuisance. But she kept these feelings to herself because regular transfusions of new blood were essential to the newsletter's continued existence. Several years ago, she had indulged her dislike to the extent of farming out the job of finding these shy, elusive creatures. It was specialized work, better done by promotional companies whose entire existence revolved around the creation of tempting offers for the millions and millions of readers on their mailing lists. "Choose any FIVE publications for a special, three-month trial . . . only $20." The resulting names and addresses were forwarded to the publishers lucky enough to have been selected, along with a nominal contribution toward the cost of fulfilling that three-month subscription.

Wendy had drummed into everyone at Custom House that trial subscribers had to be given the royal treatment. "We want them to spend more money. We want them to convert from three-month trials to one- or two-year subscriptions. Therefore we have to fill their orders promptly, while they're still interested."

To fill an order you had to have a name and address. For two days now there had been no names, and Iris, the data entry manager, was concerned. So Wendy's day had begun with a call to New York. She discovered the promotional company had coded the responses wrongly so that readers expecting a copy of *Merchant Princes*, and a three-month trial subscription to "Banks & Banking," would instead be receiving the Spring catalogue of a well-known clothing store.

Quel dommage, she reflected with unwholesome cheer, then reproached herself. After ensuring that the error would not be repeated and negotiating a reduction in December's promo fee, she rang off.

Anyone who wanted to understand the world of money and banking read Owen's newsletter, and its subscribers included banking insiders, corporate borrowers, sophisticated money managers and well-heeled private investors. Owen wrote about banks of all kinds—central banks, full-service banks, private banks, credit unions and S&Ls. He wrote about the common law confidentiality practiced in Commonwealth countries, the legislated privacy and secrecy of Swiss banks, and the encroachments on privacy arising from the U.S. war on drugs. He discussed banking services, banking products and bankers themselves.

Over the years he had acquired a reputation as an accomplished interviewer. He had interviewed bank presidents, corporate treasurers, central bank officials and real estate promoters with licenses to operate S&Ls. He preferred if possible to let the interview speak for itself; sometimes, on reading what they had said to him, his subjects wished he had not.

Wendy's morning included a meeting on a new special report consisting of excerpts from the best of these interviews. Afterward, Polly, the graphic designer, stayed behind.

"This is that paper," she said, passing a blank sheet of paper to Wendy, now back at her desk. Postage was by far their biggest fixed cost, and the printer had suggested a new, lighter paper as a way to reduce the weight of the monthly mail-out, consisting of an eight-page newsletter, a promotional flyer, a return envelope and the outside envelope holding these pieces.

"Too much show-through," said Wendy skeptically, as she fingered the paper. It was remarkably thin, almost tissue-like.

"He says it won't," replied Polly. "He says it has a very high clay content."

"I'd like to believe him. What do you suggest we do?"

"I guess we could try it on the next issue?" said Polly uncomfortably.

Wendy repressed her exasperation. She was encouraging the graphic designer to take on greater responsibility, but all Polly wanted to do was lie low behind the light table and play with her graphics software.

"Why not ask him to print a few sheets of this on the end of the January run and let us see them," she suggested, and Polly brightened and went away to issue the instructions.

Wendy was reminded of her own ignorance some twelve years ago. She'd been working for Sharp Response Marketing, earning a pittance. It was a stopgap, she'd said to Keith, until a decent magazine job came along. Frank Sharp provided a fulfillment service for small magazine and newsletter publishers, everything from editorial (Wendy's job) to typesetting, graphics, layout and design, mailing and list management.

She had no interest in the graphics or printing side of the operation; she knew nothing of list rentals or fulfillment. She had seen the stacks of computer-printed address labels at work, and the baskets of returned envelopes from subscribers who had moved or died. She had sometimes wondered in passing how each individual label got onto its envelope. She concluded that Sharp must employ row upon row of people each with a pair of scissors and a pot of glue to do nothing each month but transfer computer labels to their individual envelopes. She didn't really know or care; she just put in her hours and went home each night. Keith was a geology professor and they were glad of the extra income.

Nowadays, she thought ruefully, editing filled only a tiny proportion of her time, and even then she did little beyond copy tasting or overall structural or content suggestions. But she didn't regret a minute of the past decade and when Owen insisted several years ago that everyone learn as much as they could about each other's jobs, Wendy approved. The company was too small for rigid job descriptions. Everyone had to be able to back up at least one other person.

Polly poked her head round the door asking about the January issue: "I still don't know what visuals it needs," she said. "Arthur said he hasn't got the copy yet."

"Owen's been delayed," replied Wendy, and Polly nodded and left. Wendy got back to work. By now the copy for January's issue, about Asian economic recovery and the prospects for the new European currency should have been in production, with Arthur and Polly working their editing and graphics magic. Instead, Owen had called two days ago, warning her it would be late. He was waiting for data from their stringers in Tokyo and Frankfurt, he said.

She worked on steadily through the day, in her normal routine. Following the call from the *Star* she conferred with the receptionist. "What's all this about Bermuda?"

Judy could not shed any light on the Bermuda rumor. Yes, she had kept the itinerary up to date, and no, no one else had mentioned Bermuda. Only one other person had called that day for Owen's itinerary: Tug Sheppard. "Owen's friend," she reminded Wendy.

Owen's schedule was available to almost anyone who asked for it. He travelled so extensively that the receptionist maintained a quarterly itinerary complete with phone numbers, and many a subscriber had had a long chat with the publisher in Frankfurt or Zurich, Singapore or Tokyo. Owen enjoyed these conversations when he was away from home, although there was a sizable list of subscribers, current and past, who were categorically never to be given his number. If necessary, Roger or Colin, the two researchers, dealt with these people. Wendy dealt with the worst cases. They formed what she privately called The Stupid List: people with more money than sense, whose investment decisions were governed by the signs of the zodiac, tides, numerology or games of chance.

Mid-afternoon, while she was perusing an array of promotional flyers for upcoming financial conferences—even though Owen declined all offers to speak at them, Wendy liked to know who and what was hot—Judy buzzed her: "Sara Newton would like to see you."

* * *

Sara had come down slightly from her high after lunch. When she first got off the phone, it had been hard to think clearly at all. She found Pam and Trish watching her expectantly.

"They've found him!"

"We know," said Pam. "You said so three times."

"Is he single?" asked Trish, young and blonde.

"I'll find out," Sara laughed. "His name's Owen Adair, he lives at the Pointe, he's some kind of publisher, in Brand's Mill. They found him! I can't believe it."

Pam had been leafing through the phonebook. "Custom House Publishing, you said." She looked up, impressed. "The Pointe! When are you going to meet him?"

"Jackson wants me to go there right away with Tom."

"Oh wow!" Trish clasped her hands, "That's so romantic! I can hardly wait to see the paper."

Sara began to consider that aspect and as she waited for Mike to return from lunch, she resolved that neither she nor Tom would play any part in the Star's peepshow. For one thing, she was uncertain how Tom might react to the news, and for another, she wanted to thank this man privately, not under the glare of flashbulbs and avid, scribbling reporters.

"They'll want to make a circus out of it," she explained to Farraday on his return, following him into his office. "They'll be swarming all over Tom at school—."

"Oh sure. You want to get him out of there and choose your own time, huh?"

"Something like that."

"So get out of here." He waved her thanks away and added as she went to the door, "And Sara—" she looked back. "Give him a handshake from me, okay?" She promised with a smile, and back at her desk she phoned her sister-in-law. Bob and Ronnie lived north of the city.

"I'd leave them next door, Ron, but Jackson would find them, and I don't want Tom pestered."

"No problem. Better pack their PJs, though. There's snow in the forecast."

Sara retrieved Tom and Janey from school and managed to postpone an explanation until they'd returned to the car. Janey clambered into the rear. In the front, Sara reached for Tom's hand.

"They've found the man, Tom." He glanced up at her, then away.

"What man?" This from the back seat.

Sara hugged Tom and resisted the urge to say, "Dad's spirit was inside him, Tommy."

"The man who saved Tom?" Janey's head appeared over the back of the seat.

"Yes, darling."

"Are we going to go and see him?"

"Not today."

"Is he nice, mum?"

"I don't know, Janey. I think he must be."

"Aren't we going to say thank you?"

Tom stared at the dashboard.

"Yes, but not all at once."

"How come?"

"Because I think he may be shy, darling."

Shy was a closed book to Janey. She looked out the window. "Where's all the reporters?"

Sara smiled at Tom and smoothed the hair back from his forehead. "I thought I'd visit him, and see what he's like, and then if you want you could come next time. How would that be?"

"Okay." He shrugged carelessly.

"And me!"

"And you. Now buckle up, Jane."

Janey climbed down and settled back in the rear seat, and Sara pulled out.

"Does he have braces, mum?"

"What?"

"Like Barry Bachman. Tom said Barry's braces make him shy. What's his name?"

"Owen Adair. That's a nice name, isn't it?" She reached over and touched Tom's cheek.

Not until she was driving back from Ronnie's did she have time to think through Jackson's proposed meeting at the Pointe, and the more she thought about it, the less she liked the idea. What if he was indeed shy? Or antisocial? She pictured their meeting under the scrutiny of Jackson and his cohorts. It would be stilted and awkward, and soon over. And then what? Never to see him again, unless they happened to cross paths at the grocery store? What if he didn't shop for groceries? Would she have to camp outside bookstores on the off chance of meeting him? Or airports? Jackson had said he traveled a lot.

She stopped in at home to change into something more appropriate to the occasion than the casual wear favored at Farraday's. Adorned ten minutes later in a charcoal grey skirt and a lilac silk sweater set knotted at the waist, she set off again down South River Road. Peering through the dull light as she approached the Pointe, she could make out a white van with the *Star*'s logo on it, parked near the front entrance. Her mind was suddenly made up. *Absolutely not,* she decided, and the road veered round to the right and the entrance was behind her.

Brand's Mill had undergone a facelift in the past two years. Formerly a collection of houses and shops clustered round an old bakery and watermill, it had succumbed to an attack of twee. Now most of the buildings were Tudor, half-timbered black and white, and antique shops outnumbered tea shoppes but only just.

Custom House Publishing occupied a sixties-style two-story office building that had recently been painted but was otherwise unaffected by this cosmetic makeover. The ground floor held an office supply store and a sandwich bar. Sara walked up to the second. Behind a broad glass wall was a foyer with a reception desk, and beyond that an open office with a number of desks. She opened the glass door and walked in.

"I'd like to see Mr. Adair, please," she said, having given this careful thought. "It's a personal matter."

"He's not here. Could Ms. MacIntyre help you?"

That suited Sara just fine, and she was invited to take a seat. On her right a couple of comfortable chairs sat either side of a coffee table, on which several newsletters were displayed. She turned one over and found on the back a list of personnel. Managing editor: Wendy MacIntyre. So now she knew whom she would be meeting. A book lay next to the newsletters: Merchant Princes by Owen Adair. She turned it over and there he was. She sat gazing at the somber, strong-featured face of Tom's rescuer.

"Can I help you?"

Sara scrambled to her feet to face a woman of forty-five or so, with a good-humored expression framed by a halo of fine, unruly brown hair, and large glasses. "I'm Wendy MacIntyre," she said.

They shook hands. Sara had not been able to think of an easy way to get past this moment. "Has the *Star* been here today?" she began, and saw the other woman's attention sharpen. When Wendy asked what she meant, Sara explained that they had called her after lunch. "My son nearly drowned in the river two weeks ago. He was rescued by someone who just disappeared. Now they says it's Mr. Adair, and—"

"Do you mean the River Rescuer?" said the receptionist. "Do you mean Owen is the River Rescuer?"

"That's what they told me." There was a beat of silence, then Sara found herself suddenly being guided past reception to the right as Wendy briskly established what she wanted to drink and relayed this information to the receptionist, whose name, Sara learned, was Judy. They walked past several desks into a corner office, and Sara was invited to sit down. Judy arrived while she was removing her coat and deposited two mugs of coffee on the desk. She took Sara's coat then waited expectantly. Wendy sipped her coffee and studied the younger woman.

"So you think Owen may have saved your son."

"It's Tommy, isn't it?" said Judy.

"Yes," said Sara to both of them.

"I had a call earlier today from some nitwit at the *Star*. He seemed to think Owen was in Bermuda. Would you know anything about that?"

Sara shook her head.

Wendy glanced at the receptionist. "I wonder if he was even in the country when it happened."

"Yes, he was," said Judy, "he went to Singapore on the twenty-sixth. The rescue was on the twenty-third." She looked at Sara. "I know he did it. I'm sure of it. Tall dark and handsome?" she quoted. "It fits, sort of."

Wendy stared at the receptionist, mystified. Then she began to laugh and quoted Jackson. "'I heard he was short with horn-rimmed glasses.' Twerp. Bermuda, indeed. Too much imagination for that line of work." Sara watched and listened, holding her coffee mug with both hands and enjoying its warmth.

Wendy turned to her. "Were you supposed to meet the reporter here?"

"I was supposed to meet him at the Pointe. That's apparently where Mr. Adair lives." And as they both nodded, Sara went on, "I really wasn't comfortable with that. It's hard enough to know what to say to him or how on earth to thank him without having Jackson breathing all over me. And in any case . . . he doesn't seem to like publicity and I certainly don't want to add to it. But I do want to thank him," she finished firmly. "I must."

Wendy gazed at her thoughtfully. Finally, "Judy, go back to the front desk and stay there. If anyone from the media calls, put it through to me. Don't let in any strange bodies—"

"As if," said Judy.

"And please don't say anything to the others just yet."

Judy left and the two women began the process of evaluating each other. Wendy began. "You must have been through a lot lately," she said, and Sara obligingly told her about the past two weeks, about Tom and Janey, her background and work, and River Reach. Then it was Wendy's turn.

"Do you know anything about newsletters?" she asked Sara.

"I get one with my electricity bill. And the school does a thing every month or so."

Wendy nodded. "There are literally thousands of newsletters, Sara. Maybe even tens of thousands. Put out by companies and industry associations, as well as schools and churches. They're cheap to produce and free. But there are hundreds of subscription newsletters as well." She picked up a selection of back issues from a book case behind her desk, and passed them over to Sara. "If people are prepared to pay for information on a subject, it's a candidate for a newsletter. You can subscribe to newsletters on sport fishing, for instance or furniture finishing. Dirt bike racing. Communications deregulation or banking. As a publisher, you just have to find enough subscribers to make it profitable."

Sara leafed through the newsletters. Few pictures; just column after column of words with some graphs and charts. "Would you get more subscribers if you did it in magazine format?"

Wendy smiled. "You mean, color photos and ads, not just text? Magazines are expensive to publish, Sara. The growth in newsletters has pretty much matched the decline in general-interest magazines. Remember *Colliers*? And *Look*? *Harpers? Saturday Evening Post?* It's the age of specialization. People want information focused on their particular interests, and those interests may be too small a niche for anything except a newsletter."

Investment and financial newsletters, Sara learned, had been around since the nineteen-twenties, but many had started up in the seventies. The financial convulsions of the late nineteen-seventies and early eighties were a further stimulus, when gold reached $850, and silver $50. Interest rates rose nearly to twenty percent, and hyperinflation seemed a genuine threat. More and more people sought to understand these events in an effort to protect their savings.

"How do you find subscribers," Sara wanted to know, and Wendy told her all about list rentals, where you looked for publications whose readers might like your newsletter, then rented their lists and sent those subscribers a special offer in the hope of enticing them to try it.

"You have to spend a lot to get trial subscribers. Keith always used to know when we were in the throes of a new campaign," Wendy explained, "because I became very, very bad tempered at the expense. No one was happier than he when we decided to farm the whole process out." She laughed ruefully and added, "It's still expensive, but I don't have to be so hands on."

Sara learned a bit about Keith after that, and then something of Custom House and its employees. Finally, they talked about Owen. They had moved to the easy chairs around a circular table near the window.

"It's an extraordinary thing, this rescue," said Wendy.

"You didn't seem very surprised by it. Nor did Judy."

"No." Wendy gazed thoughtfully outside and after some moments she said, "I've been thinking about that. Owen's a risk-taker, that's why it doesn't surprise me."

She turned to face Sara on the sofa. "This isn't really for publication, because we don't like to refer in print to embezzlers and theft and so forth, but it's common knowledge in the company and I don't see why you shouldn't know."

*   *   *

Sharp Response Marketing was a thriving concern in the early eighties. Frank Sharp handled fulfillment for ten newsletters, four of them industry publications with huge mailing lists, and the remainder small subscription operations. Desktop publishing was scarcely more than a gleam in Steve Jobs's eye back then, and Sharp's operations were centered around his IBM mainframe, which handled the mailing lists, and his Merganthaler typesetter.

After working for papers in New York and London, Owen Adair wanted to start his own newsletter. He had gravitated toward business and later banking because he had a facility for explaining the forces underlying trade and commerce, and an interest in the ways people sought to make money. He had returned home with knowledge, experience and a wide range of contacts under his belt, and he had big plans for his future.

Sharp quoted him a monthly fulfillment fee, one that covered editorial and graphics through printing, mailing and modest but steady promotion. They found several publications whose subscribers Owen thought would look favorably on his work, and Sharp rented those lists and promoted to their readers while Owen wrote each month the hardest-hitting, most incisive copy he could turn out. He used his savings to help fund the first two years of the newsletter. By the end of that period he had some twenty-five hundred subscribers.

This was nowhere near enough to be self-sustaining or to enable him to grow and expand as he had planned. After some reflection he flew to New York. He'd learned by now that to build a substantial subscription list you needed a first-rate promotional package mailed to top-quality lists, coupled with irresistible premiums and a competitive price. He visited one of the best direct mail writers in the business and convinced him to take on "Banks & Banking." Then he flew to London where, using the contacts he'd acquired in his *Financial Times* days, he succeeded in landing sufficient financing for a massive promotional campaign, one big enough to vault him into the big leagues.

He returned home and explained his plans to Sharp and Wendy. During the next six weeks he would complete the manuscript of a new book, *Merchant Princes*, a history of the best-known merchant banks in London and New York. This would be one of the promotional premiums to be offered in the mail-out, along with two special reports which Wendy would put together using material from the past two years of the newsletter. While the promo package would be created in New York, Sharp would handle the list rentals and million-piece mailout.

Over the next two months they prepared for the campaign. Owen began feeding chapters to Wendy, in between researching and writing current issues of the newsletter and updating the material for the special reports she was assembling. He also found time to consult with Sharp on the lists they were going to rent.

Wendy was impressed with *Merchant Princes*. Broadly speaking, it was nothing more than a series of rags-to-riches stories set in London and New York. But Owen had brought alive the world of commerce as practiced in the eighteenth and nineteenth centuries by immigrant European merchants. She like the book so well that, without saying anything, she sent off a set of galleys to a colleague at *Esquire*.

The promotional mailout took place in mid-November and two weeks later, Sharp was able to deliver a verdict.

Based on the early returns, he told Owen, the campaign would generate a 1.5 percent response. This was respectable but only half what Owen had hoped for. They would have roughly ten thousand subscribers once the dust had settled, rather than the seventeen thousand Owen had wanted.

Shortly thereafter, Sharp left on vacation. He never returned. Six weeks later, with inquiries coming from employees and other customers, Wendy went through his desk and was shattered to discover seventy-five hundred response cards in the bottom left-hand drawer: he'd absconded with half the funds from the promotion and hidden the cards where he knew she would eventually find them.

She called Owen and asked him to come into the office. His appearance shocked her: his fiancée had left him, and he was evidently spending much of his time either drinking or drunk. He had turned in quite passable copy for the last issue, but this one, when she glanced at it later, looked like pain on paper.

She sat him down and put the bundles of cards into his hands and onto the desk before him. The prospect of his having to print and mail double the number of newsletters with half the revenue made her quail, and she could scarcely believe her ears when he gave the ghost of a laugh.

She thought he'd lost his mind. He looked up at her and laughed again. "How about that?" he said. She asked if he understood what she'd told him and he answered, "Sure. We got a three percent response. I was right all along."

It seemed to put new heart into him. He went away to call London and beg for a moratorium on his loan. Wendy did some serious thinking about her future and talked to Keith, and then she put together a plan. A few days later she presented it to Owen.

Instead of taking his business to some new fulfillment house, she said, why not form his own company? She would run it, continue to edit and produce his material, and they could cover much of the overhead by taking over Sharp's other newsletters, if his customers were agreeable. Wendy knew little about the fulfillment side of the business, she said candidly, but she would learn it.

Owen thought about this proposal and liked it. The call from *Esquire* decided him. The editors wanted to reprint two chapters of *Merchant Princes*, and they agreed to include full subscription details in Owen's byline.

He renegotiated his bank loan, formed Custom House Publishing with Wendy as managing editor, took out a second loan later the same year and accepted outside writing assignments to pay his own expenses. He moved into a smaller apartment and found a place that sold hamburgers cheaper than McDonald's.

He gave Wendy a ten percent interest in 1988. In 1991, the company turned the corner, and in 1992 found itself awash in profits. The shareholders declared a dividend in November of that year, after Wendy had restrained him from dispensing fully eighty percent of the profits to their twelve employees. She and Keith put a downpayment on a summer cottage while the majority shareholder purchased his apartment at the Pointe.

*   *   *

The short winter afternoon was over, and Sara could no longer see outside. "Would he really have given away all the profits like that?"

"Yes, I think he would." Wendy traced a pattern on the arm of the sofa. "It offended me, Sara. He had sacrificed so much and worked so hard. To give it all away like that . . . I wanted to hit him." Sara laughed, and Wendy's expression lightened. "I had the accountant on the phone before you could say dividend. Fortunately, he made Owen see sense."

"Did you ever recover the money Sharp stole?"

Wendy shook her head. "The police caught up with him two years later in Costa Rica, but it was history. Owen didn't seem to care. He'd written it off right from the start."

She got to her feet. "Let me show you round, then we'll call him. Owen never likes to be thanked, but he'll just have to learn to take the rough with the smooth. It's time he met you, and the press must surely have finished with him by now."

5

The *Star*'s society editor, Monica Stephanopoulos, stood on the steps at the entrance to the Pointe and watched as Owen Adair sprinted along the road, veered off into a flower bed, dodged a rhododendron and disappeared round the side of the building, with Jackson and the photographer in pursuit.

She turned her attention to the cab driver, who stood at the trunk of his cab, holding in his arms a large box. Like her, he had been gaping after Adair and the reporters.

"What kept you?" she asked.

He came toward her with the box. "We been all over hell's half acre lookin' for this." He continued past her into the building. She surveyed the deserted landscape and followed him inside.

Newsletters, in Monica's view, were a subspecies of junk mail, and she had been annoyed at being diverted from her daily round by a direct mail merchant. However, she knew the Pointe's developer, so while the photographer drove and Jackson called Sara Newton, Monica had established with two well-placed phone calls that a guard called Arnold Dexter worked the day shift. Jackson speculated that Dexter might have been his morning informant and this was confirmed when they arrived at the Pointe. He recognized Dexter's voice through the intercom, and watching through the glass, Monica noticed the tension in the guard's face.

Now on the inside, she waited until he had dealt with the cab driver, then she confronted him.

"Is there another way in?"

"I have to ask you to leave ma'am—"

"Listen, Dexter. Your boss is a friend of mind. Do you want him to learn you were prepared to sell out an owner? Now: is there another way in?"

She got the information she wanted, and bullied Dexter into leaving her with Adair's possessions in the elevator. He rallied sufficiently to demand two hundred dollars and her promise of silence, and thinking he might have future value, she complied. Then he made himself scarce.

*　　*　　*

Owen Adair leaned against the wall coughing painfully. He stood in the windowless corridor of the arm connecting the main apartment building with the pool, saunas and racquets courts. His heart hammered, his legs were trembling with fatigue and he stared blindly at the opposite wall, astounded at himself. He struggled to regain his breath, thinking resentfully of the inevitable reports. He'd soon have no credibility left at this rate. *Should have stayed in bed*, he thought. *Why didn't you just stay in bed?*

He hadn't been outside in nearly two weeks; a strange lassitude had kept him idle while the pain in his chest grew steadily worse. He had cancelled the Singapore trip himself, guiltily reluctant to involve the office, but that sacrifice had failed to appease the invader within his chest. This morning, when even the small effort of going downstairs for his mail had exhausted him, he knew finally that he must see a doctor. He'd been about to seek Wendy's advice when he remembered Dr. Byrd, the spinal-cord specialist who was also a subscriber.

He'd looked up Byrd's number and phoned, catching him on the point of leaving for Bermuda. The doctor had been kind enough to come up to the penthouse, where he'd listened to Owen's breathing, arranged an appointment with a cardio-pulmonary colleague, and had even taken him to the hospital. During the next two hours Owen had been examined, x-rayed and cultured (sputum and blood) before the cardio-pulmonary specialist, Dr. Spence, an ascetic man in his late-fifties, had delivered his verdict. Owen had wanted to pay him.

"You must take that up with Doctor Byrd," said Spence briefly, as he gave the nurse a prescription. After she'd gone, Owen had waited in a haze of escalating discomfort while Spence continued writing, this time on a foolscap pad.

"I'd really like to pay you, doctor."

"I'm not in the habit of debating my fee, Mr. Adair." A silence, then: "You once gave Doctor Byrd some investment advice. It seems he profited greatly by it."

"I gave him information, not advice."

"You neglected to bill him, in any event." He finished writing, tore off the page and folded it. "It sounds highly unprofessional to me, but doubtless you know best." Owen was stung, but before he could reply Spence was passing the sheet across the desk. "Give this to your nurse." Then an orderly had entered with a wheelchair, and Owen was helped into it, over his protests, and taken down to the cab.

They'd nearly reached the bridge when, wondering what was in store for him, he read the nurse's instructions, and it was then that he discovered his treatment required cough suppressant and a humidifier, neither of which he possessed. The search for a humidifier had bordered on the epic, and they had toured the drugstores of the downtown area before an enterprising clerk had phoned around and located one at an outlet not far from the hospital.

Then at last they headed homeward, and Owen had put his head back, closed his eyes and tried not to cough. He couldn't shake Spence's comment. Was it unprofessional not to have charged Byrd, he wondered. "I'm not in the advice game," he muttered, and waved off the cab driver's inquiry. "Sorry. Nothing. I'm fine, thanks."

Spence's comment was particularly irksome because Owen prided himself on his professionalism. He'd set out to become a good journalist and by any standard he'd succeeded; and his business judgment had been confirmed numerous times. Beyond that true estimate he seldom ventured, avoiding introspection by the simple expedient of focusing on other people. He'd discovered the technique at 19, as a means of overcoming the shyness that had afflicted him throughout his childhood, and he proved unexpectedly adept at it, having both intuition and a keen ear for nuance. Other people became a refuge against himself, and the quality of his business interviews was a rich dividend.

To Owen, other people were uncharted continents, rich in promise. If he thought of himself at all, it was as an apple with a worm in it, a warped streak that periodically threatened to overturn all his achievements. That—he averted his eyes from the frozen stream and playground as they drove down River Road—that business was a prime example of the warped streak, and he had been nagged by a sense of guilt about it ever since.

They threw away the wrong part, didn't they? The sentence entered his mind unbidden and he wondered if it was the product of delirium, and Spence's observation throbbed like a sore tooth and he wondered if he should have charged for the information he'd given Byrd.

As the cab pulled into the driveway at the Pointe, he reminded himself that he must make up the guest room bed for the nurse, and call Wendy. The sense of guilt intensified. He scarcely registered the three people clustered at the front doors, starting slowly up the steps while the driver went round to the trunk.

"Mr. Adair? Owen Adair?"

Two men and a woman advanced toward him. He was blinded by a flash.

"You're Owen Adair, aren't you? Flick Jackson, sir. The *Star.*"

All morning, Owen had assured himself that he really didn't mind if he was recognized. The reality was otherwise. Their avid, intent gazes filled him with disquiet and for the second time in as many weeks he obeyed an impulse. He fled.

Where the strength in his legs came from he could never say, but he managed to stay ahead of them down the driveway and through the flowerbed. He shook them off at the three-foot drop round the corner of the building, hearing the two men stumble and fall behind him. He sprinted along a gravel path toward the connecting arm, inserted his security card and entered.

He had recovered sufficiently now to get himself upstairs, and he pushed himself off the wall and made his way slowly along the corridor to the apartment building. The door opened into the small mail room behind the elevators and he passed through into the vestibule, hearing one elevator in use. The doors of the other were open and he stepped inside, then stopped. The female reporter stood at the rear next to his humidifier and suitcase.

She smiled professionally, relieved Owen of his security card, inserted it in the slot and pressed "Penthouse."

"You can't escape us that easily, you know. I'm Monica Stephanopoulos."

As the elevator rose, she studied Owen, leaning against the opposite wall, head sunk on his chest. He looked terrible, she had to admit, his face grey and sweaty.

"What have you got to hide?"

He shook his head. "You just . . . caught me by surprise."

"It was you who rescued the boy from the river, wasn't it?"

He nodded.

She assessed his overcoat. Cashmere blend. Wet it would weigh a ton. "What were you wearing?"

He raised his head and regarded her. "Did they pull you off the society page?"

"That's right." Had he recognized her name? Most people did, but she wasn't sure about this man. "Were you wearing that coat?"

By the time they'd entered the penthouse she had established what he was wearing and why he'd been walking by the river that night. She took in the spacious living room, the vaulted ceiling with a skylight running along its length, the grand piano to the left. He sank down on an off-white L-shaped couch before the fireplace and gestured her to a chair.

Monica removed her coat and sat down, took a small recorder from her bag and put it on the coffee table, on top of the *Wall Street Journal*.

"Why did you do it, Owen?"

"You can't just stand by when a kid's in trouble."

She wanted more than this banal response but he leaned back looking tired and ill.

"Did you walk home?"

"Sure."

"How long did it take you?"

"I didn't notice the time, just wanted to get inside."

"Are you saying you suffered no ill effects?"

"Not until now."

She scrutinized him, then tried again. "What went through your mind, Owen? When you entered that freezing water? What were you thinking as you—." She stopped. He was shaking his head in bleary amusement. "Owen, this town has been turned upside down looking for you. Do you realize that?"

She watched as he tried to focus on her.

"Sara Newton is really dying to meet you."

"Who?"

Where on earth had he been? Monica reached for her bag and took out her cell phone. "Listen, darling, I'm going to do you a favor." That provoked a faint grin, which she ignored.

"Mrs. Newton will be here any minute. I realize you're sick but I suggest you see her now. Get it over with, Owen. That way, we can wrap up the story complete with happy ending." And the *Star* would have its exclusive. "What do you say?"

Owen stared at the coffee table, trying to think. Would this get rid of her more quickly?

His nod coincided with the ringing of his phone, and he leaned forward to pick it up as Monica punched a number into her cell phone, and walked along the hall to talk to her cronies and take a peek at the rest of the penthouse.

It was Tug on the phone, and Owen forgot the interview and listened with a kind of wistful pleasure as his old friend issued an invitation to dinner on the seventeenth.

"That's a great idea, Tug. Sure I'll come."

He could hear Tug's surprise. "You're sure, Owen?"

"Sure I'm sure." Then he remembered. Liz had rejected his gifts. *Not nice. Not good. Poor old Liz. Good old Tug, though.* "Say, Tug—."

"Yeah?"

"I forgot. Have to change my mind. I've got pneumonia. Probably going to be out of commission for a couple of weeks." *Couple of weeks, couple of weeks, couple of weeks. . . .* He was suddenly deathly tired, and he told Tug he'd be fine, had to go, the nurse was arriving shortly.

Monica's voice broke in as he disconnected. "Fantastic!" she said into her cell phone, coming back into the living room. She shut it and threw a bright smile in his direction. "She'll be here any moment, Owen."

He gathered his strength once more. Monica became solicitous. "Would you feel better climbing into bed?"

But he was not quite delirious, because she heard amusement in his voice as he answered: "I think not."

*   *   *

Jackson sat with the photographer in the van as darkness fell. He had tried Sara Newton at work and home, without success. At ten past four, a dry cleaning delivery van pulled in and Jackson slipped into the building behind the driver.

Monica had learned that the shift changed at four and midnight, and he introduced himself to the night guard, Drummond, and tried to find out Adair's condition on the night of the rescue. But Drummond had nothing to say, and when Jackson persisted he was manhandled to the door and ejected.

Hoch called soon after. He had received the copy and film they'd couriered downtown. There would be no mention of Adair's hundred-yard dash: the *Star* did not want to be accused of harassing a local, and extremely sick, hero. Jackson protested that he couldn't be that sick or he'd have been kept in hospital, but Hoch overrode him, instructing them to get a picture of the mother and boy at Adair's bedside. But they waited in vain for Sara Newton. Eventually, Monica came downstairs, dictating into her phone, and they drove off. Scattered snowflakes shone in the path of the headlights.

*   *   *

"Good evening, Drummond."

"Evening, sir. Mrs. Jorgensen." Drummond smiled as the Jorgensens left, then bent once more over Mrs. Warburton's luncheon guest list. Thus he failed to notice Sara, who smiled her thanks at Jorgensen for holding the door, and stepped inside.

She'd never been to the Pointe, though Sam had had a client there once and she knew it by reputation. She looked around curiously. No homely piles of unwanted flyers in this foyer; no stacks of free community newspapers. Just a spacious lobby in Florentine marble, with recessed lighting and two huge facing mirrors in dull gold antique frames.

The traffic up the River Road had been heavy and it was now after six. Wendy had called and Owen had agreed to see her, and had promised to leave word with the front desk. He had sounded very relaxed, Wendy said. She buried her hands into her coat pockets and walked toward the guard.

Drummond looked up and his cop's mind registered: Caucasian female, early thirties, dark hair, five-seven, fine-boned, grey eyes.

"Ma'am?" Russet wool coat and hat, black boots, black shoulder bag and a white muffler. Slender: one-thirty maybe.

"I'm here to see Mr. Adair."

"Are you Mrs. Newton?"

Relief flooded through Sara's body. He hadn't forgotten, then. "Yes, I am."

The guard studied her. "Mrs. MacIntyre called ten minutes ago. Wanted to know if you'd arrived." He straightened some papers in front of him. "We have a situation here, ma'am. Mr. Adair's got pneumonia. I'm just waiting for the nurse."

Earlier in the day, Jackson's news had lifted a weight from Sara's heart. Now it descended once more. "Is he—how is he? I mean, should he be in hospital?"

"I don't know, ma'am. Probably." He smiled slightly.

"Has he seen a doctor?" The guard nodded. "Then he probably has some sort of medication. Is anyone with him?"

The guard eyed her. "I'll tell you, ma'am, there's no one. He's just waiting up for the nurse."

"Could I ask your name?"

"Drummond."

"Mr. Drummond, please let me see him. Please let me help him until she arrives."

Drummond had been considering this option since Mrs. MacIntyre's call. "I thought he sounded a bit odd," she had said, after he had explained the position. There had been a silence, then, "Is he delirious, do you think?" Drummond thought he might be. Also stubborn and pigheaded, but he didn't say that. Another silence, then Mrs. MacIntyre had said decisively, "Sara Newton seems sensible and level-headed and she wants nothing to do with the press, which rates a big plus in my book. If she offers to help, I think you should let her. "

This conversation passed through Drummond's mind as he appraised the woman in front of him. He liked the look of her, and he knew he would feel a lot better with someone upstairs, just until the nurse arrived, wherever the blazes she was. He came to a decision, checked the board and reached for his beeper. "This way," he gestured, and Sara accompanied him to the vestibule. They entered the elevator and he studied her as it rose. Sara was oblivious, her mind on the knowledge that Tom's rescuer had come down with pneumonia.

The doors opened and they stepped out into a foyer with a metal utility door at one end. Facing them were wide oak double doors. Drummond tapped and they waited. He knocked. No answer.

"Wait here, please." He inserted his master card in the slot, and opened the door. The lights were on and he disappeared to the left, leaving the door ajar. To the right Sara could see a hallway and across from it, stairs leading upward.

She heard a low-voiced exchange, followed by silence, then a thump against the wall to her left. She made up her mind and stepped inside, looking round the door. Adair was coming toward her supported by Drummond, one arm round the guard's shoulders. He raised his head, muttered something to her and stopped, swaying in front of her.

"Come on, sir," said the guard.

A phone began to ring.

Sara stepped aside to let them pass, then closed the door. "I'll get it," she said to Drummond and he took Owen along the hall. She found the phone on the coffee table and picked it up.

"Hello?"

"Thank goodness someone's there! How is Mr. Adair?" A female voice.

"Who's calling, please?"

"This is Natalie Sheepwash. I told the doctor's office I'd be there by three, but my patient fell and sprained his ankle and then I was delayed in traffic. How is he?"

Drummond returned a few minutes later to hear Sara saying goodbye. She put the phone down and looked at him, then at a sheet of paper in her hand.

"That was the nurse." She raised her eyes and said, with a trace of defiance, "I told her not to come." She turned away and took off her coat. "How is he?"

"Why'd you tell her that?"

"Look, Mr. Drummond. I've nursed two kids and a husband through all the standard ailments. She lives on the east side, she hadn't even left home, and the traffic's terrible." The snow had been falling more and more heavily for the last hour.

Sara referred to the sheet of paper. "It seems Doctor . . . Spence has a poor opinion of nurses. He left full instructions." She straightened up under Drummond's gaze. "Please don't be angry. I'll take good care of him, I promise. She'll come tomorrow morning, when it's light."

Drummond was thinking there might be worse fates, if you had a fever, than to be nursed by Sara Newton. He said only, "He's kind of restless. Worried about you. I said I'd show you where everything is."

She picked up a bottle of pills and a thermometer lying on the table. "He thinks I'm the nurse, doesn't he?"

Drummond nodded. Sara thought for a moment. "Better leave it like that for now. Is he likely to have a heart attack when he learns the truth?"

"I don't think so." He grinned, then turned for the door. "I have to check around downstairs. Better give me your keys and I'll put your car underground." She found her car keys and asked him to bring the spare pair of shoes she kept in a plastic bag under the passenger seat.

She took the pills and thermometer and looked along the hall at two facing doors at the far end, then enquiringly at the guard.

"The one on the left, ma'am." She had nice eyebrows, he thought. Not thick like a lot of girls. Elegant.

They weighed each other and Sara smiled. "Sara."

"I'm Mac. Nice to meet you, Sara."

*   *   *

Owen's eyes opened as she approached the bed. She shook down the thermometer. "Open, please." He opened his mouth and she inserted it, felt his forehead, and thought fleetingly of taking his pulse but remembered that she hadn't got a second hand on her watch. Instead she walked briskly round the bed and investigated the bathroom.

She found an empty glass, sticky with orange juice, and took it with her back to the bedroom. His eyes followed her. She went off down the hall and returned with a jug of water and a clean glass, putting them on the bedside table next to the pills.

He had a temperature of 103. She hid her disquiet, put the thermometer away and picked up the pill bottle.

"Did Drummond show you the guest room?" His voice was weak.

"Don't worry about that, Mr. Adair," she said, feeling her way into the role. "I'm used to finding my way round strange homes. Now. When did you last take one of these?"

Several hours ago, he thought. She gave him two pills, supporting his head while he drank some water. "Try to finish it. We must drink lots of water, Mr. Adair."

He managed most of the glass, then lay back and watched as she rearranged the big pedestal easy chair in the far corner to face the bed. She experimented with the swagged lamp behind, switched its trilight on low, then came back and turned off the bedside lamp.

He was staring fixedly at her. She tried a professional smile and pulled the covers up over his shoulders. "Everything's going to be just fine," she said.

Owen had passed the long hours waiting for his nurse in preparing himself for every eventuality, but this vision of lilac and legs, with a perfume of tantalizing delicacy, conformed to none of his imaginings. Fevered in body and mind, he suffered a perturbation of spirit.

"Did you bring a bedpan?"

Sara opened her mouth and the words flowed out. "You know, I was delayed with my last patient and I just rushed out of the house and left it on the kitchen counter." She gave him her best clinical look. "Do you want to go to the bathroom?" He shook his head. "Fine. When you do, I'll give you a hand."

She saw the whites of his eyes and he fell into a paroxysm of coughing, rolling on his side with a spasm of pain. She kicked herself mentally and whisked away to get the cough suppressant from the coffee table. The bottle had been opened and there was no spoon in sight so she searched hurriedly for one in the kitchen.

He was lying on his back when she returned but the coughing had stopped. She gave him a spoonful of the medicine, then capped the bottle and put it with the other things. She sat on the side of the bed, then stood up hurriedly. Mothers might sit on the bed but surely not nurses.

"Would you like to try a little soup, or some more juice?" A slight shake of the head. "Then I want you to relax and close your eyes and try to sleep."

He turned on his side and Sara went out, leaving the door ajar.

*   *   *

She ran her fingers over the satiny finish of the piano, a Baldwin grand. It curved round a fig tree and a black leather armchair facing out toward the city. The piano was angled to give the pianist a view of the living room or the city lights across the river. She'd seen them earlier, when she arrived, but now the driving snow blotted all light, even from the River Road below.

She drew the curtains. High up in the vaulted ceiling a paneled skylight extended the length of the living room. She shivered, looking up at it, and found the switch turning on the fire in the grate. That was better. She sat down on the big L-shaped couch and gazed at the painting over the fireplace, of an alpine lake under a summer sky, pleasure boats dotting the water and an elegant hotel behind. The execution was meticulous in its detail. In the left foreground was a crumpled sheet of thick letter paper, covered in fine copperplate writing.

Trompe l'oeil, she thought; you could almost swear that crumpled letter was real. She wondered what was written on it.

Her gaze went to the staircase and she decided to save the second floor for later. The main floor consisted of the living room and a dining area to the left of the fireplace. Off the hallway were a utility room, the kitchen, a toilet and the two bedrooms. She'd explored all the rooms, then returned to the living room, hung up her coat and straightened the mess on the coffee table, a large circle of glass on a marble pedestal. The bills she left in a neat pile. An early Christmas card was now sitting on the bedside table where he could see it if he woke.

The table sat on a Persian rug in the square formed by the fireplace, couch and two easy chairs upholstered in the same off-white fabric. Between them, a side table held a tall lamp with a dark-green glazed base.

Sara gazed pensively at the fire thinking over all she had learned today. Owen was a man of some achievement, an admirable man even. He could have been a thief or a murderer, it would have made no difference—she was eternally indebted to him regardless—but the reality was far more agreeable.

She leaned back on the chesterfield and decided she liked his taste in interior décor. She approved of the kitchen's granite counters and light oak cupboards, and she definitely approved of the bathrooms. The warm, textured quarry tile of Owen's bathroom impressed her favorably, as did the aquamarine marble of the guest amenities.

How awful, she thought, to be indebted to a man who went in for black tubs and red lighting; or exposed piping and Tiffany shades; or those vulgar verses some people liked to stick on the wall so that you couldn't avoid seeing them when you sat on the pot. Not that it would have lessened her gratitude—you couldn't hold a man's bathrooms against him when he'd saved your son's life—but even so. . . .

The door opened and Drummond returned. "I'll tell you, Sara, that's a four-star blizzard coming up out there." He gave her the car keys and the bag holding her shoes. Then he glanced up and she watched as he walked over and pressed a button on the wall near the dining room table, round the corner from the fireplace. A panel sighed into place over the skylight. "That's better, huh?" He sat down on the opposite arm of the couch. "I have to warn you, if you don't leave tonight, there's a chance you could be stuck here awhile."

Sara pulled off her boots and slipped her feet into the shoes. "Mac. Were you on duty the night he rescued Tom?"

"Yeah. How about I show you round?" He stood up but Sara made no move.

"How was he?" She waited, but Drummond was silent. "Did he walk home?" She looked at him straightly. "I'd like to know."

He sighed and sat down. He rubbed his chin. "Tell you somethin', Sara. I never seen anyone like that." He'd told no one of that night and it was a relief to speak of it now.

Owen had arrived home just after nine-thirty, he said, and when Sara stirred he cocked an eye at her. "The accident happened around seven, that right?"

She nodded. "How far is it, Mac? Do you know?"

"Three point six miles. I clocked it one day last week, to find out." They both thought about that, then Sara shivered. "Go on."

"I just happened to look up, and saw him on the first step and got ready to unlock the door. I must have looked away or something but when I looked back, thinking he was at the door, he was still in the same place. Just standing on the first step, swaying slightly. I couldn't figure it out. Couldn't see his face, he was looking down at the steps. Then his one foot came up and kinda eased down on the next step. By then I'm at the door. I went out and caught a-hold of him and he was like a block of ice. And grey!" He fell silent and shook his head, remembering.

"I asked him what happened and he mumbled something, couldn't make it out. I brought him in and I'm going too fast for him and he starts arguing, trying to pull away from me, all disoriented like. I finally got him up here and got his clothes off. You know something? His pants were frozen solid from mid-thigh down, stiff as boards."

He stared at his hands, brooding, then went on. "I saw a piece in the paper a couple days later, about hypothermia. The Cold-Hearted Killer, they called it." He glanced up at Sara and she nodded, recalling the article.

"They listed all the things you aren't supposed to do. Know something, Sara? I did 'em all. I did all the wrong things. Makes my blood run cold just thinking about it." He told her how he'd run a hot bath and given Owen a couple of shots of scotch. "It was two hours before I could get him into bed. He said he was okay and I left him."

He lapsed into silence again, then resumed: "He came downstairs three nights later, and—" he stopped abruptly and Sara thought she saw a flicker of anger cross his face, then he went on, "It was the same night that article came out and I showed it to him. Know what he did?" Sara shook her head.

"He laughed. I mean, he threw back his head and roared with laughter. Said I wasn't to know."

"You weren't, Mac."

He shook his head, unconvinced.

Sara laced her fingers together in her lap. "He caught pneumonia because of Tom. I wouldn't wish that on him for all the world. But since he has got it, I'm very, very glad I'm here, Mac. And if I have to stay 'til this storm passes I'll be even happier. I can't ever repay him, but at least I can help him now when he needs it."

Drummond regarded her silently. "He'll be okay, Sara," he said at last. "He keeps himself in good shape, works out in the pool and the weight room."

He took her off to the kitchen then, to explain the internal phone system. Owen had an account at a twenty-four-hour market half a mile away. Sara checked the fridge and made up a list. They phoned it in and after a lengthy consultation with the produce manager she decided on seedless grapes, a few bananas and a box of Mandarin oranges.

There was a half-eaten roast chicken in the fridge and Sara realized she was ravenous, so she carved some chicken and made a small salad. Mac refused to join her; he had his own dinner downstairs, he said. She decided chicken soup might be useful, so she phoned the market and added onion and carrots and celery to the list.

Owen was sleeping deeply when she checked on him, and though she didn't like the sound of his breathing she couldn't think of anything she could do for it. Then, returning along the hall, she noticed a large cardboard box against the living room wall and it proved to be a humidifier, a ten-gallon metal box on castors. Mac unpacked it and pushed it into the kitchen and they filled it with the kettle then rolled it, with some difficulty, along the hall to Owen's room and plugged it in. Sara felt better watching the mist rising from it, so they returned to the kitchen.

Over dinner, Sara learned about Mac's daughter Dolores and her entertainment-lawyer husband and their two kids in L.A., and Mac heard all about Tom and Janey, and then about Bob and Ronnie.

She found a piece of Brie for dessert, and a half-full bottle of Chardonnay. She phoned the market, catching them just as the order was being made up, and added a tub of Häagen-Dazs French Vanilla to the list. She caught Mac's grin as she replaced the receiver.

"I'll pay him for it if he doesn't eat any."

"I'd sure like to watch you doing that, Sara."

She sat down and poured a glass of wine. "There's something I'd like to ask you, Mac." She turned the stem of her glass between her hands, avoiding his gaze. "Please don't be offended but . . . you said he was waiting up for the nurse. Couldn't you have let her in?" She tried to keep her voice neutral.

He regarded her silently, then said, in a tone matching hers, "I offered, Sara, but he said he wanted to wait up."

There was something here she didn't understand but the guard had to go, so she followed him to the door and stood watching while he pushed the elevator button. "When do you go off duty, Mac?"

"Midnight, if Daly arrives. But I won't be going home. I'm here for the duration, like you."

"Where will you sleep?"

"We got a bed downstairs, off the office. I'll tell Daly about you, so call if you need anything. It's all part of the service." The doors opened and he stepped in and turned.

"Goodnight, Mac."

"Night, Sara. Sleep tight."

*   *   *

The wind howled round the penthouse walls. Sara dozed from ten until one, curled up in the armchair in Owen's room with a blanket over her. He grew progressively more feverish as the night wore on, throwing off his blankets, muttering and turning in bed. Sara made him drink as much water as she could. He was never more than half-conscious, returning each time into fitful sleep. His skin burned to her touch and she was afraid to think what his temperature must be.

He became exhausted by about five, and she left to make herself a cup of tea. When she returned he croaked for water and drank two full glasses. They both slept then, until about eight.

6

Sara returned from her shower to find that Owen had been to the bathroom while she was gone. He lay in bed watching the snow swirl in pockets near the lower corners of the window, and when she saw the bathroom light on and the door wide open and looked at him, he smiled slightly and she seemed to see a gleam of triumph in his eyes. She laughed and shook her head—she'd planned to use the opportunity to change his bed—and picked up his empty juice glass. He'd eaten a few grapes, she was pleased to see.

"What's your name?" he asked, when she'd taken his temperature. His fever was still high. She studied the thermometer, trying to recall Nurse Sheepshank's first name, then suddenly ceased to care. She'd ease into the truth, he had to know sooner or later.

"Sara." She pulled up a cane-backed chair and sat down, smiling at him reassuringly.

"Married?" His eyes fell to her ring finger.

"Widowed." Surely he knew now? But he turned on his side to see her more easily, and his expression remained the same. She began to talk casually of River Reach, the house, the kids, and wondered if he was listening, until she said, "You have a beautiful piano. I gave Tom one of those electronic keyboards last year and he just loves it."

"Any fool can play those things," he said impatiently, then asked, after a pause, "Who's Tom?" and she knew he hadn't made the connection.

"My son," she answered and went on to tell him about Tom and Janey and their school and their likes and dislikes.

His eyes began to close, first briefly then for longer moments, and finally she stopped talking and stood up, whereupon they opened and he gazed up at her and said, with certainty: "You're the mother. Aren't you."

She smiled and sat down again. "Yes, I am. Sara Newton." He didn't seem unduly disturbed by the fact. "I'm so glad to meet you. And I promise not to make a fuss."

He reached for the water glass and after he drank he drew himself up in bed and leaned back against the pillows, and she could see him trying to gather his strength.

"Please don't worry, Mr. Adair."

He shook his head. "Owen. I want you to listen carefully, Sara. What I did was nothing. I really mean this. Anyone would have done the same. You can't stand idly by when a child's in trouble. I assure you, it's no big deal."

"It is to me."

He shook his head. "I don't want you to feel all overburdened about this. Listen. You know what it was? It was a reflex. That's all. It was instinctive. No thought, no planning, just a reflex. So please, just forget about it."

Sara stood up and came to his side. She stooped and took the bottom sheet and gave it a firm tug, and he looked startled. "You know," she said, "I did consider that. I thought, I'm very grateful to him, more so than I can ever say, but after all, anyone would have done the same." She drew him up to a sitting position. "That's what I thought until I actually went down there." She plumped the pillows and lowered him back again. "I asked Ellie Griff—the woman who helped you that night? I asked her to show me exactly where it happened."

She pulled up the top sheet and blankets, straightening them, and walked briskly round the foot of the bed, still talking. "I climbed down that wall and crossed all the boulders right to the edge of the river. And that's how I know you're wrong, Owen." She busied herself with the bottom sheet, then the top.

"You had time to reconsider. You had time for second thoughts, climbing over those rocks. I certainly did. I stood there and listened, and I looked at that black, terrifying water, and I thought, I couldn't do this."

She returned to his side and looked down at him. "I couldn't do this, not for any child but my own. That's what I thought, and that's what most people would have thought." She tweaked the sheet and blankets over him, just so. "It took a brave, generous man to rescue my Tom," her voice trembled and she hardened it. "So don't tell me you acted instinctively," two quick pats to the blankets, "because I know better. Now go to sleep."

She picked up the empty juice glass. She thought he'd closed his eyes but he was staring past his nose at the neat fold of the sheet over the blankets. She left.

* * *

Sara finished reading the *Star* article and glanced again at the picture of Owen looking startled and unwell on the steps in front of the building. She raised her head to find Mac gazing at her.

"He's in pretty bad shape, Sara. You sure you can manage?"

"These people," she lifted the paper, "like to exaggerate. Doctor Spence would never have allowed him to come home if it was as serious as they make out. He's much better this morning, Mac." She forbore to mention her fear during the night. "He's being cared for by a fully qualified registered nurse under the direction of Dr. Henry Spence. It says so right here." She smiled at the guard. "And I'm under the direction of Nurse Sheepwash, so the chain of command remains unbroken."

She read the short interview by Monica Stephanopoulis while Mac pulled out a toothpick and chewed on it. He had his suspicions about Monica's entry, but he doubted he'd be able to prove them.

Daly, the night man, emerged from the office hauling a large mail bag. "They brought these as well. Letters for Mr. Adair." He glanced outside, a pink, cheerful little man. "I doubt they'll be bringing anything else." The *Star* van had come by at five a.m., but three feet of snow had fallen now with no sign of easing. The wind was still battering the building.

Sara opened the neck of the bag and pulled out a handful of letters, some of them opened. They were addressed to "Shane" or "The River Rescuer" c/o The *Star*, an accumulation of mail over the days following the rescue.

She chatted with the two guards a few minutes longer, then took the newspaper and sack of mail upstairs. Owen was asleep and the chicken carcass was simmering nicely, so she settled down with a cup of coffee at the kitchen table to sample the letters. The phone rang again, and Owen's voice kicked in after the first ring with a laconic "Back soon. Leave a message." Sara pulled a pad toward her and added the caller's name to the list.

Last night she had made a policy decision, given the *Star*'s penchant for muck-raking, to pretend she was the nurse if anyone called. She had discovered the answering machine when a phone rang upstairs and she'd run up to hear the message followed by Wendy's voice: "Sara? Pick up if you're there."

Sara had updated her on Owen's condition, and since the upstairs business line was unlisted, she had decided to move the answering machine downstairs. This morning she was glad she had.

When she had finished reading the letters from the *Star*, she returned upstairs with her coffee. She'd explored the second floor last night, finding a large study and a den lined with books, many of them biographies. In daylight she discovered that the den overlooked a roof garden, now shrouded in snow. The study lay under the same skylight as the living room, with a desk overlooking the river. A computer, fax and photocopier were ranged along the wall behind, with built-in bookcases extending waist-high round the other three walls.

She was halfway through *Merchant Princes,* which she'd started last night. It was easy to see why Wendy had liked it, and Sara was immersed in the world of commerce in the eighteenth and nineteenth centuries. She liked Owen's writing: it was easy and unpretentious, and flipping through back issues of the newsletter she glimpsed a wry, self-deprecating humor and thought of Tom, glad that he would soon meet this man.

*   *   *

Some businesses and schools opened that first morning, but all closed early, and most people stayed at home. They watched TV, listened to the radio and read the paper. Many of them thought about Owen while writing their Christmas cards or doing their Christmas baking.

One person who did not think of Owen was Tom Newton. He sat in the den flipping through the TV stations and feeling depressed. He wasn't aware of feeling depressed because you don't get into things like depression or introspection until you're ten or eleven, and sometimes not even then. He just felt kind of low, without knowing why.

He didn't want to play with his cousins in the basement. He didn't want to do much of anything. He'd spoken briefly with his mother when she called, after Aunt Ronnie and Janey. "How's my boy," she'd said and he could tell she was a bit worried so he answered "I'm okay, mum." He searched for something to make her feel better. "We had pancakes for breakfast. They were great." "Lucky you," she said, and went on to say she was stuck at the guy's place and Tom must mind his manners with his uncle and aunt and make sure Janey did, too, and Tom said he'd watch out. Then she said, "Mr. Adair seems like a nice man, Tom. I think you'd like him." Tom didn't much care, but felt he'd better not say so. "How about if I write him a thank you letter?" His mother was big on thank you letters, he knew. But she'd been kind of vague about that, so they left it up in the air.

Now he studied the videos in the wall unit, wondering what he was going to do stuck here forever. Kid's stuff mostly, then his eyes lit up. *Die Hard*. He'd seen that before, it was great. Then he heard a stamping sound from the kitchen, and heard his uncle's voice and he ran out to find that Uncle Bob had tried unsuccessfully to reach his clinic a couple of miles away. Now he was home and when Tom came into the kitchen he said, "How's my favorite nephew?" That always made Tom grin because he was the only nephew so he pretty much had to be the favorite. Uncle Bob faked a punch. "How about helping me shovel the walk?"

So Tom dressed up warmly and they spent the day doing important guy things outside and in the garage.

*   *   *

"If he'd drowned, would you have sued the city?"

Sara lifted her head and found Owen watching her curiously. *Now what?*, she thought. "Sued the city?"

He nodded. She turned away and emptied the saucepan of water into the humidifier. One more, she estimated, eyeing the water level, and returned to the bathroom to give herself time to think.

She was at her wits' end. Owen was in poor shape, but nothing she suggested seemed to please him. He wouldn't rest, he wouldn't eat, he didn't want to talk—or hadn't until now—but neither did he want her to leave. She'd looked in just before six to find him awake and watching the weather report on the TV built into the wall facing his bed. She hunted through his closet for a change of clothes while she took his temperature, finding a dark-blue tracksuit and a pair of socks. His temperature was down a degree, and she tried to tempt him with some banana and ice-cream while they watched the news. The gravest item concerned a school bus with twelve junior-high band students and their teacher, missing since three p.m. Emergency crews were out in force, hampered by the wind, driving snow and freezing temperatures. Owen had been more concerned about Sara, despite her assurances that she was just fine.

"I'm having a great time," she had said cheerfully. She relayed Wendy's best wishes and told him of his other calls: one radio and two TV stations, and a host of friends. He seemed surprised at all the calls, but uninterested. The sack of mail from the *Star* earned the same reaction, and when she offered to read some of the letters he shook his head fretfully. "Put them by the front door. Wendy can have them couriered to the office."

"Try to rest," she'd suggested, but he didn't want to rest. He suddenly began to cough, the dry hack that hurt Sara almost as much as it did him. She administered the cough suppressant, then remembered the humidifier. The water level was low and she used a saucepan to top it up. "This will help, Owen, it just takes time. But you can feel the difference in the air, can't you?" She disappeared into the bathroom for more water. "I gave Tom hell for going outside the skating area," she said as she returned. "I can't tell you how angry I was." He lay watching her, while the wind whined in the silence, and after her third or fourth trip he came out with his question.

She emptied the saucepan once more, then put it down and joined him, sitting in the cane-backed chair. "I suppose I might have sued the city if it was their fault. But it wasn't. It was Tom's." She eyed him. "Why do you ask?"

He was silent for a while. Finally, "It reminded me of a case I once read about, of a boy playing in a municipal dump, clearly signposted off limits. He suffered a spinal injury and his parents sued the city."

Sara considered. "I don't agree with that," she said finally. "People have to take responsibility for their own actions."

OWEN'S DAY

He shifted restlessly. "It's a matter of judgment, not just responsibility. People resent being exposed to risk. Ever notice? Even when it's their own fault, they resent it."

"Honestly," said Sara. "You'd think there was some unwritten constitutional guarantee against personal injury."

He looked at her in a pleased way. "Why, I think the same."

"I know." She slid down in the chair and propped her feet on the side of the bed. "I read it in one of your articles." He peered owlishly at her and she added, "I hope you don't mind. I've been reading quite a lot of your work."

"Are you really a nurse?"

She crossed her legs. Ronnie had once observed that Sara could look good in sackcloth and ashes, and even in Owen's tracksuit with the cuffs rolled up she managed to convey an element of style. "Don't I look like one?"

He nodded thoughtfully. "The kind who'd leave a bedpan on the kitchen counter." She laughed.

His mood seemed slightly lighter, and she considered how to keep him distracted. More than anything, she wanted to talk about the rescue, in the way that one relishes rehashing disaster once it is averted. But he'd shown no interest in the subject, and she decided to approach it in a roundabout way.

"You've made quite a study of risk, haven't you?"

After a while he said, "I believe we have to take risks if we want to get ahead."

One of his articles, "Of Mice and Men," had argued that banks and businesses were guilty of a caution so excessive it amounted to timidity. She mentioned this. "You said it's easier to make your mousetrap comply with the regulations than try to build a better one."

95

"Easier and safer." He gazed at her. "What do you do, if you're not a nurse?"

"I'm a secretary. So—are you saying businesses don't take enough risks?"

"It's much wider than that." He reached for his water glass. "Ever heard of Walter Wriston?" Sara shook her head. "He used to be chairman of Citicorp. A very wise man. He gave a speech once in Chicago, years ago. Made a big impression on me."

He drank some water, then Sara made him get down under the covers, worried about the cool moist air of the room.

"Was he the reason you specialized in banking?"

He thought this over. "I don't recall. My mother wanted me to be a lawyer."

Sara was amused. "So did my dad. He's one himself."

"Oh my." He gazed at her interestedly and she laughed.

"Was your mother a lawyer?"

"A dental assistant. She just wanted me to take up a good, well-paying profession. Law, medicine, dentistry, something like that."

"Tell me about this speech."

Owen marshaled his thoughts. "Nowadays, thanks to the media, we hear about every accident, disaster and infectious outbreak that occurs anywhere in the world. Wriston argued we're beginning to see disasters as the norm instead of abnormal. We're becoming too timid to take risks. Worse still, we insist on a fresh regulation to plug the dike every time a disaster happens, as though disasters could be eradicated like disease. And as he rightly pointed out, the eventual result of all these regulations will be no more progress, and worse still, no more freedom either."

"But disasters do happen."

"Sure they do. But issuing another regulation won't stop them. What it will do, what regulation has done, in my opinion, is impair our judgment." Sara looked skeptical and he went on: "We have this attitude that, well I've paid my taxes, government's supposed to stop this kind of thing happening, I don't need to think about it any more. And so we don't. We stop thinking for ourselves. But judgment's like a muscle. The more you exercise it, the better it gets. It has nothing to do with intellect or genius; so-called stupid people can exercise good judgment, just as intellectuals can behave like idiots."

That rang a bell and Sara recalled a piece about the collapse of Baring's Bank and Orange County's losses from ill-advised and risky investments. While there had been a general call for greater regulation of the financial markets, Owen argued that the losses under regulation would be far greater. When investors discover that a financial sector is government regulated, he explained, they don't exercise proper care. And when they get burned, they demand compensation. The article had been titled "Dumb and Dumber." She mentioned it now.

Owen nodded and turned on his side. "You develop good judgment through personal experience. Sometimes it's painful experience. Regulations and government guarantees and bail-outs act like a screen between us and our environment. They obscure these relationships and that impairs our judgment."

He turned again restlessly. Silence fell between them, save for the whistling of the wind round the windows. Studying him, Sara decided Ellie Griff was wrong. His features were too strongly defined to be handsome. But it was a good face, she thought, a face with character.

"You like taking risks, don't you."

"Not me. But I see the need for them."

"You've taken two big ones that I know of." He stared at her. "Tom. Your bank loan."

He nodded. "That was a calculated risk. I knew I had to do it to get ahead, you see?"

Sara was suddenly curious. "Rescuing Tom. Was that a calculated risk?"

"That was an impulse," he said irritably, "I told you. Look, I'm not talking about jumping in rivers. I'm talking about innovation and experimentation, about backing your own judgment and going out on a limb instead of cowering in a corner or sitting on your fanny waiting for someone to give you a guarantee."

"Risk is risk," said Sara thinly.

"I don't think so. Doing asinine things with a microwave or stepladder, then suing the manufacturer when you get hurt, isn't taking risks, it's acting like an idiot. We're becoming a nation of nincompoops."

"Oh? So the only good risks are business risks, like borrowing money? Saving children's lives is the act of a nincompoop?"

He became angry. "I'm just saying people these days exhibit lousy judgment and it's getting lousier. A driver who's drinking coffee and talking on his cell phone has nobody but himself to blame if he gets scalded. Or sideswiped."

Sara felt cold all over. "Sam—my husband wasn't doing either of those things." She stood up as the words pushed out of her. "And all the vigilance in the world couldn't have saved him. Bad things happen to good people, you know, through no fault of their own. It has nothing to do with judgment." She picked up the sack of letters and left.

*   *   *

Owen woke twice in the night, first at about one-thirty. Sara came out of a light sleep to hear a stifled groan. She crossed immediately to him, pulling the blanket over his shoulders. He turned and muttered something and she stooped: "What?"

"If I die—"

"You're not going to die, Owen."

"—just shut the door and go down to Drummond. He'll find you a place to sleep."

"You're not going to die." She wiped his face with a damp cloth. "If you die, I'll sue the city."

If she had wanted to distract him, she succeeded. His eyes moved to her face for a long moment, then his features relaxed in a faint smile. Eventually he lapsed once more into sleep.

At four she was wakened by coughing and found him lying on his side, his face distorted with pain. "Sh," she said, and made him take some medicine. "Try to relax, Owen."

He lay silent and gradually his breathing eased.

"Sorry I said that," he muttered. "About drivers."

"Don't be. I shouldn't have upset you."

"How long ago?"

"Two and a half years. And there's no need to be sorry for me. I've done more than enough of that myself."

She settled him comfortably, made sure his glass was filled and as she was about to return to the armchair, he spoke again. "You're lucky in one way."

She looked down at him.

"You had a clean grief. Not corrosive. You couldn't blame yourself."

*   *   *

Drummond opened the door of the reception room and Sara walked inside. Occupying nearly half of the second floor, it was dominated by two huge crystal chandeliers. Sofas and chairs were clustered around an ornate fireplace on one side, and in isolated groups near the windows. The furniture and the marquetry hardwood floor gleamed in the sullen afternoon light. He switched on the lights.

"Oh Mac! What a beautiful room."

"Mrs. Warburton gives it a workout. She does a lot of committee work, so she has her lunches and teas here, 'stead of upstairs. Suits her husband better that way."

Sara walked to a window overlooking a patio. The falling snow obscured the view, but Mac had said the grounds were terraced down to the river, broken by rockeries into small private enclaves of lawn where one could sunbathe alone or with others.

He'd shown Sara the pool and jacuzzis, the tennis and squash courts, and the weight room. Then they'd returned to the apartment building and come up to the second floor. She'd looked in on the movie room, just like a miniature cinema, the billiards room and a small, fully equipped office.

She walked over to examine four tapestry medallions along one wall before rejoining Drummond at the entrance. They visited the library next. "The management puts in a standing order for five copies of every book on the *New York*

Times best-seller list. After a couple of years, we just send four copies to a used book store and keep one."

Next door was the smoking room. "Some of the spouses don't like cigar smoke, so you get people down here of an evening. I like a cigar myself." He pointed to the ceiling. "We've got an extractor fan system in there, so the smell doesn't hang around."

It was its own private world, reflected Sara as they returned to the elevator. She had a cup of tea with the two guards, in the kitchen of the office behind the front desk. They were having an easy time of it: half the owners were away at this time of year, in the Caribbean or south Pacific. The guards would each get several days off once the blizzard passed; Dexter, Dunn and Driscoll would take over.

"Strange that all your names start with D," said Sara, and they exchanged a look. Daly was the first to speak.

"You ever heard of an intolerable irregularity, Sara?" He pronounced the words with care.

She gazed from one expectant face to the other, then said, somewhat mystified, "Do you mean, like constipation?"

They gaped at her, then both guards roared with laughter. She'd stolen the wind from their sails without even meaning to, and they loved it. Drummond slapped his knee while short, round Daly sat at the table shaking with mirth.

Sara waited patiently. They'd been sweet to her and she was glad to have amused them; no doubt they'd explain in their own good time.

"Consti—ha, ha, ha!" Drummond pulled out a handkerchief and wiped his eyes, while Daly tried to compose himself. Eventually they told her about the Alewayos. Mr. Alewayo was African, a retired diplomat of some kind; Mrs.

Alewayo was English; and they were both starchy. Their daughter had married an IBM executive and they'd moved to the Pointe to be close to her.

One night several years ago Mrs. Alewayo had phoned downstairs in the throes of some crisis, and during the course of the conversation she'd discovered that the guard's name was Simmonds. A few days later the management received a letter from Mr. and Mrs. Alewayo complaining about the intolerable irregularity in the security arrangements. The Alewayos did not wish to be unreasonable: Simmonds could legally change his name—they suggested Dristan or Donnelly; alternatively, he must be replaced with someone more suited to the position.

The management apologized for its oversight, transferred Simmonds (and Thompson, the other irregular) and replaced them with Dunn and Driscoll.

"The rich really are different, Sara," said Mac. "Whatever they want, they get."

"Betcha they don't get constipation," said Daly, and on that uproarious note Sara left them.

*   *   *

"Could I try some soup?"

"Of course you could!" Sara went away, pleased, and returned with a bowl of chicken soup on a tray. Owen sat up against the pillows and she fed him, because he was too weak to lift the spoon.

He'd slept all day and was feeling better. The blizzard was expected to abate some time tonight, according to the evening news, but the busload of children still hadn't been found. Owen was more concerned about Sara. She told him about her tour of the building and found herself telling him of her job and a little of her background, hesitantly at first for fear of tiring him. But he would ask a question whenever she paused, and gradually she relaxed and talked freely of her childhood and family. She told him about summer holidays and summer camp, and about her grandmother, the black sheep of the family, who had run off with a golf pro when Sara's father was ten, had subsequently remarried many times but was still known throughout the family as granny (now great-granny) Hargreaves.

She told him about high school and college, and her decision to forego the law; and about the Thanksgiving when her dad, roaring drunk, had carved the turkey with great tears rolling down his cheeks while he blamed himself and Sara's mother for the fact that she was a failure. "Kids don't stand a chance, he said, unless they come from broken homes. It toughens them for the real world." She stood up to demonstrate Bill carving the turkey under the influence, and Owen laughed.

He wanted to know what she did after finishing college, so she told him about Sam's practice and all the discussions they'd had about his setting up on his own, and how Sara had been fine with that as long as they had clear goals and a business plan. "He was doing his internship when we met, and he took his licensing exam just before our wedding. He stayed on one more year while I did my third year of business, and then we took the plunge."

She told him how family referrals had saved their bacon the first two years, with one renovation after another. And how she'd used the file room as a nursery when Tom came along, and about slim profit margins and cash flow problems.

Then Sam landed a commission for a sporting goods store and another one for a house, and they were off and running.

She fell silent, absorbed in the memories. "They said he never knew what hit him," she said at last. "There hadn't been anything in my life to prepare me for it. Some people have illness or even death to contend with from an early age, but I didn't. Sam and I had our ups and downs, in fact we nearly split up about eighteen months before he died, but we got past that." She looked up with a slight smile. "We thought we had it made."

"I didn't mean to suggest that disasters never happen."

"I know. You're just saying we shouldn't let them rule our lives. And I agree with you...." She picked up the tray and got to her feet.

"Will you come back?" asked Owen. "I mean, if you haven't got anything else to do."

She looked at his gaunt face and turned away. He'd saved her from her blackest nightmare and she wanted nothing more than to hold him to her heart and pour out her thanks. But he didn't want that, and she told herself that he was ill, she must be patient. So she prepared her dinner and took it in to his room on a tray, telling him he'd have to talk because she couldn't talk and eat.

So Owen told her about his years in London, of working for the *Financial Times*, and going stalking in Scotland as the guest of the chairman of one merchant bank while he was interviewing the chairman of another, also a guest. Owen's deadline meant he had to continue interviewing while they were out on the hills, and with his nose in the peat, he'd asked a question at the wrong time and the deer had taken flight. Both chairmen had glared at him and ignored him for the rest of the day.

"Over there, the deer are top dog. They're the same color as the hills, there's no trees to hide behind, and every time the wind shifts, they know exactly where you are. We spent four more hours crawling up hills and lying in bogs and waiting for the wind to shift before we finally got him."

He went on to tell her how, five years later, he'd presented himself before the host chairman, who'd taken one look at him and said, "You're the silly bugger who startled my stag." Owen had made a split-second decision. "It gets worse," he'd said. "I'm here to borrow a half-million dollars." This had evidently been the right approach, for the chairman had invited him to sit down and explain. "So it worked out all right in the end," said Owen to Sara.

She finished a mouthful of lamb chop. "No thanks to Frank Sharp."

Owen was philosophical. "You know, I should have seen that coming." She looked skeptical and he added, "Oh yeah. Desk-top publishing was just getting going then, with new software applications coming out every day. Sharp was saddled with huge payments on his IBM mainframe and his typesetting equipment, losing business all round. I should have seen it coming," he gazed absently at the TV, "but I had other things on my mind."

"Wendy mentioned that your fiancée left," Sara said gently. "That must have been a very bad time for you."

He was silent for a long while, and she began to regret her comment. Then he said, "The loneliness was frightening, you know?" Sara knew. He went on, "For a long time I thought she'd taken all the warmth and laughter out of my life."

105

Another silence. "I was wrong about that. She didn't take those things because she hadn't brought them." His smile held the memory of pain, Sara thought. "She was just— decorative. She was the most beautiful thing I've ever seen, Sara. Like a work of art. I don't usually go by appearances, but she was an exception."

"What did she do?"

"Do? Gloria? She didn't do anything. She just took." He looked wry. "We were very compatible, because I'm good at giving. You always blame yourself in these matters but people are what they are. Gloria was made to adorn a room, to give pleasure to the eye. That's what she did." He paused. "You'd probably call her a gold-digger. Ruby did."

Ruby Jablonsky had been one of the callers yesterday. The solitary card on the beside table was from Ruby, she learned. Owen had met the Jablonskys through their daughter, Betty. "We didn't have a lot in common, but I liked her, and her family. She was the youngest of five kids, the only girl. We used to go out there for dinner on Sundays. Families are interesting, don't you think?"

"In what way?"

"In their variety. Some families, you always take your shoes off when you enter the house. Some families always say grace before meals. Some go around hugging each other and saying 'I love you' all day long."

"Some do all three," Sara said gravely.

He considered. "I would have to say they're seriously dysfunctional," he said at last and she laughed and asked him about his own family. But Owen was an only child. His parents had died while he was in college. "They were much older than most parents, they married late. In our family," he went on, "people never dropped in. They visited, but only if they were invited. Now, the Jablonskys had an open-door policy. It used to amaze me. Ruby never could tell you how many were coming for dinner but if anyone extra turned up, she'd just throw another potato in the pot and hey presto."

*   *   *

On and on the storm raged. After two nights in the armchair Sara was longing to sleep in a bed and when Owen drifted off he seemed less restless than on the two previous nights. She looked in on him at eleven and decided to sleep in the guest room across the hall. She left the door open in case he called, woke up at three to total silence, and found him sleeping quietly. She returned to bed and slept dreamlessly 'til morning.

7

Sara wakened to a world of white and blue. The darkened living room seemed almost to have an air of suspense about it, like a theater as the lights dim, and when she drew the curtains and retracted the skylight cover the sunlight poured in, flooding into the corners, refracting off the glass and polished surfaces, and she pirouetted and made a deep curtsy to the fig tree, and laughed.

She looked out at the world. The River Road stretched below her, white and unmarked for miles. Even the river itself seemed harmless on this morning, and she went to make the coffee, catching the tail end of the news when she turned on the radio. Snowplows were out all over the city and suburbs, then in a recap of the lead item she learned that the school bus had been miraculously discovered, its occupants cold and hungry but otherwise fine. Sara glanced over the swing doors to the window beyond the dining area, and thought that nothing bad could happen on a day like this.

Owen claimed he felt much better and proved it by eating half an orange, five grapes and a piece of banana. She told him Nurse Sheepwash would be arriving later that day and he rolled his eyes. "Think she'll bring a bedpan?"

"Count on it," said Sara. He wanted to see his faxes and printouts of his e-mails, and she decided it wouldn't hurt and went to get them. The phone rang as she returned downstairs and incautiously, thinking it might be Ronnie or Bob, she answered it.

"Good morning, nurse," said a female voice. "Doctor Spence wishes to know Mr. Adair's condition."

"He's much better," said Sara. "I think the antibiotics have really kicked in. His temperature's down and he managed to eat a little breakfast."

"Could you give me his pulse and temperature readings for the past two days, please?"

Sara was taken aback. She hesitated, then said, "Look, I'm not the nurse. She'll be here later on."

"Who are you?"

"Sara Newton. Please don't be angry with—"

"Oh Mrs. Newton! That's so—gracious, I don't know what to say. How long have you been there?"

"I arrived just before the storm broke the other night. The nurse was held up, so I stayed to help."

"Goodness me! Aren't you wonderful! Did Mr. Adair give you any trouble?"

Sara looked out through the dining room window. It didn't matter now. "The first night was frightening. He had such a high fever, and I felt so isolated." The nurse was sympathetic and Sara unburdened herself further, then finished: "But he's much better now. I said he could move to the living room couch for a while later on. Would you ask the doctor if that's all right?"

"You must keep him in bed, Mrs. Newton. You can't fool around with double pneumonia."

Sara was suddenly doubtful. "Is that Nurse Jensen?" She remembered the name from the *Star* article.

"Nurse Jensen hasn't made it in yet. I'm assisting the doctor until she arrives. Now, Mrs. Newton?"

"Yes?"

"It's none of my business, but I wouldn't tell the press who you are. You know what they're like."

"I'm not going to," said Sara. "I'll just pretend I'm the nurse and refer them to you. But I don't think they'll be interested in Owen, do you? With all the storm news?"

The nurse agreed she was probably right, and Sara rang off and took Owen's messages along to the bedroom.

At the offices of the *Star*, Monica Stephanopoulos and Flick Jackson put down their phones. Jackson grinned: his hunch had paid off. He'd tried Sara's home without success ever since the Adair interview and had broached the matter with the editor this morning. Seated on the edge of Jackson's desk, arms folded, Hoch gazed placidly at Monica.

"You nearly lost her on fooling around with double pneumonia," he said in mild reproach. Monica gave him an unfathomable look and walked off. Hoch picked up Jackson's pad and studied his notes of the conversation.

*   *   *

Owen spent a pleasant morning dealing with his messages. With Sara's help he faxed his European and Asian stringers concerning further data for the January issue, and sent instructions to the agent handling his negotiations to purchase a small book publishing company whose backlist Owen liked. When they'd finished, he told Sara to submit a job application and he'd see what he could do.

"Stick it in your ear," she said sweetly and went to make his lunch. She was trying to decide between tuna and egg when she looked up to see him passing the kitchen entrance in his bathrobe. He refused to return to bed, and rather than stand there arguing she helped him through to the living room. He sank down on the L-shaped couch and his expression changed as he looked up at the wall above the fireplace. Festooned across it, strings of greeting cards fell in waves from near the ceiling down to the painting of the alpine lake.

"They're from your admirers," she said. "They wanted to thank you. And so do I."

"We settled all that." He seemed at a loss. "Where did you get that string?"

She'd sought Mac's help yesterday and he produced the box of Christmas decorations they used for the lobby. She found just what she wanted: a ball of thin green twine and a box of tiny red clothespins. She pegged the cards to the twine, and Mac brought her a stepladder so she could put up the strings.

"What do you think?" She wanted him to approve.

"Did you keep the envelopes?"

"What do you want with the envelopes?"

"I have to thank them."

"No, you don't, Owen. You've already done your part. They wanted to thank you. Most of them wrote letters." She nodded toward a pile of letters on the dining room table.

Owen was more interested in his painting. He asked her opinion of it, and without waiting for an answer began to tell her of his explorations in the world of art. He was a newcomer to the field, having become interested only last year after visiting the Rijksmuseum in Amsterdam.

Sara listened politely. She had loathed the picture since discovering the contents of its crumpled letter.

"It's a style called *trompe l'oeil*," explained Owen. "That means deception."

"Really? How interesting." If she had been candid, she would have said, "This is a timid piece of work, not at all worthy of a man who saves small boys from certain death."

"In a way it follows in the tradition of the Dutch still life. But *trompe l'oeil* is mostly an American form. Edward Harnett was a leading exponent a hundred years ago." He turned to her, absorbed in his subject. "He was enjoined from painting currency by the Secret Service because his work was so life-like they said it qualified as counterfeiting."

"Fascinating," Sara said.

"You don't like it." He was disappointed.

"The detail is really impressive."

"You've read the letter?"

"Mm." The letter, she had discovered, had been written by a nineteenth-century debutante touring Europe with her mother. The picture held only the second page and she'd read it twice.

"Come on, I can tell you don't like it."

Sara gave him an unreadable look and began to quote from the crumpled sheet: "—his lungs are weak and so we will stay here for another month before returning to Boston. Gaston knows all about you, dear John—" her voice turned treacly and Owen laughed, "—and he *so* looks forward to meeting you— oh!" She broke off. "How could you buy a painting of a dear John letter? I was so angry I nearly fell off the stepladder."

"Then you could have sued me," said Owen deadpan but she refused to be sidetracked. "Forget the contents," he said. "Look at the technique. You can tell he was angry by the way the paper's crumpled. That's thick rag paper. Look at the creases in it."

Sara was unimpressed. He tried again.

"Shall I tell you what happened when they returned to Boston? They came down the ramp and John was there to meet them. He shoved her in the harbor and socked Gaston, then he tipped his hat to her mother and walked away."

Sara's mood improved. She regarded the picture more kindly then asked, "Is it possible her name was Gloria?"

This had never occurred to Owen and he gave it serious consideration. "It wouldn't surprise me," he agreed at last. Sara laughed and went to the dining table, returning with a handful of letters. "These are proposals, some marriage, some what I would have to call other. Lie back and enjoy." She dropped them in his lap and returned a few moments later with a blanket to find him raising an eyebrow at one of the more lurid propositions. She spread the blanket over his knees and disappeared into the kitchen.

Owen should never have left his bed that morning, and he would pay for it after Sara left, relapsing into high fever for two more days. Now he proceeded to compound his error. She had just lowered an egg into a saucepan of boiling water when she heard a mellow golden ripple of sound and she lifted her head and looked out over the swing doors at the blue sky to the strains of "Around the World in Eighty Days." She stood entranced, then her feet moved of their own accord and she drifted out into the dining room with a spoon in her hand, gazing out at the sky, wanting to embrace the world, then waltzed over to the piano and listened as though in a dream.

He changed suddenly into "Up a Lazy River," a rollicking, good-humored river, and Sara laughed and sat on the back of the couch. After one chorus, the river became "Blue Skies" and she waved the spoon and suddenly remembered the egg.

She'd forgotten to put the timer on, but it must have been boiling for ten minutes, she thought, so she fished it out and put in another as he began "Night and Day." She went back out to listen, and after a chorus he changed abruptly to a saucy "Love for Sale," played in the upper octaves, left hand ranging up and down the keyboard, and Sara remembered the second egg.

That, too, was hard boiled, judging by the water level. He'd switched to "Old Man River" by now, long flowing passages, and she wondered suddenly at his selection and went back out. But Owen was absorbed in the music, going with the flow, taking whatever came along.

This wasn't getting her anywhere, she told herself, and went off to change his bed, keeping the door wide open so she could listen. He played some more Cole Porter, then a selection of Broadway show tunes, Kern and Berlin and Rodgers and Loewe.

She was peeling the eggs when he began "Music of the Night" from *Phantom*. Sara loved that song. It was so wistful it caught at your heart, and she wandered back into the living room and leaned on the piano, gazing outside as she listened. Towards the end, she caught sight of his drawn face and remembered her responsibilities.

"What on *earth* do you think you're doing?"

He stopped playing and she came round and helped him over to the couch, berating both of them. "I should have my head examined, and so should you."

"Sorry," he said, and sank with relief into the cushions. She covered him with the blanket. "Where did you learn to play like that?" She was still angry, and it came out as an accusation.

"Lessons."

"Well there's no need to show off." He grinned and she made a face at him. "How long for?"

"The lessons? I started when I was six, stopped at sixteen."

She sat down. "Did you hate them?"

He nodded. "I think everyone does, unless they're Mozart."

"Was anyone else in your family musical?"

"No. Unless you count my dad used to play the mouth organ."

"Don't move." She went away and came back with the eggs in a bowl, a piece of toast on the side. "Did you learn classical music?"

"Of course. It's the only way." He shook his head at the food but she persisted and he ate a mouthful or two. "You learn the precise fingering for your Bach Preludes and your Scarlatti and so on and it's like being in a cage. But eventually it sets you free."

Sara thought about this, then said deliberately: "Do you think I should make Tom take lessons?" She'd been wanting to talk about Tom for three days. "He took them for a year when he was seven and complained so much about missing hockey that I let him stop. But he's awfully good with his keyboard, Owen, he really is."

Owen lay back against the cushions. "I'll sometimes hear a piece of music and something about it is just—perfect, so perfect that it's the purest, most piercing pleasure." He looked at her and she nodded. "So, now and then I'll be playing and something new will just flow out onto the keys."

"You mean, you compose your own music?"

He shook his head. "I just make things up. But I'll sometimes get that same feeling from something I created." He was silent for a moment, then he added: "That's what the lessons did for me. Gave me enough to derive great pleasure from music. That's a wonderful thing."

"Do you often play for others?"

"Oh sure."

How wonderful, she thought, to be able to entertain like that, then heard him say,

"Actually, that's a lie." He looked wry. "I suffer from stage fright. That's why I didn't do better on my exams. My hands would shake so badly."

*   *   *

The River Road was a ribbon of brown and Sara knew it was time to go. Nurse Sheepwash hadn't arrived but Bob was driving the children home and she wanted to get there before him. Mac had promised to bring her car round and she turned away from the living room window and put on her coat. She left Owen's security card on the kitchen counter with a note for the nurse and walked along to his bedroom to say goodbye. He opened his eyes as she sat down on the edge of the bed.

"I'm leaving now, Owen. You be nice to Nurse Sheepwash and I'll come and see you again in a couple of weeks." She smiled at him.

"Will you do something for me, Sara?" He reached over to the bedside table.

"Of course. Whatever I can," Sara replied, a little surprised because he'd asked her for so little.

He held out a check and she took it mechanically. "You take this and enjoy it. I can't thank you enough for what you—."

She stood up abruptly as though stung. "That's ridiculous," she said. The check fluttered to the floor and there was hurt and anger in her look, and scorn. She turned on her heel and walked out.

Owen stared at the door. He heard the living room door click shut. He turned on his side and closed his eyes, but he could still see that look. It would haunt him through his fever in the nights ahead.

*   *   *

Sara walked out of the elevator and along to the lobby. She gave Drummond and Daly a brilliant smile. "I'm leaving," she said. "Thanks for everything."

"Bye Sara, take care," said Daly but she'd already turned away.

"Here's your keys," said Mac.

She tugged at the door handle just as Daly pressed the unlocking mechanism, and it jammed. Sara's hand fell and she stepped back. Mac reached her as the door clicked and she opened it and went out into the brilliant sunshine, the guard following.

"What is it, Sara?"

She reached her car and turned to face him. "He tried to pay me. Can you believe that, Mac?"

He regarded her, a faint smile on his face. "Yeah. I'm real sorry. I was hoping maybe you'd make him see sense." He looked out toward the river. "He won't take anything, Sara. He doesn't seem to know how. He just knows how to give."

Sara lifted her face to the sky. "What a beautiful, beautiful day." She took her keys from him and half-turned. "Have you ever heard him play, Mac?"

Drummond shook his head. Sara's eyes suddenly filled with tears. "Aw, honey—," he said, and put his arms round her.

"I'm just tired, that's all."

Neither of them noticed the photographer stationed by a tree near the river sidewalk, and he got several excellent shots.

*   *   *

Bob arrived with the children soon after five and with a honk and a wave left immediately for home. Janey was full of the indignities she'd suffered at the hands of her older cousins and Sara was kept busy feeding the two of them, then doing a wash and settling them for bed.

After she'd tucked Janey in and settled her and kissed her goodnight, she went in to Tom and heard an account of his activities the past three days.

"You had fun with Uncle Bob?"

"Yeah, he's great." He lay on his side and their heads were level as Sara knelt next to his bed. "When do I have to meet that guy, mum?"

"We'll see. Maybe I'll invite him for dinner when he's better."

"Mum? Do you still miss dad?"

"We're always going to miss dad, darling." She paused, then went on, "He's watching over us, Tom. But if we do foolish things, we can't expect his help. All we do is make him unhappy. Do you understand?" What was going on inside that head, she wondered, until finally Tom nodded. She stayed a little longer then kissed him goodnight and went to the door. "Sleep well." She turned out the light.

She wondered as she made up the lunches whether there was any point inviting Owen for dinner. He didn't want to be thanked, and she no longer felt like thanking him. He'd displayed no interest in Tom, had only once referred to him directly—and then only to prove some hypothetical point. "If he'd drowned, would you have sued the city?" *Cold-blooded bastard*, she thought, slicing through a sandwich.

She remembered the calls from his friends. She was astonished that he still had any, given her own experience and Mac's. Drummond had driven her home, after arranging with Daly to pick him up when the replacement guards arrived. Sara had given him a beer while she changed with relief into jeans and a sweater. Then she'd made a cup of tea and listened as he told her of his friendship with Owen.

"He used to come down of an evening and sit in the office with his feet up on the desk and we'd talk. Mostly I talked. Owen's a great listener, maybe you noticed?" Sara nodded. "He really listens, know what I mean? He doesn't just go on cruise control."

Mac was lonely, she suddenly realized, his only child far away. She suppressed a surge of anger at Owen's behavior.

"He used to bring me things. Nothing much, just little stuff. Like I always use those small post-it notes on my clipboard, he brought me a couple blocks of those once. And a key ring, when I was complaining about how mine was too small. Stuff like that. He'd always bring something back from his travels."

He grimaced. "I hate buying gifts, Sara. But I got to thinking I'd like to take Owen to lunch one day. Figured I'd take him to Barney's. You know it?" Sara nodded. Barney's was a popular tavern on the river, well regarded for its corned beef sandwiches.

"He was real tickled about that, and we had a good time. Then he picked up the tab. I was surprised at first, and I said no way, this was my deal but he insisted. 'Forget it, Mac,' he said, 'it's nothing.' It wasn't nothing to me. When I saw he was really going through with it, I just got up and left."

"Obnoxious oaf."

Owen had come down that evening to apologize. "He told me he didn't mean to do it, but something about me paying just didn't sit well with him. I said he was always givin' me things, and he said that didn't count."

"Didn't count?"

"Yeah, because he liked doing that." He paused, then went on: "He wanted to do it again sometime, go out. Promised he wouldn't try and pay. But I dunno. . . ." He looked down at the beer can between his hands and was silent.

"He should have known better. You were in an impossible position as an employee."

He gave her a grateful look. "I know. I just didn't see how it could work between us." He fell silent, then told her about the night Owen came downstairs after the rescue. "He brought me a box of Havanas and I hit the roof. I told him I nearly killed him, said no way was I taking anything from him and we both got mad."

He stared moodily outside. "He's a fine man, Sara," he said at last. "And I reckon what he did, saving your son, that was about the bravest thing I ever heard of, and I've heard and seen a few. But he don't seem to know how to take, and that's wearin'." Later, as he pulled on his coat before leaving, he

121

looked at Sara and gave a short laugh: "I dunno, I only got a box of cigars. He gave you fifteen hundred dollars. Maybe that's a compliment."

"Not to me," retorted Sara, tartly.

How could anyone be so crass, she wondered as she undressed for bed. Watching the late news, mostly given over to the school bus rescue out in the suburbs under the clear bright sky, the beauty of that morning returned to her, and she felt another surge of anger at him for blackening her day.

The teacher had made the kids march up and down the aisle of the bus to keep warm, and had climbed out periodically to clear the snow from the tailpipe and idle the engine to keep the bus warm until they ran out of gas. Last night, he had shoveled a small space outside the door, and at first light two trumpets and a Grade Seven piccolo prodigy had climbed out and practiced their Christmas concert repertoire.

Sara saw the teacher and children tucking into bacon and beans and hash browns at the road crews' maintenance depot, then the picture cut outside to a leathery faced man standing next to a snowplow.

"I heard this noise over the engine, wasn't a knock, couldn't figure what it was. Stopped plowing, could still hear it. So I switched off an' opened the door. It sounded like one of them pipes, the kind they use to play 'Dixie'?"

"It was a piccolo," said the interviewer.

"Yeah? Anyway, I stood on the seat an' just listened an' it was the prettiest sound I ever heard." He lifted his face to the sky in remembrance. "I'm lookin' over this pure white snow under a blue sky an' I'm thinkin'—," he gave a deprecating grin, "this is God playin' a song." He paused and grunted a laugh. "Then all of a sudden I hear pom tiddley om pom? An' I said, hold on, Pete, God wouldn't go pom tiddley om pom, so I look around and about a quarter mile up ahead on the right, stuck in the middle of a field, I see the top of this bus."

The camera cut to the kids eating breakfast and closed in on two fourteen-year-old boys. "What were you playing out there?"

"Joydthworld," muttered one of them, and the other added, "Dunno what he was playing." They shot dirty looks at the twelve-year-old piccolo player, one Sigmund Smith. Black button eyes in a paper-white face. "I was improvising," he smirked, then added, involuntarily, "It just came out." He suddenly looked very young and nearly human.

"Little brat," Sara laughed unwillingly, and wondered, as she switched off the TV and went to bed, if music always sprang from such obnoxious sources. She turned out the light, reflecting that the only good thing about the day was the total absence of any news item about Owen Adair.

8

"A Mother's Anguish," screamed the *Star*'s headline, over a picture of Sara being comforted by Mac.

Trish was talking excitedly to Pam when Sara arrived at the office. "...and I'm going, 'Of *course* I know her. She works in my office' and she's all 'Are you serious?' And this man leans over and says, 'They're having an affair' and I'm ready to sock him and the bus stops and—" she glanced round. "Sara! *You saved his life!*"

Sara hung up her coat. "I did not save his life," she replied shortly. She was tired of saying it: her mother and Beth Elwing next door had both phoned this morning.

Trish stared at her. "You must have. Why would they say you saved his life if you didn't?"

"You didn't do him any harm being there," said Pam reasonably, while Sara bent over Trish's desk and read the short bulletin below the picture:

> ... Adair's nurse was prevented by the storm from reaching the luxury apartment complex on South River Road. Mrs. Newton battled Adair's high fever and her own exhaustion in the fight to preserve his life from the pneumonia that struck him down after his courageous rescue of Tommy Newton. "I just

don't know what I'd have done if he'd died," she said.

Adair's condition is described as serious but stable.

"How come you were crying?" asked Trish, handing her several messages.

"I had something in my eye." Both Beth and her mother had swallowed this, but Trish's reproachful gaze made her add, "I was just overtired, that's all."

"I guess," said Trish happily. "Who wouldn't be?"

Sara poured a cup of coffee and retired to her desk, leafing through the messages. Farraday came out and bent over her solicitously.

"You should maybe stay home and rest up, Sara."

"I'm fine, Mike!" She repressed her annoyance.

"You did a great job," he went on, as the phone rang. "He's going to be okay, isn't he?"

Trish called, "It's for you, Sara." Her eyes sparkled with excitement. "Hanna Magnussen from the Noon Hour."

The Noon Hour, Sara soon discovered, would love to have her on their show, could send a car for her, how about it? Sara protested that she really couldn't, she had a job to do and a backlog of work. After a short argument, the producer conceded defeat gracefully, and asked about Owen's condition. Sara said he was just fine.

"He's quite a guy, isn't he?" Sara agreed that he was.

"We're finding a big increase in civic awareness because of what he did. Speaking personally, I'd like to thank you."

Sara disconnected feeling churlish and ungrateful. Moments later, Trish called: "It's Flick Jackson."

Sara picked up her phone. "You listen to me, you—"

"I just called to find out if you're feeling better today, Sara. We were all worried."

This took her breath away, but not for long. "You deliberately misled me yesterday!"

"Me? I didn't speak to you—"

"You know what I mean. One of your sidekicks. That Monica female, probably."

"Sara, the public has a right to know if Owen's going to pull through. You did a great job there—"

She cut him short. "You never even told me he had pneumonia in the first place. Don't call me again, and don't expect any cooperation from me in future. I think you and your newspaper are disgraceful and my biggest regret right now is that I don't have a subscription to cancel." She disconnected sharply and became aware of her audience of three. "They really annoy me," she added, unnecessarily.

Trish turned back to her phones. "I think it's great. He saved Tommy's life and now you saved his." Sara bowed her head on her arms and Pam laughed.

The phone calls continued throughout the day. Trish was instructed to say that Sara was fine but busy right now, and to take a message. Looking through them after lunch, Sara found one from Ruby Jablonsky. She decided to return the call that evening, at home, then Trish called over: "It's Mrs. Jablonsky again."

Sara hesitated too long and Trish put the call through.

"Hello, Mrs. Jablonsky."

"Ruby, honey. Would you meet me for lunch, Sara? I'd like to know how Owen is, and that nurse won't tell me a thing."

"He's just fine, Ruby. I mean, he'll be fine in a few weeks. He's in no danger."

But Ruby persisted and in the end, reluctantly, Sara agreed to meet her, and they fixed a day.

Bob called that evening, after dinner. "You should have told me, kiddo. I didn't realize it was that serious."

"It wasn't, Bob! Honestly, he's fine now."

"Why were you crying, then?"

"I wasn't crying. I just had something in my eye."

She heard him repeat this, then Ronnie came on the line.

"Is that what you've been telling people?"

"Don't start with me, Ronnie."

"I'm not starting with you. I just want to know. Did he try to molest you?"

It was the first laugh Sara had enjoyed all day.

"That's better," said Ronnie. "So tell me what really happened."

"He tried to pay me."

"You're kidding. How much?"

Sara told her.

"Fifteen hundred dollars? For what?"

Sara explained.

"Is that all? I'd have done a lot more than that for fifteen hundred. Go *away*, Bob. Sorry, Sara. Well, I don't understand. Why cry? Didn't he sign the check?"

"Oh stop it."

"For pete's sake, the guy's loaded. If he wants to throw some of it your way—"

Sara erupted. "Owen Adair is a maladjusted prima donna who thinks everything has a price, and I frankly don't care if I never hear his name again!"

She banged the phone down. It rang moments later and she picked it up. "Now what?" she snapped, but it was Tug Sheppard phoning to thank her for saving Owen's life.

*   *   *

December moved into double figures, and Sara's life became hectic. She steadfastly refused to accommodate the media, but friends who, at her own request, had crossed her off their lists for the past two years became insistent, and she accepted invitation after invitation, to lunch, to dinner, to parties.

She became inured to the inevitable questions about Owen, responding briskly and brightly and changing the subject as soon as she decently could. After a few days, she was able to view him dispassionately. He was rich, successful and remote, preoccupied with the rarefied world of international finance, the unwilling agent of Tom's rescue—for which she was grateful—but a man with whom she had nothing in common. She had discharged her obligation to him; as far as she was concerned the matter was ended, and as the Christmas season picked up pace he receded further and further in her mind. Her days were filled with social engagements and Christmas shopping, with work sandwiched in between. She rediscovered the pleasures of partying: at a Christmas bash hosted by a firm of architects who had been colleagues of Sam's, she found herself flirting outrageously with one roving unattached male and laughed inside because she was having a ball.

On the fourteenth, she dutifully met Ruby Jablonsky for lunch as agreed, combining it with shopping at Ellis Mall. They had arranged to meet at a garden restaurant on the second floor of the mall. Sara was ten minutes late and came off the escalator burdened with carrier bags, scanning the outside tables. A hand waved in the corner and she walked over.

Ruby was a plump woman with faded blonde hair, wearing what Sara uncharitably thought of as a K-Mart jersey suit, and loaded with gold: bracelets and watch, rings and several chain necklaces. She had a vodka tonic and a cigarette, and shrewd blue eyes.

"You look just like your picture, Sara," she said as Sara put the bags on a chair. A waitress materialized with a speed alien to Sara's experience and she ordered a glass of white wine. "Just leave the menus," Ruby told the waitress, "we'll order in a minute."

"She'll never return," said Sara, taking off her coat.

"You've been through a lot, honey," said Ruby with a smile.

"Not really," said Sara brightly. "The press exaggerate."

Ruby sipped her drink without comment as the waitress returned with Sara's wine. Then she went on: "It was a real thrill for us to find out how well Owen's done. When we met him his business was just beginning to make money, and now look at him."

Sara had resolved to keep her opinion of Owen to herself, so she settled in to describe his condition and the Pointe in detail. Ruby's pleasure was unfeigned. "Wait 'til Sol hears this. My, he's done well for himself." They consulted the menus and ordered, and she went on to talk of her children and grandchildren, one anecdote leading easily into another, and slowly Sara relaxed. When the waitress came with their orders she discovered why the service was so good. The Jablonskys owned the Kitchen Korner chain. She knew it well—there was a store in Ellis Mall—and she recalled Ruby's Christmas card. "You've got a baker's dozen and Sol retired this year and Mike runs the business."

"That's right," said Ruby, pleased. "Aron's in charge of purchasing. I stopped working five years ago, but I thought we were going to have one of those palace revolutions if Sol didn't get out soon."

Sara began to warm to this untidy, unpretentious woman and they discussed the perils and pleasures of family businesses. Ruby was impressed with her education. "I never went to college, Sara. I had to wing it the whole way." They finished lunch and she lit a cigarette. "I wish Betty could have met you. I always hoped she'd end up running the company. I never said that to Sol, of course, but it used to irritate me the way he just assumed Mike would take over, Mike and the other boys. I told Betty, you can do anything you want to, honey, and sure enough," she finished wryly, "she did. She's married with four kids." She noted Sara's amusement and shook her head with a reluctant laugh.

Betty had met Owen two years after Gloria left him. "Sol and Mike thought he was a keeper, but I never did. Betty was good therapy for Owen, but she never understood him." They had only gone out for a few months, and the Jablonskys hadn't seen Owen since, but they still remembered him with affection. Sara discovered they were a busy, productive family, straightforward in their likes and dislikes, honest according to their lights, and loyal. Nothing was too much trouble for people they liked, and they liked Owen very much.

"I see his company is still in the same building. He was having trouble with the building inspector when we met him, something about his inventory being too heavy. Vern fixed that for him." Vern was the youngest Jablonsky son, a lawyer. "Clar helped him out with his accounting software, and Mike took him for a round of golf at the club one weekend to introduce him to a couple of contacts." She turned to Sara. "The Jablonskys aren't good for much except hard work, everyone's always got five things going at once. You know what they say, it's easy to get ahead if you know the right people?" Sara nodded. "We don't. We just know a lot of people. But it usually works out the same in the end. The thing is, it's easy to help out that way, especially if you like someone."

"He must have been grateful," said Sara, curious to know how Owen had reacted. Ruby studied her cigarette thoughtfully.

"He wasn't so much grateful as amazed. He was just amazed that anyone would do anything for him. Sol told him it's no trouble, we'd do the same for anyone."

"Your card really gave him a lift," Sara said. "He told me a little about you and your family. It was obvious he was very fond of you all."

Ruby was pleased. "We're such a ramshackle bunch, I used to wonder what he made of us. Everyone talks at once, do you know what I mean? Except for Clar, he's the quiet one." Clarence was the third son, an accountant. "There's always one you worry about, isn't there? Clar wasn't going anywhere with that firm, but he'd never say anything. Then Owen sat down with him one evening and Clar talked and talked. I guess it went to his head because he set up on his own soon after, and never looked back."

She added reflectively, "I phoned Owen about six months later, just to let him know. He wouldn't take any credit. He'd just listened, he said, nothing more. You must have asked the right questions, I told him, but he said that's his business, asking questions."

The waitress came and they ordered coffee. After she'd taken their plates, Ruby studied the younger woman. "Owen's a generous man, Sara. Did you know that?"

Sara avoided her glance. "He told me he was good at giving." She mentioned Gloria Lake and Ruby snorted. "Pond scum, honey. Do you know what I mean? It looks pretty in the right light, but it just lies there doing nothing." Sara laughed as she went on: "We had a line of arborite once called Morning Lake. Green with flecks of gold in it. I always called it Gloria Lake myself."

Silence fell, and they gazed out at the crowded restaurant and mall. Finally, Ruby said, "Mind telling me why you were, uh, anguished, honey?"

Reluctantly, Sara told her. Ruby was surprised. "He paid you? Money? That's not like Owen at all." She gave Sara a penetrating glance, then shifted her gaze to a nearby potted plant. "What you have to understand is that Owen loves giving gifts. It's kind of a habit of his."

Sara wasn't really interested. "What do you mean, a habit?"

"He just is always giving things. Or he always used to. Every time he came to dinner, every time we did anything for him. It drove Sol up the wall and that's why I finally said something. I sat Owen down at the kitchen table one Sunday evening and had a heart to heart with him. I told him, listen honey, we think of you as one of the family, you don't have to bring presents. Oh it's nothing, he said. Besides, he enjoyed doing it." She glanced at Sara. "He did, too, you could see that. I think that's why he loved Gloria. She let him give to his heart's content. Plus he'd been brought up that you always take a gift when you visit other people's homes. Did he tell you anything about his family?"

Sara reflected. "He was an only child. His mother was a dental assistant. I don't know what his dad did."

133

"He had an appliance store in Minton. His mother was kind of rigid, if you want my opinion." She sipped her coffee. "They never had much money when Owen was growing up. I'm not sure why, with both parents working like that. But I never got a chance to find out, because he and Betty broke up and we never saw Owen again."

The waitress brought the bill and Ruby opened her bag, looking for her wallet. "I'm guessing Owen feels pretty low about that check, honey, but you don't want to hold it against him. Everyone's got faults. I used to tell Sol, Owen's gifts don't matter, what he did for Clar—that's the only gift that matters." She glanced at Sara. "I guess you can relate to that, can't you?"

That's all very well, thought Sara mulishly as she drove back to the office, but I'm tired of feeling grateful to a man who won't even discuss my son, and my son's life and what it means to me. To hell with him, she concluded as she pulled in, twenty minutes late and hoping Mike would be later. She was disappointed: all three were waiting for her in high anticipation.

"Guess what." Farraday grinned.

"Did you hear the radio?" Pam took one look at Sara and answered her own question. "She hasn't heard."

"Heard what?"

"You'll never guess who called," said Trish, eyes sparkling.

*   *   *

"The most wonderful thing, Mr. Adair! The mayor's assistant just called." Nurse Sheepwash placed the tray holding Owen's lunch across his knees, plumped up the pillows behind his back and beamed at him. "You're being given the freedom of the city!"

Owen stared at her dumbfounded.

"Do you know what that means?"

He shook his head.

"You get free parking for a whole year! Isn't that nice?"

"There must be some mistake," he began.

"Of course there's no mistake. Drink your bouillon. There's a ceremony on the twenty-third—now relax, I've told them you can't possibly attend. It's at City Hall, and the mayor's assistant said they'll do a camera hook-up or some such thing to you here. Oh Mr. Adair, it's just wonderful!"

Nurse Sheepwash was so patently delighted that Owen hid his consternation and addressed his lunch—beef bouillon, nutritious bean salad and a tiny healthful whole-wheat roll—while she sat down on the cane-back chair, leaned forward and continued: "They were going to give you a civic merit award, whatever that is, but public response has been so strong that they upgraded it to freedom of the city. You'll be getting a scroll and a medal and free parking and free admission to all civic facilities." She clasped her hands. "I'm so excited for you! I just don't know what to say!"

In that, she was not alone.

*   *   *

The *Star* was unimpressed with the Mayor's proclamation. An editorial headed "What's Wrong with City Hall?" concluded: "The announcement carries all the hallmarks of Mayor Franklin Briggs' administration: it is cheap, grudging and inadequate. This caring citizen deserves better, and we hereby serve notice that in the hearts and minds of our employees and our readers, December twenty-third will be Owen Adair Day. Fie on you, Franklin!"

Even the staid *Dispatch* weighed in: "While we generally applaud City Hall's fiscal prudence, we are astounded by this failure to proclaim a day in honor of Owen Adair. The city is quick to honor its ball players and rock stars; why not its Good Samaritan?"

On December sixteenth, the Mayor's office issued a fresh bulletin, declaring December twenty-third Owen Adair Day. Preparations kicked into high gear.

*   *   *

"It's Wendy MacIntyre," said Trish, and Sara picked up her phone. "Hello, Wendy."

"Hi, Sara. Isn't it great about Owen's Day?"

"Fantastic!" Sara smiled at Trish, who turned back to her phones.

"You'll be attending the presentation, won't you?"

"Yes." They discussed the details, then Wendy said, "You were right about the letters."

The morning the blizzard ended, Sara had phoned her about the sack of letters from the *Star*. "He ought to read them, Wendy. So if he asks you to take them, could you make some excuse?" Wendy had agreed, and now she brought Sara up to date. "He's had eight more sacks since you left. He wanted us to take them but I told the nurse we were too busy. She left half an hour ago and he called and asked me to go over and help him deal with them."

"Good," said Sara. Casting round for something else to say, she asked, "How does he like having a day named for him?"

"I don't think he knows." A short silence, then: "He was scheduled to fly out today for the Christmas break. If I tell him the news I'm afraid he might just do that."

"Has he finished his article?"

"No, not quite. But he could e-mail it from Cayman."

Great idea, thought Sara. "Well—see you on the twenty-third. Thanks for calling, Wendy."

She rang off, and turned back to her computer screen thinking, not for the first time, that she must be the only person in the city who did not think Owen Adair was a great guy.

"Ronnie's on the line," Trish's voice penetrated her thoughts, and she picked up the phone to hear that her sister-in-law had been trying to get a copy of the Shane photograph of Sara and Tom. "You may think you look like a sheep, but Bob's crazy about it. I want to give him a framed copy for his office."

"So call the paper."

"I did, but they won't release it to anyone but you. Would you call the photographer? I've got his name and number."

"I swore I'd never speak to those people again—"

"You should never say never, Sara. It's fatal." Ronnie went on to offer anecdotal evidence that saying never virtually guaranteed the opposite outcome. "Some people even believe that saying you'll never do something means you subconsciously want to do it, but I wouldn't go that far."

"Good," said Sara dryly.

"You don't have to speak to the reporter."

"Ronnie—"

"Do you want to break your brother's heart?"

Sara gave in, and with Ronnie's thanks in her ear called the newspaper. No problem, said the photographer, and promised to drop off a glossy plus a negative in the next few days. Wasn't it great about Owen's Day? Fantastic, said Sara.

Trish came back from lunch with an Owen Adair Day T-shirt: powder blue with a black silhouette of a man carrying a small, limp body over rocky ground. "He looks like one of those GIs at Iwo Jima or something," said Pam admiringly, and Trish told her where she could buy one. A local T-shirt manufacturer had offered to supply the city with free Owen's Day pennants in return for an exclusive vendor's license on T-shirts, and little blue and white flags were now fluttering from all the metropolitan lampposts underneath the red and green Christmas lights.

"Fantastic!" said Sara brightly, and thought longingly of New Year's.

*   *   *

That evening she dined at the Sheppards'. Tug had invited her the night after the blizzard and Sara had been caught without an excuse. He asked her to come early, before the other guests, and when she arrived at their rambling home north of the bridge, her coat was taken by the maid while the Sheppards made her welcome and sat her down with a drink.

"Tell us everything," said Liz, and Sara recounted her story, including Mac's description of Owen's condition on the night of the rescue.

They discussed the award briefly. The Sheppards would be away: they were flying out on the twenty-first, taking their boys to Whistler for Christmas. Then Liz wanted to hear all about the penthouse, so Sara launched into a room by room description, and then the other guests began to arrive.

Tug got to his feet. "Listen, Sara. Owen'll want to give you something for taking care of him. Don't worry about that. He likes giving things." He turned to greet the couple entering the living room.

Liz laughed shortly. "Just hire a hall," she said as she stood up.

The guests were a mixture of business contacts and friends, four couples and a stocky, energetic individual in his late thirties, who turned out to be an auto parts manufacturer. "Oh right—Sara Nightingale," he said with a grin when Liz introduced him. "Zack Lapierre." He turned to Liz. "Your grandmother get home alright?"

"She never left, Zack." To Sara: "Gran lives in Staple. You remember the train wreck? The evacuees returned home today."

"That was weeks ago!" Sara was astonished. "What took them so long?"

Zack explained while they helped themselves to drinks from the tray being handed round by the maid. The Crisis Management Committee, he said, had painted themselves into a corner. "They were the ones calling for an evacuation. It turned out to be unnecessary but they didn't want to admit that. So they got into this thing with the railroad about guaranteeing peoples' safety before allowing them to return home. No way the railroad was going along with that, so they kept batting it back and forth until everyone lost interest."

The derailment was the principal topic of conversation in the room, and all the participants came in for some blame: the railroad, the chemical companies, the media and the various government agencies. Zack had a realist's view of politicians, regulators and government agencies. "They act out of self-interest, just like the rest of us. Trouble is, most people have trouble remembering that."

The comment seemed to strike a chord with Tug as they went in to dinner. "You know, Zack, you're absolutely right."

"Oh Tug, don't let's start that now." Liz looked anxiously round the table, but she was too late.

"What are you trying to say, Tug?" asked Herman Philpott, the guest next to Sara. He had introduced himself to her as they sat down, a rather ponderous man in middle age.

"It's so easy to blame someone else," explained Tug. "The railroad should have maintained the rail better, and the chemical companies should have been more careful, and the media shouldn't be so sensational and on and on." He shook his head. "The whole thing's an embarrassment. There was no danger. I was there. We went to a meeting in the morning and there was absolutely no danger. But that afternoon, these bureaucrats come round alarming the residents, and everyone decides to leave town. A guy'll express his opinion and no one listens to him. But as soon as he says he's from the CMO, why then of course he must know something. Well, Bee wouldn't budge. This reporter shows up, wanting to know why she's not leaving. She was sweeping the kitchen floor when he arrived, and I thought she was going to sweep him right off the porch. 'I'll leave when someone can give me a good reason to leave,' she says."

He looked at Herman with chagrin. "I'm embarrassed because I was ready to leave along with the rest. We're like lemmings, most of us."

"Tug thinks Gran stayed because she's pioneer stock," added Liz. You know, more independent?"

"I don't care. They shouldn't transport dangerous chemicals like that." The speaker was a large leathery woman sitting across from Sara.

"You're the expert," said Tug to the guest on his left. "How should they transport them? Gwen's a research chemist," he explained as Sara glanced along the table at the woman, in her late 40s with a plain, intelligent face.

"Anyone would think that train had been carrying mustard gas, or methyl isocynate." Gwen sipped her wine. "The fact is, it was carrying ordinary industrial products for the most part. But just mention the word 'chemicals' and the public goes into a tailspin. People have become paranoid about the subject ever since we learned how to measure particles per billion."

No one had a ready response to that, so Tug invited her to explain.

"It really began back in the fifties, with Rachel Carson's book about DDT. *Silent Spring*, do you remember?" Several guests nodded. "Then we had thalidomide, Love Canal, Three Mile Island, PCBs and so on. Many impressionable baby boomers absorbed these events and came to the conclusion that chemicals per se were bad. Then in the seventies we learned how to measure particles per billion and discovered that almost everything contained carcinogens. Everything." She looked round then table. "The fact that these were trace elements somehow got overlooked in the press coverage."

Someone observed that science, having added fifteen years to the average life span, was now intent on preventing anyone from enjoying them.

"Science isn't doing anything of the sort," retorted Gwen. "People are doing that all by themselves."

"Whatever," said Liz. "I buy organically grown vegetables and I'd rather not hear that they have carcinogens."

"All right," said Gwen equably. After a pause, she asked, "Which do you think is more hazardous to your health? Living with a smoker, or drinking two glasses of milk a day?"

"Is that a trick question?" asked Herman Philpott after a silence.

Gwen smiled. "Suppose you knew there was one chance in a million of contracting cancer from saccharine. Would that stop you using it?"

"Why take unnecessary risks when you don't have to?" Herman looked round the table. There were murmurs of agreement.

"All right," Gwen went on. "Consider this. The risk of contracting HIV from a blood transfusion has been estimated at one in four hundred thousand. Yet some patients have actually preferred to exsanguinate because they don't like those odds."

"Exsanguinate?" Zack grimaced. "There's a word."

"You can't be too careful these days," said Herman.

"That's just my point," replied Gwen. "You can. You can become so obsessed with long shots that common sense goes out the window. It's called statistical homicide."

"I know what you mean," said Zack. He finished eating and leaned back. "This guy used to worry about air travel. He found out the odds of being on a plane carrying a bomb were one in a million. He didn't like that. But then he discovered that the chance of a plane carrying two bombs was so remote they couldn't even calculate it. So whenever he flew he always carried his own."

After the laughter died down, Gwen went on: "In point of fact, the biggest cause of death in North America isn't AIDS, heart disease, cancer, smoking, pesticides, drinking or driving." She smiled and finished eating. "It's household chores. That was delicious, Liz." She added, with a twinkle in her eye, "It might interest you to know that the risk of food poisoning from seafood is twenty-five times greater than from beef."

"Dear Gwen. Thank you for sharing that thought with us." Liz nodded to the maid, who began to clear the plates.

Sara looked enquiringly at Gwen. "So which is more hazardous, milk or second-hand smoke?"

"Milk," answered Gwen.

Liz looked upset. "I don't believe it. You're just saying that because I won't let you smoke in the house."

"I'm saying it to provide a little perspective. The EPA estimates the risk of contracting lung cancer from second-hand smoke at one in thirty thousand." She looked round the table. "What does that mean? In practical terms, is that a high risk, a low risk? One study found that you have a greater chance of contracting lung cancer from the natural carcinogens in milk, if you were to drink two glasses a day all your life."

The atmosphere had become a little strained, and Zack tried to ease it. "Listen, plenty of people worry about chemicals. The railroad could have done a better job explaining what they were carrying. Half the chemicals on that train were harmless."

"I don't care." The leathery woman opposite Sara spoke up again. "I'm sick of all these disasters. You can't open a paper these days without reading something terrible."

"It's funny," Sara said thoughtfully. "We keep thinking of it as a disaster because that was our first impression. But no one was killed or even hurt as far as I know."

"That's not quite right, Sara," said Zack. "Three thousand baby chicks were killed. A generator failed during the blizzard and the chicken farmer had been evacuated so he wasn't there to fix it. Now he's suing the CMO and the railroad and anyone else he can think of."

Liz was amazed. "That must be Mr. Bergamini! Tug saw him that same day, didn't you, Tug?"

"You see what I mean?" said Tug. "There we are: Bergamini, me, Bee and this guy from the public works department who's been drafted into the CMO. He didn't know anything more than the rest of us, but who did Bergamini believe?" He shook his head. "Lemmings. That's what we are, most of us. Just lemmings marching over the cliff."

Gwen patted his hand consolingly. "Poor Tug. I think you mean sheep, not lemmings."

"Is that supposed to make me feel better?"

"You're not alone. Most people would behave the same."

"Do I have to repeat myself?" he asked her, and watching from the other end of the table, Liz was pleased to see her husband's habitual good humor restored.

The talk round the table became general. Herman launched into an Amtrak anecdote, while the large leathery woman leaned across the table and engaged Sara's attention. She had blonde hair scraped back from her face and a tanned, unlined skin stretched tight across her cheekbones, and she explained at some length that Owen was a dear friend and she missed him terribly. Could this possibly be Gloria, Sara wondered, and laughed immoderately at Herman's punch line.

"Eden Philpott," said Liz later, as Sara was preparing to leave. They walked down the hall toward one of the guest bedrooms. "She's the wife of Tug's biggest customer, so we're stuck with her. Owen used to bring out the best in the old bag. He was a lifesaver for dinner parties, Sara." They entered the bedroom. "Get Tug to tell you about the shyness book sometime—Oh dear . . ." She gestured distractedly as they stopped before a pile of coats on the bed.

Sara moved forward. "I see it."

"I suppose Annie ought to hang them up," Liz watched as Sara delved into the pile, "but she always says she's got better things to do and naturally I always agree. Good help is so hard to find, isn't it?"

Sara agreed that it was. "It must be due to the household chores mortality rate."

Liz apologized for Gwen. "We're old friends but I honestly think she comes out with these statistics just to upset me."

Standing before the mirror, Sara felt a wave of depression flood over her. Liz reverted to the subject of Owen. "Tug misses him. So do I, bless his heart. I wish he'd get himself married but I suppose he's too busy making millions."

"Why did you say I should hire a hall?" They were returning to the front door. Liz looked skyward.

"Let's just say he's absurdly generous and leave it at that." But she sighed and went on: "He never turned up without a gift. Not just wine or flowers or the latest Belgian chocolates. Wonderful gifts, some of them." She shook her head. "Annie dotes on him. He bought her a CD player once, after she sewed a button on his jacket."

They stopped before the door. "That's not why she dotes on him," Liz went on. "I know people who throw money and gifts around to compensate for being obnoxious, but Owen isn't like that and I don't know why he does it."

Earlier, Sara had felt a stab of remorse for her thought about Eden Philpott and Gloria, and now she felt another one. She held out her hand, but Liz was taking a jacket from the hall closet. "I'll walk you out to your car," she said, insisting over Sara's protests.

It was snowing lightly when they came outside. Sara had parked on the street, and they picked their way through the thin icing of snow on the driveway.

"It's my fault we don't see Owen any more."

Sara didn't want to hear. "Why do you say that?"

"I used to dread his arrival. His gifts were always so damned perfect. It drove me wild." She hugged the jacket round her as they reached the car. "I finally threw a box of French soap at Tug one night and told him to straighten Owen out, but he wouldn't. So I did. I told him if he brought one more gift Tug would deck him. That was an awful thing to say, Sara, but I was driven to it."

Sara could easily believe it. "What did he say?"

"Oh, we all laughed about it, and Tug said afterward that Owen wasn't offended."

Sara unlocked her car door and turned, waiting.

"But I never saw him again. Tug does, for lunch or a game of squash, but I haven't seen him since he moved to the Pointe, and that's four years ago. He just makes an excuse and won't come."

Sara was glad it was dark because her cheeks suddenly felt hot. "I'm sorry," she said lamely, and held out her hand. "Thank you for a wonderful dinner, Liz."

They exchanged compliments of the season and Sara climbed in the car. There was a tap on the window and she rolled it down. Liz bent over. "Do you like Owen, Sara? You didn't say."

Sara's throat tightened but she met the other woman's gaze. "Yes. I do." Liz smiled and stepped back, waving and hurrying back inside.

Snowflakes shone in the beam of the headlights as she drove homeward, reminding her of another night two weeks earlier. She'd been happy that night, driving up from Custom House to the Pointe to meet Tom's rescuer. She remembered the plans she'd made before she had even met Owen, to thank him and introduce him to Tom and Janey, to her parents and Bob and Ronnie and the rest of the Hargreaves clan who were dying to meet him and thank him.

As she turned in at River Reach, she finally admitted the truth: his check hadn't offended her. It had hurt her. He had hurt her, because she'd liked him more than she'd realized.

She took a long hard look at herself, and realized something else: that she was becoming brittle and mean-spirited. Owen could teach her a thing or two about kindness, she thought, remembering his concern for her throughout his fever. She recalled his music, and his humor, and she hated herself for that bitchy thought about Eden Philpott because he'd been hurt by a beautiful, decorative, empty woman, and while Eden Philpott might be empty she could not help being neither beautiful nor decorative.

She turned on the gas fire in the den and sat there with a glass of wine. You could tell a lot about a man, she mused, by the company he kept. She liked Ruby and the Sheppards, she'd enjoyed meeting Wendy, and she liked the atmosphere in that office. She'd spoken to several other friends of his on the phone, and all of them had prefaced their remarks with some version of "I haven't seen Owen for ages." Yet they'd all phoned to find out how he was, and they all spoke of him with affection. All these people respected Owen, all of them saw too little of him. Was that because of his gift-giving?

Half an hour ticked by and still she sat, lost in thought. She had meant to ask him so much and instead she had talked about her life, on and on, much as Ruby's son Clarence must have done. It had done her a power of good, too, she realized. She thought with chagrin of all the questions she could have asked. . . . She began to think he had a point about regulation impairing judgment. The Staple incident seemed to display poor judgment all round, and the CMO's intervention had just complicated matters. . . . He had no one. . . . How could so considerate a man be so crass?

*　　*　　*

On Saturday, still in a hair-shirt mood, Sara decided to shovel the driveway. Ray Elwing from next door came through the hedge an hour later to find her enjoying the sun and the exercise. She laughed at his disbelief and cleared another lane, reaching the end of the driveway in a spurt of energy as snow piled up over the top of the shovel. She heaved it sideways, banking it against the hedge, and paused for a breather. Another five lanes, she calculated, maybe six. Better than aerobics. She took a deep breath and sat against the bank for a moment.

"Mum!"

Janey was wrestling with a large ball of snow, trying to lift it onto the larger base for her snowman in the middle of the lawn. Sara left the shovel and went over to help her, and together they lifted it into place. Then they rolled a third ball for the head, and Sara put that on top and helped Janey find some pebbles in the flower beds under the eaves of the house. Then, after the snowman had eyes and a nose and mouth, she flicked snow at Janey and they had a mini-snowball fight until Sara wrestled her down and tickled her. Janey sat up and threw back her head and laughed the way she did everything, with gusto, and Sara left her tramping a space round the snowman, and returned to the driveway.

A car came along the road and pulled in at the kerb. Flick Jackson climbed out, and Sara straightened up and watched as he trudged through the snow toward her.

"Hi there," he called cheerfully and waved at Janey. He handed Sara a manila envelope. "Your picture. I was coming out this way so I said I'd drop it off." In fact, the editor had told him to do so.

"Oh. Thank you," Sara took the envelope.

"I spoke to Mrs. MacIntyre at Custom House yesterday. Owen's much better."

"Yes, I heard."

"Been to see him lately?"

"No." This sounded abrupt even to her ears, so she added, "He's not allowed visitors."

"The nurse has left. I wanted to get his reaction to the Mayor's announcement. You know, naming a day in his honor."

"I'm sure he's thrilled," Sara said. She half-turned, toward the house. "Thanks for bringing this. . . . "

Jackson looked round the yard. "I saw the kids skating down at the park. Wasn't it closed off?"

"Yes. Some of the parents wanted it open again." She forbore to add that she'd been one of them and had spent an hour trying to make Ellie Griff understand that you couldn't wrap kids in cotton wool.

"Aren't you worried?"

She turned away, but not before he saw a flash of hot anger in her eyes. "Sorry. Dumb question. When are you taking Tom to see Owen, if you don't mind me asking?"

Sara stared at him. Finally she said, "After Christmas sometime, when he's fully recovered." She added politely, "And I won't be notifying you in advance, you may as well accept that. It's a private matter, between Tom and Owen." She held his look and at last he gave a rueful half-laugh.

"Yeah, I guess. See you." He trudged away toward his car and Sara watched until he drove off before taking the photo inside.

9

On the afternoon of December twentieth, Owen ventured upstairs to his study for the first time in nearly three weeks. Wendy had faxed the January issue for his approval, and he collected the edited made-up pages and dropped them on the desk, glimpsing a flash of blue as he sat down. He found a post-it note stuck to the blotter. The message was short: "Should you be up here?" Sara must have left it, he realized, and he smiled and fell into a reverie.

"I am sure we're both grateful to Mrs. Newton for her timely assistance," were Nurse Sheepwash's first words as she entered his bedroom on the afternoon of the eighth, and Owen had been too feverish to debate the inadequacy of the word "grateful." In any case, he was given no chance to respond, for she deployed her thermometer and proceeded to define the rules of play. He had expected a rawboned woman with chapped lips and red hands; he was nonplused by this small, trim figure with square shoulders, a square chin and calm, inflexible determination. Nor, he soon discovered, had she left the bedpan on the kitchen counter, and she deployed that, too, with a clinical detachment Owen strove to match until he realized that his feelings were utterly irrelevant to her; thereafter, he relaxed and thought of other things.

He thought about Andrew Byrd, the Bermuda-bound specialist whose investments had turned out all right; and he thought about Spence's charge that he'd been unprofessional, a comment that still annoyed him. He thought of Mac Drummond and of all the friends who had called to wish him well. Most of all he thought about Sara.

He did much of his thinking in the mornings, while Nurse Sheepwash read to him. She had conceived the idea that hearing from his well-wishers would speed his recovery and once the sacks of mail began arriving she would read a random selection of letters. Owen didn't want to hear the letters, nor see the bouquets of flowers she brought in, but his wishes were ignored, and so he thought of other things while "Congratulations" and "Get well soon" washed over him. But some residue of this tide of benevolence must have stayed with him, because when he saw the sacks ranged against the wall by the front door, he did not call the courier service; he phoned Wendy instead.

That was on the sixteenth, the day the nurse left. She had whisked him off to the hospital that morning, wrapped up and in a wheelchair, and Spence had expressed restrained approval of his progress and agreed that he could manage on his own provided he stayed indoors, preferably in bed, and did nothing foolish for the next three weeks. Owen said stiffly that he had no intention of doing anything foolish, and the nurse wheeled him home again.

Wendy congratulated him on the Freedom of the City award. "Media hype," he said dismissively, having had two days to become accustomed to the idea. "They're always hard up for news at this time of year." He wondered fleetingly at the note of apprehension in her voice, then his eye fell on the sacks of mail by the door. "I wondered whether you could spare the time to help me with all this mail." Glad to, Wendy had replied, and suggested bringing Iris and Spider as well.

He returned to bed after the nurse departed, remaining there for most of each day, writing his article on the laptop while the others toiled away in the living room.

He was feeling much stronger now and had walked slowly upstairs without pain. He finished reading the January issue and faxed his minor corrections to the office. Then he turned his attention to the first of two pleasurable tasks before him. Of the four couriers who had arrived today, one had brought a sealed envelope from his bank. He opened it and withdrew 10 cashier's checks. "I'd feel more comfortable inserting the payees, Owen," his manager had pleaded, but Owen told him to relax and stop worrying. Now he fanned the checks and leaned back, drawing a stack of letters and brochures toward him, short-listed from the numerous requests for assistance among his hundreds of cards and letters. There were two think-tanks he liked the sound of, several foundations, and an intriguing organization involved in "microfinancing," something new to Owen. It seemed they lent start-up amounts to small businesses—most conceived by women—in the inner cities and the Third World, and he made a note to investigate this further as a potential article. Presently, ten sealed, stamped and addressed envelopes lay on the desk before him. He sat in thought for a while, imagining how the money would be used, aware it was only a drop in the bucket to these organizations but knowing they'd get some mileage out of it and pleased by that prospect.

Eventually he rose, went to the den and put on a couple of CDs, Tchaikovsky and Prokofiev, adjusted the sound for the living room speakers and returned downstairs. He began to smile as he entered the living room because he still wasn't used to it.

The room seemed to radiate good will, an almost palpable warmth spreading outward from hundreds of Christmas cards, covering all the walls, the valances above the curtains, the mantel and the piano. Over in the corner, between the piano bench and the doors to the roof garden, stood a Christmas tree, delivered three days ago with a note from the Firefighter's Union: "Any time you want to change jobs, call us." Owen had helped Iris to decorate it and now its lights twinkled and winked at him. His gaze roamed leisurely over the cards. He'd made himself read each one before Spider hung them, and he recognized some of them now. He thought of all the homes in which he'd spent Christmases past, homes in New York and Connecticut, and London and the English countryside. None of them had ever had a display quite like this. . . .

He stood in the middle of the room, hearing their voices still. They'd finished earlier but already he missed them: in the space of four short days they'd become like a family to him.

*   *   *

He had heard them arrive that first afternoon, using the security card left at the front desk by Nurse Sheepwash. He went through later and found them hard at work round the dining room table. Two of the eight sacks had been opened and the table was piled high with letters and boxes.

"Show him the loot, Spider," said Wendy, while Iris fussed over him then went off to the kitchen to make him a sandwich. Owen sat down in the corner of the couch and smiled at his partner.

"I'm fine," he reassured her. "Much better." Spider arrayed the boxes before him: brownies, a whole fruitcake from Mary Cavanaugh ("P.S. It'll keep for weeks."), a huge gingerbread man with the iced message, "We love you Owen the Hendersons," and cookies of every kind, mostly broken into small pieces. Owen peered into a box of chocolate chip offerings ("I hope your better soon, Simone Wieczorek, age 10. P.S. I made them all by myself") and Spider held out a box of orange coconut fragments.

"These are great," he said, and Owen sampled them. Then Iris brought him a cup of coffee and a sandwich, Wendy gave him a stack of cards and they returned to the dining room table, Spider at one end opening the sacks and passing the envelopes to Wendy and Iris, then dealing with the packages himself.

"Keep any return addresses," Owen told them, "I want to thank them."

"That isn't necessary, Owen," said Wendy. She turned around in surprise. "No one expects it."

"That lady who invited him to Acapulco expects it," said Spider.

"That was no lady, dear," observed Iris comfortably but Owen insisted on responding to every return address. Wendy had ordered five hundred thank you cards from the stationers and yesterday he spent an hour signing these and passing them along to Spider, who stuffed them in the envelopes and dropped them in a box to be sealed and metered at the office. "Should I put in a sub flyer?" he asked. Iris nodded approvingly and Owen laughed.

"I think not," said Wendy tartly.

Spider was the youngest Custom House employee. He had started part-time in the mailroom after school and when old Darcy retired, Owen and Wendy had interviewed him together, as they did every prospective employee. Owen had studied the uncommunicative, nondescript youth and glanced at the name, "Philip Bitzi," on the application. "We've already got a Phil. How would it be if we called you Spider?" Spider had hunched his shoulders and mumbled something affirmative, but thereafter, Wendy discovered, he lived for Owen's infrequent appearances in the office.

At sixty-eight, Iris was the oldest employee and the first person Owen had hired after Wendy. She was the data entry manager, responsible for maintaining and updating the subscription lists, a plump motherly figure who occasionally presented an incongruous sight in a steel-studded black leather biker's jacket, a present from her grandsons. This she wore whenever she had to do battle with careless data entry clerks or spotty programmers on the software help line. On weekends, Iris gave Tarot readings for a large and growing clientele, so all in all, she led a full life.

They worked away around the table while Owen read his cards. When he tired of that he would close his eyes and listen to the office gossip. Roger and Arthur, the senior researcher and editor respectively, were still sniping at each other; Polly, the graphics artist, had finally set a date for the wedding after five years of indecision; and Colin, the second researcher, was conducting a torrid affair with Shirley, one of Iris's data entry clerks. Iris was fed up with them.

"So I said tell me where TZ is, Shirley, because I'd like to know. It says Houston, she said. So I said Houston is in TX, Shirley, not TZ. I don't think she checked them at all."

"Tell her to leave the nail file at home." Wendy sounded preoccupied. "You can't proofread address labels when you're filing your nails. Here's another endorsement request."

"Wouldn't that be a violation of her rights, dear?" Iris called everyone "dear."

"Do I have to send Colin's faxes?" Spider spoke through a mouthful of food. "It's not in my job description."

"I've already spoken to him about that." A pause. "We'd better start a separate pile for endorsements." Another pause. "If I see you eating one more of those brownies, I'll have to revise your job description." Owen smiled and returned to his cards.

At four, when the short daylight hours had passed, they drew the curtains and sat round the fire with coffee, herbal tea and Coke, sampling the baked offerings.

"You know, dear," Iris leaned earnestly toward him, that first afternoon. "That was just a wonderful thing you did, saving Tommy Newton."

"No it wasn't, Iris," said Owen. "It was stupid and reckless and not part of the game plan. I could have been killed."

"I know, dear." She looked momentarily distressed. "That's why it's so wonderful."

"Iris, if I'd been killed, you'd have been out of a job."

"The point is, you weren't," said Wendy.

"No, the point is, I could have been."

"But you weren't."

"It was an irresponsible thing to do."

"Oh no, dear. It was beautiful. And brave and giving."

Owen stared at the two women in annoyance, then Spider weighed in, around a mouthful of the Hendersons' ginger-bread man. "We could go on selling books and back issues even if you died," he pointed out. "It might've even been better." He appraised the living room with the eye of an auctioneer or a tour guide. "People'd pay to see this, I bet. Like Graceland."

Wendy had difficulty repressing her laughter at the expression on Owen's face.

Once the sacks had been opened and sorted, Spider began hanging cards pegged onto the green twine. Cards of every description: large and expensive, small and cheap, and homemade. The latter fell into two categories: portrait of the artist, with or without family; and portrait of Owen. Of the latter, his favorite came from Cindy Meyer (age nine). It featured a long skinny blue body topped by a mass of curly black hair and a wide grin showing a great many teeth, all clenched.

He was at a loss to understand the kids' cards. He had always considered children a pitiable species, small and helpless, easy prey for monsters and perverts. It sickened him that the world had become so unfriendly to them and he gave them a wide berth to avoid causing alarm. He had braced himself for a succession of pathetic pleas from helpless victims, but these had failed to materialize.

"What do you make of this?" he asked Iris one afternoon, holding out a small card of a snowman surrounded by a family of rabbits. Iris opened it. Inside, in stick letters, it read: "Owen Adar. Hero of the Year. Megan Cafferty. P.S. I'm 6 and I can skate."

"I remember," Iris smiled. "Sweet little thing."

"What does she want?"

"Want? She's only six, dear."

"I know she's only six." He'd frowned.

"She's proud of being able to skate and she wanted to tell you."

"Why?"

"I don't know, dear. Maybe it's her best thing." She smiled and handed the card back. "Children aren't complicated, dear. Not like adults." She rose and returned to the table.

Her best thing. Owen had thought about that a lot.

It was Spider who broke the news about Owen's Day. He'd been up the stepladder, working on the long wall between the front and patio doors, while Owen and Iris were stringing the Christmas lights on the tree. They broke for coffee and joined Wendy in front of the fire, while Spider finished hanging a string of cards and climbed down from the step ladder. He took off his sweater, revealing a bright red T-shirt, stopped in front of Owen and struck a pose.

"Ta-daaaah!"

"Spider!" said Wendy.

"You weren't ever going to tell him."

Owen stared. The T-shirt had a silhouetted picture surrounded by the words "Owen Adair Day, December twenty-third."

"Neat, huh?" said Spider.

Owen looked at Wendy. "Don't you think you're carrying this a little far?"

"Me? It's nothing to do with me." She could see he still didn't understand. "It's the city, Owen. It's not Custom House."

"I could have predicted it, dear, if you'd let me do a reading."

Owen fell silent. The idea that the city would actually design a T-shirt and name a day in his honor was so irrational he felt a twinge of fear. Then he had a comforting thought. "When are the next civic elections?" Media hype coupled with political hay-making: now that made sense. He was merely the poor sucker caught in the middle.

Wendy seemed to read his thoughts. "It's got nothing to do with politics, Owen. If you were taking your calls, you'd know." At Nurse Sheepwash's request, Owen's calls had been forwarded to the office.

He said nothing. You spent your life doing your job, observing the law, paying down the mortgage and no one said a word. One feckless, impulsive action and suddenly you were a hero? He went over to the dining room table to deal with the endorsement letters. Wendy joined him.

"How long have you known about this?"

"Three days. I was afraid you'd leave town if you found out."

He said nothing, glancing at the letters one by one, scribbling "no" against each request, trying to concentrate, to quell the fear. This thing was like a juggernaut . . . "Budgie food?" he burst out at last. Wendy began to laugh. "Budgie food? I can understand scuba gear, I can even understand thermal underwear—"

"Please say yes to that one. Please—"

"—but budgie food? For God's sake!" and he scrawled NO against Brady's Budgie Biscuits and threw the pen down.

"I don't know what the world's coming to," he began, but Wendy was in the grip of a *fou rire* and he watched sourly as she tried to support her head on one hand, then glimpsed his expression and flopped over, laughing her head off. He left the table and sat down before the fire, scowling at the cards on the mantle. Christmas cards. Tarot cards. The whole world was going mad.

Eventually, she recovered her composure and he returned to the table. "The scariest trend these days isn't domestic abuse or teenage gangs or AIDS," he said, lowering his voice so that Iris wouldn't hear. "It's this unholy alliance between technology and the occult. It scares the pants off me."

Wendy agreed cheerfully that it was simply shocking, and pushed over another stack of letters. "It has to do with the search for meaning and value in life," she observed. "There's nothing new in that." She continued sorting the dwindling pile of mail and looked up a while later to find his eyes on her.

"Do you want me to start taking my calls?"

"You'd never get a thing done." She was silent for a moment. "I'll tell you what I'd like," she said at last. "I wish you'd come into the office more often. I know there's no reason to, but we miss you." He grunted.

She gazed round the living room. "I really thought we'd see more of you when you moved here."

"You don't need me."

"I know. But the office is a better place with you there." She gazed at him, chin on hand. "When you're not being rigid and dogmatic."

"Who's rigid?"

"You are, sometimes." She nodded towards the living room. "This is such a wonderful outpouring of gratitude. Why can't you lighten up and enjoy it? You can't imagine how proud we are. Arthur's taken to throwing his chest out. I saw him walking to his car the other day and he actually strutted."

"Arthur always struts. When you're only five foot three you have to strut or someone might beat you up." He finished dealing with the endorsements and joined Iris at the tree, and they hung decorations while he kidded her about her fortune-telling prowess. "If you can tell me when the Dow will hit fifteen thousand, I'll give you your own column," he said, and Wendy observed that if they were going to upgrade the quality of their predictions, it was time to increase the subscription price. Owen winged a decoration at her as Spider looked down austerely from the ladder. Later, feeling reckless, he even played a couple of Christmas carols while the others sang. Afterward he apologized for all the mistakes. "What mistakes," they said, and that was that.

Now, on the afternoon of the twentieth, he stood in the middle of the living room, his glance moving slowly over the walls, the mantel above the fireplace, and he smiled to see the little snowman card, "her best thing," then shook his head. People were amazingly kind but he felt like a fraud.

He walked over to the dining room table. It was bare now except for three packages delivered earlier this afternoon: a tulip-shaped vase for Wendy, who loved flowers and who had been delighted to take most of Owen's bouquets; a Calvin Klein jean jacket for Spider; and an illustrated history of Tarot cards for Iris.

When Owen told Sara he was good at giving, it was no more than the truth. Despite his wealth he was not ostentatious. His gifts were frequently small and always thoughtful and well chosen. But they were unremitting; that was the bad part.

He couldn't see this. Gift-giving was for him a natural response to the upwelling of affection and gratitude he felt around people he liked. If someone expressed the wish that he would please for God's sake stop bringing a present every time he came over, Owen would comply: by not coming over. It was not a matter of pique. If his gifts were not wanted he was hamstrung. He had nothing else to give, and so he would plead other engagements when invited out. As his business prospered, work and travel gradually supplanted the company of friends, and until now he had not noticed the loneliness.

The matter of the employee bonuses had had a similar effect on his presence in the office. He had returned from two months in Europe to find the company so busy, renewal rates so robust (for, as he'd said to Wendy, the only way they would ever get rid of the loan was if the subscribers for whom they had paid so dearly chose to renew their subscriptions) and his employees so productively and gainfully employed that he felt that familiar upsurge of gratitude and wanted to reward them. Wendy had restrained him, but afterward he had realized he must keep his professional and personal lives separate if he wished to preserve his business. Nowadays he went in to the office only once or twice a month.

As for bonuses, he confined himself to annual checks along guidelines laid down by the accountant and endorsed by Wendy. He had never given any employee a gift—and he knew he should not start now, but this was a special case and a special time of year, and he'd reached the decision last night and was glad of it.

He had accounts at several stores throughout the city and after some hours of pleasant thought, leafing through catalogues for ideas, he had hit upon these three items and phoned round first thing this morning. He drew the Tarot book toward him and began his Christmas gift wrapping. He'd courier the packages to the office tomorrow.

For a man who could be so insightful about others, Owen's lack of self-knowledge was startling. Beyond the certainty that there was a worm in the apple he knew little more than that he loved giving gifts and hated being indebted. "The Adairs aren't beholden to anyone," his mother had said on numerous occasions and Owen approved. He was sometimes inflexible about it, Tug had taught him that, and occasionally, as with Mac and Sara, it crept up and bit him in the leg.

He finished wrapping the cards and began on the vase. He would start going in to the office regularly. He'd keep a rein on his personal predilections, but he was going in to the office again. And as soon as he had recovered he would visit Sara. He could still see that look when he'd given her the check; it had haunted him through the fevered nights following her departure. To offer money after what she'd done! How she must despise him. Yet her kindness through his fever had made the most profound impression on him. He'd been trapped in a place deep and dank and dark. He'd been helpless, in sweaty pajamas with a vile taste in his mouth, and each time, out of the darkness, a cool hand and a kind voice had calmed his fear. He could never put into words what her presence had meant to him; instead, he'd tried to pay her.

He had to make amends to her, and more than that he wanted to see her again, even though she was encumbered with children. He wanted to see her, and hear her voice again and catch the scent of her perfume. Her voice . . . Owen set great store by voices. Gloria's voice had been true but thin, like a tiny bell. Betty's had been flat and a little irritating, truth be told. But Sara—Sara's voice was like—he stared at the living room—like Brahms' second piano concerto; as richly textured as Black Forest cake.

He shook himself and got on with the Christmas wrapping. The doorbell rang just after he'd finished Spider's jacket, and he crossed the living room puzzled that the front desk hadn't warned him. Then he thought with a surge of hope that it must be Sara and flung the door open wide.

"Owen, darling!" said Monica Stephanopoulos, and stepped inside. "You're vertical!"

*   *   *

Hoch was not happy at the turn of events. His story—the story he had broken and nurtured and fanned and encouraged until it had all the legs he could wish for in a Christmas diversion—this story was taking an unpleasantly familiar turn. Television had got into the act, and now the *Star* was losing its edge. Adair would receive his award on TV; people would watch the event rather than reading about it; Briggs would make political capital from it; and the *Star* would gain nothing.

He called Monica into his office and gave her an instruction: get Adair out of his apartment. He added two variations on that simple theme: get him to agree to attend the ceremony; and get him out before, the sooner the better.

Pursuant to this challenge, Monica phoned Antonia Warburton to request an interview. No one listening to her could have guessed how galling this was, for Mrs. Warburton loomed large among the correspondents of Hilary Gray, pathetic insipid Hilary Gray of the *Dispatch*, and Monica was compelled to promise several plugs for her worthy but tedious charities in return for the interview. However, she had acceded gracefully because in addition to Hoch's demands, she had her own agenda for Owen Adair.

After leaving Mrs. Warburton's apartment on the ninth floor, she had discovered to her dismay that the elevator would not respond when she pressed any of the buttons from ten upward. So she walked through the utility door at the end of the foyer and staggered up eleven floors to the penthouse. It took her fifteen minutes to recover her breath, time she spent thinking black thoughts of Dexter. He had flatly refused to assist her: one of the other guards suspected his earlier involvement, he said, and he was afraid of losing his job.

Now, as Owen closed the door behind her and gestured to a chair, she exclaimed over the cards, expressed her delight at his recovery, and asked his reaction to Owen Adair Day.

"What can I get you to drink, Monica?"

It had been years since anyone asked Monica that question: all the world knew she drank white wine from eleven 'til three and whisky sours thereafter, but she agreed to make do with scotch on the rocks and reviewed what she knew of Owen while he went to fix it. Jackson was doing a backgrounder for tomorrow's paper and she'd scanned it quickly before leaving. He appeared to have led a blameless life: honors student, no athletic or musical ability, unmarried—she took the drink from him and smiled her thanks.

"How did you get in, Monica?"

"I had an interview with Toni Warburton, do you know her? And I thought afterwards, Gosh I wonder how Owen's doing? So I just popped up to see." She ignored his grin and sipped her drink. "Pianos really make a room, don't they?"

Owen agreed gravely that they did, and she went on, "I'll come straight to the point, Owen. I really expected you to be prostrate with pain—" she made a meal of the words and he laughed, "but since you're not, don't you think you could attend the presentation in person?"

He shook his head. "I'm under doctor's orders. The TV people are coming tomorrow to check out the lighting or something. Everything's set up."

"I know, I know. But how can we have Owen Adair Day without the guest of honor?"

"That's your problem." He eyed her without sympathy. "I'm not allowed outside for another two weeks."

"But darling! You wouldn't be outside! We'd send a car for you, we'd drive you downtown, you'd be underground at both ends! And people would be so thrilled to see you."

Owen already knew that. Both Spider and Iris had observed wistfully that it would have been great if he could have been there.

Monica continued: "You probably wouldn't have to say a word. And I know the room where they're making the presentation. It's tiny. There's only space for Mrs. Newton and her son and a pool camera and two reporters."

Mrs. Newton. . . .

"What do you say?" coaxingly.

"I'll think about it." He eyed her. "Anything else?"

Monica shook her head and reached for her drink. "That's all, darling." She let her eyes roam around the room for a moment, then said, "Your parents married late, didn't they?" Owen nodded and she asked, "Is that why you haven't yet married? This isn't for publication, darling, I'm just curious."

He regarded her with amusement. "Playing matchmaker, Monica?"

That was exactly what Monica had in mind, for she was a matchmaker *par excellence*—but not of the romantic variety.

She hadn't a romantic bone in her body; work was the whole of her existence. Her day started at roughly 10 a.m. and finished at one or two the following morning, hours which had led to the departure some years earlier of Georg Stephanopoulos, who, when asked his views on holy matrimony said he couldn't see the point. She smiled back at Owen and shook her head in response to his question. He gazed at the fire and said suddenly,

"Sure, okay. I'll go to the ceremony."

"*Darling!*" Monica finished her drink, pulled out her cell phone and called the paper before he could change his mind. Owen fixed her another drink. He was under no illusions about Monica: she was a gossip columnist and he was grist for the mill. But she was good at her job, and he enjoyed her company, so when he'd returned with her refill and she said, "Don't you think it's time you did something for your town, Owen?" he replied amiably enough,

"I already do something for my town, Monica. I pay my taxes, obey the law, stay out of trouble."

She waved this away. "You could be a major force for action on any cause you care to lend your name to."

"Not interested."

"Oh come now! Everyone's interested in something. How about cancer research? Or the environment? Or the symphony?" He was studying her curiously and she went on: "You know, government funding for projects and groups, no matter how worthwhile they are, is drying up. Nowadays, any organization wanting money has to appeal directly to the public, and believe me, the competition's intense."

Owen was aware of it and approved: if taxpayers had to decide what they wanted to spend their money on, they were apt to spend more carefully than government agencies, and had no one to blame but themselves if they did not.

Monica went on: "Listen Owen, there are a hundred foundations and causes and organizations out there, all battling for media space and consumer dollars. The actual work gets done by drones, and maybe ten percent of the people on the boards and committees are drone representatives. But the other ninety percent? They're the movers and shakers, the power brokers, the celebrities, the names. You're a name. Now, if you were some bozo who'd never done anything with his life 'til he happened to haul a kid out of the river—well, I'd say enjoy and *ciao*. But you're not. You've got an international reputation, you've made a pile of money. With that background plus your name, which is priceless—thanks partly, if I may say so, to my newspaper—you could make a difference to any cause you care to help."

Owen shook his head. "What is it with you people anyway?"

"What do you mean?"

"You just don't give up, do you? Someone does one little thing and you blow it up out of all proportion—"

"Darling, we don't make the news, we just report it."

Owen disregarded this. "And now, now that you've built me up, you want to get as much mileage out of me as possible."

"No." Her denial was emphatic. "I'm not saying this because you'd make great copy, you wouldn't. You're too good to be true." He laughed and she made a face, then continued: "I'm saying it because in my business you get a feel for the kind of people who can make a difference, and in my judgment, you're one of them."

Owen wasn't to know that this kind of matchmaking had made Monica, unofficially, one of the most influential people in the city. In the non-profit sphere she had single-handedly shaped more boards of directors than even she realized, by dropping a word here, a suggestion there. Any publicist desiring a plug in her column was required to supply her with three items of information in return, and as a consequence, on any given day Monica was a treasure trove of unused but valuable tidbits. It was she who had suggested the lead singer of the rock group Metal Pedal to the MS Society board, having learned that the singer's older brother had multiple sclerosis. The MS Society board had tottered backward at her suggestion, but the lead singer had proved to be a welcome injection of fresh blood and the Society was doing well.

Knowing none of this, Owen said merely, "Aren't you nice. What's in it for you?"

"It wouldn't do me any harm to be the person who opens the right doors for you. I admit it. And make no mistake, Owen, you need to get next to the right people, and they're not necessarily the ones who'll be all over you at first."

He gazed at the fire. "The answer's no, Monica. Thanks anyway."

"Why not?"

He shrugged. "For one thing, it doesn't interest me. For another, I'm no good with people."

She stared at him. "How are you no good?"

"Thirdly, you overestimate my value—or the value you people have tried to make of me. In any case, I have a business to run, and—"

"That's nonsense. You're never there. Wendy MacIntyre runs it, not you."

"Even so. I'm not interested," he met her gaze, "and that's final."

She looked disappointed, and sipped her drink in silence, while Owen leaned back against the cushions, hands behind his head. "Ever read Jane Jacobs?"

"Who does she write for?" She stared suspiciously at him over her glass and he laughed.

"She's not a columnist. She lives in Toronto. She's written several books, mostly on the quote civilized art of maintaining creative cities." He smiled. "Nice turn of phrase, don't you think?"

"You mean, like artists' colonies?" Monica was unimpressed.

"Good heavens, no." Owen sat up. "Jacobs argues that the wealth of a nation, its economic activity and growth, is generated by cities." He leaned back again. "I don't have much time for politics, personally, but it wouldn't surprise me to see a devolution of political power from the national to civic arena. Maybe then we could get away from one-size-fits-all federal regulations."

This wasn't getting her anywhere, Monica thought. "It's getting so decent people don't want to run for political office anymore," she observed. "Now, maybe that's bad, maybe it's good, I don't know. But just because they don't go into politics doesn't mean they can't help their communities in other ways." She shot a meaning look in Owen's direction, but he was gazing at the fire. "If they don't, then eventually nothing's going to get done."

She'd sandwiched her own purposes between Hoch's twin demands. She wasn't giving up on Owen by any means, but for now it was time to move on to stage three. So she finished her drink and prepared to leave. Owen accompanied her to the door.

"You're wasted on the society page, Monica."

"No, I'm not. I'm very good at it. By the way, how's Sara Newton these days?"

"I imagine she's fine," he said, opening the door. He turned to find her staring at him, plainly puzzled. "What's wrong? Why shouldn't she be fine?"

"No reason. I'm just surprised you haven't spoken to her since that day."

"Since what day?"

She laughed with exactly the right tinge of regret. "I guess you wouldn't tell me, though, even if you had. But she certainly was upset."

Owen's patience was running out. "Upset when? What are you talking about?"

"The day she left, of course. She was crying, I assume because of your condition. That's why I'm surprised you haven't spoken to her since then." His eyes were still, and she added, with perfectly feigned sympathy, "I'm sorry, Owen. I thought you knew."

10

It was the last day of school and Tom was waiting for his ride with Janey and the Elwings when he saw Randy Casilio crouched down under the big tree by the kerb. Randy had his back to him but seemed to be poking at something on the ground. Tom left the group and went to join him, and Janey tagged along.

"Watcha doing," he called as he drew near. It paid to ask first with Randy because he got up to a lot of stuff you weren't supposed to. Tom was no saint, but he liked a little advance notice so he could decide for himself whether he wanted to break the law instead of just getting sucked into it.

Randy's head turned and he drew back so that Tom could see he was poking at a dead cat with a stick. "Look! It got run over," said Randy. He picked up the cat's tail and lifted. The hindquarters came off the ground, splayed and flattened.

The cat meowed.

"Cut it out!" Tom went straight for Randy and shoved him hard. Randy fell backward, then scrambled up and shoved back. "You cut it out!" But Tom was crouching over the cat and ignored the blow. Janey squatted at its head, watching raptly.

"Is it alive?" she asked.

"Sure it is," said Randy. "It can't feel anything on its back but see, look." He poked at the cat's shoulder and it flinched. "Quit it, Randy!" Tom said angrily.

The hindquarters were matted with slush and blood, the head and shoulders more or less unmarked.

"Tom, look!" Janey pointed and Tom saw that the cat had only one front leg. Randy said, "Yeah I know," and speculated that the missing leg was a birth defect or a long ago injury.

It meowed again and Tom stared at its eyes. Half closed, they stared back at him. He suddenly scrambled round the tree, pulled off a glove and grabbed a bit of relatively clean snow. He breathed on it as he returned to crouch before the cat, and the snow was already melting from the heat of his hand. He held it under the cat's mouth and its tongue came out and rasped against his palm.

He watched intently, absorbed in the sight and feel of that tongue. Randy's voice receded, and the cries of children playing, and the traffic noise. Then the tongue stopped.

He looked into the cat's eyes, and there was a moment and then another moment. The cat was there and then it was gone and Tom knew instantly when it happened, though the eyes stayed open, half-lidded.

A chill touched his heart and he drew back. The cat was gone, really gone and—and Janey was tugging at his arm, "Come on, Tom," and he heard Brad calling his name. Mrs. Elwing's car was idling in the schoolyard and the others were already climbing in. He ran after Janey.

*   *   *

They went tobogganing with Brad and Tony after they got home, in the field with the small hill a few blocks over. It was a pretty pathetic hill but better than nothing, and afterward they came back the short way, cutting through the Thompsons' yard and emerging opposite the Elwings'.

"You guys coming in?" said Brad, who was twelve and responsible for Tom and Janey. He back-pedalled down his driveway looking at Tom, who shook his head.

"Maybe later, okay? I want to practice the keyboard." Sara didn't like them being on their own but she would allow it occasionally as long as Tom checked with Mrs. Elwing. "Tell your mum, okay?"

Brad nodded and waved and Tom, with Janey trudging behind, pulled the toboggan along the road to his own driveway, divided by the hedge from the Elwings'. They turned in, and there was a car parked on one side of the drive, tight against the banked snow. A man with a carrier bag was walking up to the front door.

They watched curiously as they proceeded along the drive. He rang the bell and waited, then rang again. Tom and Janey stopped near the closed garage, by the nose of the car, and Tom took Janey's hand. "If I say run, you run." The hole in the hedge through to the Elwings' was behind them.

The man left the carrier bag at the front door and came down the steps then halted, seeing them. He was very tall and he immediately lowered himself into a crouch and said "Hi. Please don't worry, I was just leaving."

Janey suddenly knew who it was and even Tom, who had avoided looking at the pictures, knew too.

"Tom! It's Mr. Adair!"

"I assumed your mother would be home. I just brought some presents by. Maybe you'd tell her I was here." Owen kept his voice even, cursing himself for frightening them.

Janey let go Tom's hand and took a couple of steps forward. "Mr. Adair? I'm Janey." Tom had most unjustly been the focus of attention lately, and she wanted to fix that.

Owen saw a dark-haired, dark-eyed, rosy-cheeked child. It was his first encounter with a six-year-old, and no contest. He felt a smile growing wide and said: "Hi. I'm pleased to meet you."

"Who are the presents for?"

"They're for all of you. One for each of you." He had to stand then because his legs were weak, and he swayed a little with dizziness. "I'll be going now," he said and came along the path toward his car.

Janey looked at Tom. Tom was in a turmoil, unsure about the presents but very sure his mother would want him to be hospitable to Mr. Adair. He suddenly wanted that, too.

"Tom?" A woman's voice called out beyond the hedge.

"Hi, Mrs. Elwing," Tom called back. "We're just going in for a snack, okay?"

"Okay, honey. See you later." They heard a door close.

Janey beamed and ran to the front steps to explore the carrier bag. Tom looked at Owen.

"Would you like to come inside?" As Owen seemed doubtful, he added: "Mum'll be home soon." Then he glanced over and saw Janey trying to drag the bag down the steps. "Janey!"

"Let me get it," said Owen and walked over to take the bag from the little girl.

Janey had a simple rule on presents: big and heavy was better than small and light. Owen's presents were only medium big but they were very heavy. She looked up at him.

"What did you get me?"

Owen smiled. "It's a surprise." He added, "It's nothing, really." That puzzled her a great deal.

*   *   *

He'd spent an uneasy night. He'd attempted three letters to Sara, thought long and hard about phoning, and finally, before he dropped off to sleep, resolved to go and see her.

Wendy had phoned this morning, to say that the Mayor's office was delighted at his decision to attend the ceremony. They wanted to move it up to noon, if Owen was agreeable, and made it clear that they, not the *Star*, would send a limousine for him.

"Are you sure about this, Owen? We're thrilled, of course, but aren't you overdoing it?" He'd been tempted to agree but one couldn't keep changing one's mind.

Now he sat obediently in a chair at the kitchen table, his mind automatically registering details. Tom had taken his coat and Janey ran out and returned moments later minus her outer garments. Tom opened the fridge then looked over at Owen:

"Uncle Bob always has beer. Would that be okay?"

"Thank you very much," said Owen politely, and Tom brought out a can of Coors Light.

"Guess what we saw after school," said Janey, sitting down at the table.

"What?" asked Owen.

"A three-legged cat," she said, impressively. "It got run over and Randy Casilio was poking it with a stick and Tom went and stopped him." She related the cat incident while Tom took out two mugs—plastic, Owen noted, and wondered if the Waterford crystal fruit bowl would be welcome.

"Cats go to heaven, don't they, Mr. Adair?"

"I don't see why not," said Owen.

"Do they go to cat heaven or people heaven?"

Subscribers' questions were occasionally way out in left field but Owen had learned to his cost that a superficial answer could land you in a lot of hot water, so he gave careful consideration to this while Tom brought the two mugs of milk to the table, then doled out cookies: one for Janey, two for himself, with Owen declining.

"I'd say that might depend on whether they were strays or not."

This opened up a whole new line of discussion and he gave Janey his full attention, sensing that Tom was content to sit and listen while he ate his cookies. Janey concluded that the three-legged cat was a stray because it had no collar.

"Would it get its other leg back in heaven?"

"It might, I guess. Unless it was born like that, and maybe even then, too."

Janey munched her cookie and thought about this. Then: "Mr. Adair?"

He smiled at her.

"Was Tom like the cat when you found him? All floppy like I told you?"

Owen shook his head. "Tom was much worse off." He sensed Tom's eyes on him and watched Janey's grow round. "He only had two legs."

She stared at him uncertainly, then Tom began to laugh. His heel banged against the chair leg and he laughed and laughed. Janey's features relaxed and she looked up at Owen and saw the twinkle in his eye. "That's funny," she said.

"I was hoping you'd think so," said Owen, meaning it, and she gave a shout of laughter and he watched both children enjoy the joke and the kitchen suddenly seemed brighter.

He studied Tom covertly. The boy seemed sturdy and well set up. "What's your favorite sport?" he asked.

"Hockey," said Tom, and Owen realized he should have guessed that.

"What do you like at school?"

Tom liked maps and stuff and places. "We did South America last week. Know what they call plains in South America?"

Owen said he had no idea.

"Pampas," said Tom. "Know what I call 'em?"

"What?" asked Owen, with a quizzical look.

"Huggies. Get it?" Tom snickered and Owen shook his head with a laugh and glimpsed fleetingly, as through a crack in time, a long-forgotten nine-year-old universe.

"Mr. Adair?" said Janey.

He cocked an eyebrow at her.

"Do you have an appendix?"

"Aw, shut up, Janey." Tom was uncomfortable.

Owen was impressed that she even knew the word. "I do indeed. Don't you?"

She nodded. "Do you think daddy has his appendix back, in heaven?"

It was asked matter-of-factly and Owen quelled his unease as he considered his answer. "The question is," he said finally, "do you think he wanted it back?"

Janey thought about that as Owen watched her, and neither of them noticed Tom staring down at the table, his face somber.

"Uh uh," she said at last, "'cos then he might have to go to hospital again and have it taken out." She finished her milk and climbed down off her chair and Tom's chair scraped against the tile floor as he suddenly stood and turned and ran out, his face distorted.

Janey stared after him, shocked, then her eyes closed, her mouth opened and out came a loud wail.

"Hold your foot up."

The wail stopped. She opened her eyes and saw him watching her intently. His gaze dropped to her feet and she looked down, then back up at Owen. He was waiting. She lifted one foot.

"Why?"

He smiled. "My daddy used to say that to me sometimes."

"Why?"

"Because—" he hadn't thought of it in years, "I guess because he wanted me to stop and think before doing something foolish."

Tom came back with traces of tears on his cheeks. He stood at the table and spoke to Janey. "I have to talk to Mr. Adair. It's—it's business." So Janey put her foot down and took her mug to the sink then left, after Tom promised to call her when they were finished.

He remained standing, looking down at the table, and Owen waited patiently. Finally, Tom spoke.

"Granny said dad's happy being in heaven. But I always thought he'd come back one day. If we ever needed him or even just to see us. Or so we could see him." He stopped, then sighed deeply. "But now I know he won't because—because I saw the cat." He raised his head. "When that cat died ... it was dead. Deader'n a doornail. It was ... just nothing." He paused, then added: "Dying's scary."

He put his head down on his arms and his voice was muffled but certain: "Daddy isn't ever coming back."

Unsure of what he should say or do, Owen remained still and waited patiently until finally, Tom raised himself up and looked him squarely in the eye. "Mr. Adair? I'm glad you were there, at the river."

"It was my pleasure," Owen found himself saying, and suddenly held out his hand. Tom took it and they shook, smiling at each other in a most friendly way.

*   *   *

Sara arrived home at ten to six, having been waylaid outside the office by two reporters who wanted her reaction to the news that Owen Adair would be receiving his award in person. Haven't they got better things to do? she thought, agreeing brightly that it was wonderful news and yes, her son was very excited. Then there was a traffic jam on the road home and she couldn't face the thought of cooking, so she called in at the mall for Kentucky Fried Chicken.

As she came into the kitchen she smelled cooking and heard Tom's keyboard and Janey singing "Silent Night," her class's contribution to the school concert. She lifted the lid of the large frypan and sniffed appreciatively. Something of Beth's? Vegetables cut large, simmering with pieces of beef.

She took off her coat and noticed the carrier bag in the hall. She stooped over it as "Silent Night" ended to clapping— who?—and opened the card on the top gift: "To Jane, Best wishes from Owen." *Damn the man,* she thought, then *I wanted to be there when they met,* then a rush of wordless relief that he was here and now they could put things right between them. But not this way, she thought, frowning as she hefted Janey's gift—a book?—then lifted another gift, to Tom, and saw a large square box in the bottom of the bag.

181

Tom started a new song, and Sara knew what it was from the preset rhythm. It was "Blue Christmas" and she and Janey always got a big kick out of it. He had a couple of false starts and she knew he must be excited. She crept down the stairs and heard his voice, high-pitched: "Listen. Listen—okay, listen—" and Owen's reply: "I am listening, take it easy." Then she bit her lip as he launched into it:

"Uh-I'll ha-ve a baloo . . . Charissmus wi-i-ithout you," in his best Elvis imitation, and Owen gave a laugh, quickly stifled, as Janey crooned: "It's elvis!" "Elvis" was her newest word and she liked saying it a lot.

"—ju-u-ust thinkin' uh-uh-uhbout you . . ." As the song went on Sara became aware of the mischievous tone in his voice, something she hadn't heard for a long time. She had to take a look.

"—won't be the samedear i-i-if you're not here with me—" Owen was sprawled on the old sofa, Janey standing next to him swaying to the beat and waving her arms, and both were looking at Tom, standing at the keyboard. Then Sara must have made a slight sound because Janey turned and saw her.

"Mummy!" She pelted across to Sara. "Owen's here!" And Sara hoisted her up with a kiss, "So I see. How's my baby?" and they walked over to Owen, looking both awkward and anxious as he stood up.

"You're looking much better," she smiled at him.

"Hi, mum!" Tom ran his thumb the length of the keyboard as Sara, still carrying Janey, sat down on the bench.

"How are you, darling?" She kissed him.

"When's dinner?" said Tom. "I'm starving."

*   *   *

Owen's concoction was overcooked, but Tom and Janey wouldn't eat KFC. Home cooking is better for you, said Janey and Owen told her she had amazing sense for one so young. Sara, measuring rice into a saucepan, observed that there must be some serious magic going on here since you couldn't pay Jane to eat home cooking when there was take-out around.

Owen sat at the table out of the way and marveled at the amount of energy created by three people in a kitchen as opposed to one. Tom and Janey set the table and told Sara all about it being Tom's idea to surprise her and how Owen had moved his car into the street and brought back the rib eye steak and onions and mushrooms and broccoli he'd bought for his dinner. And they'd supplemented this with carrots and cauliflower and tomato out of the fridge.

"And I broke the broccoli into pieces, mum," said Janey.

"And Mrs. Elwing came over and went all gushy when she saw Owen," said Tom, and Sara glanced over at Owen and laughed. Their eyes held for a moment and she turned away with a flooding gladness that he'd come.

It was so nice to sit peacefully and silently eating her dinner while Owen fielded Janey's questions and discussed hockey with Tom and she could just relax and let the fatigue dissipate. After the main course, which no one seemed to mind being overcooked and tasteless, they had Adair strudel with Newton ice cream and it was after that that Sara got a wake-up call.

Janey and Tom both had seconds and Owen took an orange from the bowl in the center of the table. Sara had just wiped up a blob of melted ice cream next to Janey's plate when she looked along the table and was transfixed by the sight of Owen's hands. They were beautiful, the most beautiful hands she'd ever seen, brown like his face, with long capable fingers and square knuckles, neither too large nor too small but just perfect for the width of his fingers, and square wrists.

She felt his glance as he smiled absently and responded to Tom's comment, and she dragged her eyes away, trying to think back, wondering why she'd never noticed before. She smiled at Janey and made some response, then covertly looked again. He'd finished peeling the orange and was pulling off segments, neatly and dexterously. A most untoward thought strayed into her mind at that point, and she thrust it away, smiling at Janey's question, and nodded.

Janey got up quickly before mum changed her mind because three helpings of dessert was unheard of. It had to be because Owen was here, she thought, and in a way she was right.

* * *

Sara sent them out of the kitchen after dinner, so after flipping through the TV channels and finding nothing but news, sports and "Ilsa, Queen of the Nazi Love Camp," which neither Tom nor Owen thought much of, they went downstairs to play hide and seek. Except for his growing tiredness, Owen could have played with them for hours: he was enthralled by them. He loved watching their active, tough little bodies; unconsciously he treated them exactly as he treated everyone, mindful only of the fact that they were younger than he was accustomed to; but this, he discovered, was the key to their most beguiling characteristic: their simplicity. They had simple wants and needs and they didn't hesitate to express them. And when Janey fell down hard and began to wail at the top of her voice, he hesitated only a second before lifting her up and holding her tight, rubbing her back because it seemed like a good thing to do. He could have held her for hours, he loved the feel of the little body, but he put her down the instant she seemed recovered, and smiled to cover a tearing sense of loss.

Then Sara called Janey to come and have her bath, so they trooped upstairs again. After Owen confessed that backgammon was the only game he knew, Tom consulted his mother and brought out Sam's leather backgammon board. They sat in the living room before the fire and Owen set out to teach him the basic moves while Janey had her bath and made Sara guess why Tom was worse off than a three-legged cat, during which Sara learned a little about the cat episode.

Janey came through to say goodnight and kissed Owen, which pleased him greatly. Tom was allowed another half hour, so they settled down to some more backgammon while Sara got Janey calmed down and finally off to sleep. Then it was Tom's turn, so they closed up the board and shook hands again.

"Guess I'll see you on the twenty-third," said Tom.

"I'm looking forward to it," replied Owen, and Tom didn't doubt him for a moment.

"Souls aren't much use," he said to Sara before she kissed him goodnight, "but I won't tell granny. That cat would have been better off losing a soul than a leg."

"We'll talk about that sometime, but not now."

"You can talk all you want, mum, but I know what I know." He looked very wise and she repressed a laugh. "I thanked Owen, mum. Guess what he said."

"What?" asked Sara with misgiving.

"He said it was his pleasure." Tom's legs kicked under the covers and he laughed.

"He must think you're a very special person." She kissed him and went to the door.

"Can I stay up? I'm not sleepy."

"Work on it." She turned out the light.

*   *   *

Owen was standing at the far wall when Sara brought in the coffee, studying the books, ornaments and holiday mementos in a glass-fronted cabinet. She put the tray on the coffee table in front of the fire, and joined him.

A ledge at waist-level held numerous family photos and he picked up one after another while she told him who they were: her parents, and Sam's, her grandmother, Bob and Ronnie and the kids. He looked for a long time at a picture of Sam on a beach with Tom. "He looks like a good guy," he said at last.

"He was a rogue," said Sara, smiling at some memory.

The living room held two big overstuffed chintz-covered couches and several easy chairs. It was gay with decorations and Christmas cards and a tree in one corner, which Owen appraised with the eye of a connoisseur before sitting on the couch before the coffee table. Sara sat on the floor opposite, near the fire, and poured them both coffee.

"I like your children, Sara."

"I know." She smiled up at him. "They like you, too. Tom," her throat tightened and she looked down for a moment and stirred her coffee, "Tom hasn't been so rambunctious for—oh, a long time. That's your doing."

He shook his head. "I think maybe it's the cat's doing." He glanced at the fire, then added, "I'm so sorry about that check, Sara."

"Oh—" she waved a hand dismissively. "Forget it."

"I just heard yesterday how upset you were. I don't know what came over me to do a thing like that."

She wanted to ask why he had to bring presents, reluctant to raise the subject, knowing she must, but he was continuing:

"I've never been that sick before. You can't know what it meant, having you there." His eyes met hers and looked away, and she knew suddenly that he wanted to join her in front of the fire and that he wouldn't, either because he was too tired or because of the children. "You were very good to me."

"How could I not be, Owen?"

He shook his head, smiling slightly. "About the presents. They're nothing, really, just a—a token of my appreciation."

"For what?"

"For what? For taking care of me, of course."

"Owen, if I'd been a stranger off the street then a token of your appreciation would be nice. But you got pneumonia because of what you did for Tom—"

"Oh now, stop it!" He stood up abruptly. "I really want you to forget about that, Sara."

"Forget about it?" She was dazed at the sudden change in mood.

"I don't want it always between us. It's history. It was nothing. Forget it."

"How can you say that?" She was on her feet too, her eyes fixed on his face. "How can you say it was nothing?"

"Because it was!"

"You've spent all afternoon with Tom. You've played with him and laughed with him and eaten dinner with him. How can you say it's nothing? 'It' is Tom. It's Tom's life. And you've never even let me thank you! How can you be so stupid?" She put a hand up to her mouth to stop her lips trembling. He took her by the arms but she shook him off.

"You listen to me!" Her voice was low and rough with anger. "This is the twenty-eighth day since you saved his life. That's—" the tears suddenly streamed down her cheeks, *"twenty-eight days that I might never have had!* How dare you say it's nothing! Don't you ever say that to me again!"

Owen was appalled. He stepped back, stumbled against the coffee table and put out a hand blindly. Sara spoke his name but he scarcely heard. He was far away from her, away from the warmth and light. His mind had plunged into the darkness of that night, into the shocking cold and fear and rising panic when he thought he couldn't hold out any longer. He felt again that thump as something hit him in the stomach, and he was suddenly covered in icy sweat at the knowledge that a yard either side and he'd never have known, never have seen. He tried to connect that limp, sodden bundle with this—with this—

He turned blindly toward the fireplace and caught the mantel to steady himself. This boy. This vital, sturdy, mischievous boy. *I want a son,* his mind shouted, *I want a son like Tom.* He was suddenly transported to his apartment, to the living room flooded with sunlight and letters and cards, and at last he acknowledged what the whole town had grasped instantly, the goodness and value of a child's life saved.

"There must be something wrong with me," he muttered. He became aware of a glass in his hand and he drank and the liquor burned in his stomach. He leaned against the mantel. It was just an impulse, he thought, and then told himself that it didn't matter, Tom was what mattered, and he'd better just be grateful he'd been there, regardless of the reason. Sara's words passed through his mind: that at some point it had become a matter of choice, not reflex, but he put them aside and turned round.

She could see his exhaustion and made him sit down while she brought him another drink. He took the glass and she sat with him, waiting quietly. He sipped the drink, then said tiredly, "It wasn't Tom I was thinking of when I said it was nothing. It was me."

"You're not nothing either."

He shook his head wearily and leaned back, closing his eyes. "My mother would have turned in her grave at what I did."

"Would she? Why?"

He opened his eyes and shrugged slightly. "She always used to tell me, You look out for yourself, Owen, no one else will."

She gazed at him, at the faint lines of bitterness round his mouth, and some hint of the conflict within him came to her suddenly, and she said:

"Maybe you were."

He looked at her. "Were what?"

"Looking out for yourself." Sara wasn't sure quite what she meant. "I mean, it isn't in some people's nature to help." She groped for the words to capture that fleeting thought. "It's like honesty. If you're dishonest, then one more lie is neither here nor there. But if you're basically an honest person then telling the truth isn't just the right thing to do, it's the only thing to do because the alternative messes you up as a person." She laughed slightly. "Sorry. It just came to me in a flash."

"Is that so?" he said gravely and she laughed outright.

"I wasn't trying to diminish what you did," she added.

He was silent for a moment, then he said, "I'd like you to tell me whatever's on your mind, Sara." He grimaced at his glass. "If it isn't too late."

She gazed at the fire and thought that it probably was too late, and hard on the heels of that came the knowledge that even so, some things deserved to be said.

"I can never never repay you for what you did, Owen," she said at last. She saw the concern in his eyes and added, "It doesn't bother me in the least. Some things can't be repaid, and this is one of them, and I don't care. I'm just so thankful you were there, and I always will be."

She looked away. He'd saved her from her blackest night-mare . . . "You didn't just save a boy that night, Owen. You saved a family. If Tom had—if we'd lost Tom, it would have blighted Janey and finished me, and so you see," she smiled at him, "you're a big fish in this little pond and we're all deeply grateful to you." His eyes were closed. She waited. "Owen?" Good lord, had he heard anything she said? "Owen?"

He opened his eyes. "Yes. Fish." His eyes creased in a faint smile. "I heard. Sara, I'm so sorry, but I've got to go home."

He refused to let her call a cab, saying the cold air would wake him. They stood in the entrance hall while he put on his coat, then turned to her, fumbling with his gloves.

"Sara—"

"Yes, Owen?" The line of her cheek was silhouetted against the light from the living room. She had no idea how lovely she looked to him.

"Sara—." He dropped a glove and she stooped to retrieve it. "Could I come and see Tom and Janey some time?"

She gave him the glove, a laughing challenge in her eyes. His mouth curved in a smile—really, it was a marvelous mouth—but he refused to say more and she thought he displayed unusual panache to brazenly assert a preference for the company of her children when he knew she knew he wanted to see her.

She laughed softly and looked away. "Would you like to join us on Christmas Eve, to sing carols? It's just family."

His face lit up. "I'd love to. I can't tell you how much I'd love to do that."

"There's just one thing, Owen."

"Anything! Just name it."

She took his hand and looked at him, suddenly grave because she had to say this, and it must be said now, without delay, or she'd never say it. "No more gifts. None at all."

11

Keith MacIntyre heard the news on the radio, and told Wendy when she came out of the shower. Wendy threw her clothes on and left the house without breakfast, stopping at the corner store for a newspaper and studying the front page as she drove. The *Star* required no concentration, no scrutiny of paragraphs of complex prose in order to grasp its message. One fleeting glance and you had it all.

"Man About Town!" blared the headline, over a picture of Owen coming out of a jewelry store—was he insane? she wondered—and across the lower half of the page: "Town About Man: Public Loves Adair" over a montage of shots of citizens and their reactions to City Hall's decision to present Owen's award behind closed doors. "They should hold it in the plaza so we could all see," said one respondent below the subhead "Briggs An Elitist."

She phoned Owen as soon as she reached the office. He seemed curiously uninterested in the furor, and when she asked why on earth he had to visit a jewelry store he replied indifferently, "To buy something."

"Owen, I think you should handle this yourself. Can I give Doctor Spence and the Mayor your number?"

"If you want," he said and disconnected. The award seemed remote and irrelevant. He felt tired and unwell and took his juice and the *Wall Street Journal* back to bed. He'd had a poor night, the second in a row, and when the phone rang he paid the caller scant attention. It was Franklin Briggs, his voice hearty and laced with professional *bon homie*. He came quickly to the point:

"There's a lot of people very happy you're recovered, Owen. I'm thinking we could make them even happier if we just move this little ceremony of ours down to the plaza. What do you say?"

Owen listened with a corner of his mind. "Because I don't like it," she'd said.

Nothing else would change, Briggs was explaining, but the location would allow more people to witness the proceedings. "None of us realized you were able to get out now, but this would be a nice touch, day before Christmas Eve. What do you say?"

"Have you talked to Mrs. Newton about it?" Owen frowned—why had he said that?—and heard the surprise in the Mayor's voice.

"Of course not. It's up to you, Owen. Nobody else. If you feel you can't do it, why just say so."

That annoyed him, for some reason. "Of course I can do it." He paused. "I won't be making a speech, though. Is that clear?"

"Absolutely," said Briggs heartily. "You just have to hold up the scroll and the medal for people to see, that's all."

Owen was suddenly curious. "Why don't you hand out keys to the city? Isn't that usually the way it's done?"

"Now look," Briggs sounded defensive, "it wasn't my administration that ended that practice. The city hasn't handed out keys for oh, ten years or more."

"Why not?" said Owen.

"Too damned expensive," came the candid reply. "Besides, they don't unlock anything." Briggs laughed. "If they did, we'd be in deep trouble."

Owen was beginning to enjoy the Mayor. "Do you expect many people to turn up?"

Briggs thought quickly. The *Star* had predicted a hundred thousand, but that was typical *Star* hyperbole: for an event they approved of, they multiplied by a factor of ten; when it was someone or something they disliked, like a Briggs political rally, they divided by ten.

The plaza would hold nearly thirty thousand, but ten was a shrewd estimate, he thought. "Well," he said easily, "it's lunchtime, a working day, I'd say we'll see a few. They won't hang around, it's too cold for that, but there's been a lot of publicity, Owen. You're a popular man. The only thing I'd caution you is, don't believe what you read in the *Star*."

Spence's call came after Owen had showered and dressed, and his mood was not improved by the nurse's "Hello, Mr. Adair. Hold for Doctor Spence, please." He disliked being put on hold by callers, he disliked Spence, and when the specialist's dry, precise voice came on the line, Owen cut him short.

"Morning, doctor. Now look, before you say anything, I'm feeling much better, and I can't imagine that being outside for a few minutes will do me any lasting harm."

"I specifically told you to stay indoors until the end of December, and to get plenty of rest—"

"Yes, well I've made the decision, and that's that."

He rang off and his mind went back to last night's conversation. "You've already brought us gifts," she'd said, and when he explained that those were nothing: "A gift is never nothing, Owen," and he'd felt an urge to throttle her.

Wendy called to express astonishment that he had agreed to an outdoor ceremony. He answered curtly. "I think I can manage to receive a scroll and say thank you, Wendy," and disconnected.

He paced back and forth, fragments of earlier remarks coming back to him. "I can never repay you . . . it doesn't bother me in the least." That had dismayed him: it was an attitude that had got a lot of Third World countries into deep financial trouble. Perhaps after all she was not the woman he'd imagined. He stared outside. "You've already given Tom a priceless gift . . . A gift is never nothing . . . You give too many gifts . . . Because I don't like it." *Because I don't like it.* She might as well have said, "Because I don't like you," he thought bleakly and his heart hardened.

* * *

Sara couldn't believe her ears when she heard of the change in plans. "Have you checked with Mr. Adair?"

"Naturally. He said no problem," replied the Mayor's assistant. "Now be sure to allow plenty of time for getting here. Could you be—"

"Did you actually speak to him?" Sara was incredulous.

"Mayor Briggs did. Would you come to my office, same as before—"

"But he shouldn't be outside," she protested. "He isn't fully recovered." Her stomach began to hurt.

"He was outside yesterday, Mrs. Newton. Didn't you see the *Star*?"

Sara had seen it, courtesy of Trish, the moment she arrived, and all she could think when she saw the picture of Owen emerging from the jeweler's was *Well, it isn't a ring,* remembering the size and weight of the box at home.

She noted the assistant's instructions mechanically and put the phone down. This was a bad idea, she was certain of it. This was terrible. She sat huddled at her desk feeling nauseous. She began to open the mail, wondering what to do, then after she'd taken it in to Mike she came to a decision and dialed Owen's number. His calls, she discovered, were being re-routed to the office, and after chatting briefly with Judy, she waited until Wendy came on the line.

"I was going to call you," said Wendy. "Have you heard the news?"

"I can't believe Owen agreed?"

"I know. He sounded as though he didn't care either way."

"What do you mean?" Sara asked with a sinking heart.

Wendy relayed her brief exchanges with Owen and added: "I honestly don't think he has any idea of his popularity. Shut up in his little treetop abode, no contact with local media."

"Do you think he's all right?"

"I don't know. The doctor's talked to him, so I assume he is." She paused. "What's going on with you two, Sara? What was he doing in a jewelry store? I've got a business to run and I'd like to know."

Sara was beginning to feel beseiged as well as nauseous. She wasn't ready to talk about Owen, not even to Wendy, who really deserved some inkling of how things stood.

Wendy relented. "Look, Sara. Owen and I have a close professional relationship, but I know very little about his personal life. It's always suited him to keep things that way, and that's fine. But we think very highly of him in this office and we don't want him to—to come to any harm."

"Nor do I," said Sara. She fell silent and finally, Wendy sighed.

"Look—you can get him on the unlisted number. And Sara—let me know if there's any change, would you?"

Farraday Construction was closing for the holidays at noon, and the morning was occupied with Christmas bonuses and matters arising from the mail. These done, Sara gazed indecisively at Owen's number. "He sounded as though he didn't care," Wendy had said.

He was angry, she was certain of it. Angry with her, as he hadn't been last night. She wished with all her heart she'd never said it, and reached for the phone to tell him he could bring whatever he liked as long as he came. She changed her mind. Things were moving fast between them and intuitively she knew this matter of gift-giving had to be tackled now, not later. She remembered his parting words. "It's Christmas Eve, I'll do what I like," he'd said over his shoulder as he left.

Eventually she did dial a number, but it wasn't Owen's. She called Ruby, seeking an ally, but Ruby's first words drove the matter from her mind.

"Hi honey, I was going to call you. Didn't you tell me Owen could play the piano?"

"Yes of course. He plays beautifully, why?"

"I guess the paper got it wrong then. But I'd be interested to meet these people, the Watsons."

Sara rang off a few moments later, and asked Trish: "Did you see a piece on Owen in yesterday's paper?"

"It's in your In tray. I told you," said Trish, adding, as Sara found the clipping, "It's kind of, like, dull? I mean, he hasn't done anything . . . "

Farraday came out of his office a few minutes later to find Sara putting on her coat.

"I have to leave, Mike." She stuffed the article in her purse. "I've got to drive out to Minton." She was gone.

Trish faced two enquiring gazes. "I don't know," she said. "He hasn't done anything. I mean, he never did...."

*   *   *

When Sara was about twelve an uncle had taken her and her brother fishing at a lake near Minton. All she remembered of the town was a short main street and a traffic light at an intersection having corn fields on two sides. Twenty years later and an hour's drive along the highway, she discovered a gentrified satellite community of low-rise apartment buildings and townhouse complexes, and upmarket dress shops. She drove slowly through town and pulled in at the gas station and convenience store.

She went inside and found a phone book. There were a depressing number of Watsons and while she was running her finger down the Gs a voice at her elbow said,

"You lookin' for Gord Watson?"

A tall, lanky youth was transferring cans of Niblets corn to an adjacent shelf. He grinned at Sara's expression. "I saw you pullin' out the *Star*. You're here about Owen, aren't you?"

Sara assented, and he went on: "I can show you where he used to live if you want. And where the Watsons live. We had that reporter in here last week, and I figured after that piece came out I should do a tour. Charge for it."

Amused, Sara asked how much he wanted. They completed their negotiations and she bought a cup of coffee and a sandwich and ate her lunch while waiting for the tour guide, whose shift ended at two p.m.

"I'm thinking about a minivan," he said at five past, as he climbed into her car.

"Wait to see what kind of demand you get," suggested Sara, and on his instructions returned along Main then turned off halfway. She was shown the high school, the location of Owen's house (which had been torn down to make way for townhouses) and finally pulled up in front of a retirement home.

"You go out along this road about two miles if you want to see the dump," said her guide.

"Why on earth would I want to do that?" Sara handed over his fee.

"Talk to Gord. Mr. Watson. You'll see."

*   *   *

Dexter looked up with an ingratiating smile as Owen approached the desk. "Great to see you up and about, sir. Feeling better?"

"Much better." Owen put four envelopes on the counter with a tiny slap. "Christmas bonuses, Dexter. Would you see that they get into the right boxes?" The guards each had a mail slot in the office.

"Sure will, sir." The guard reached for the envelopes.

"You'll see there's nothing for you there. I'm assuming Monica paid your bonus this year. No need for me to."

"Sir?"

"I thought of raising this with the management, but we can settle it between ourselves, don't you think?"

Dexter looked as though he'd been bitten by a stuffed toy. "Now wait a minute, Mr. Adair. Has Drummond been telling you some nonsense about—"

"I haven't spoken to Drummond. Don't say something you might regret, Dexter. Monica Stephanopoulos was waiting in the elevator with my suitcase, the day of the blizzard. You had to have let her in."

"I couldn't—I don't—" Dexter began to gabble.

"Oh, I think so. Now, if I'm being unjust you just say the word, and we'll put the question to the management and let them settle it. Would you prefer that?"

He waited through a feeble protest until Dexter fell silent, looking down at the desk, reddening.

"I thought not. The way I see it, Monica must have paid you to let her in. So you haven't lost out." He turned to go. "And Dexter?" He glanced back. "You take care that never happens again."

Dexter was about to give a facile assurance when his eyes were caught by Owen's. He said nothing, feeling unnervingly transparent. "Yes sir," he muttered at last. Owen nodded and returned to the elevator.

He got out at the second floor, seeking diversion of some kind. He found it in the library, where Hank Garrett was peering at the titles for something to read after his swim. Garrett was a wiry man in his late fifties, with pale blue eyes and a seamed face. A mining engineer three times divorced, he'd just returned from Colorado. Owen's name meant nothing to him and they settled down to a cosy chat about the price of gold, extraction costs per ton, underground versus open-pit operations, stoping methods and the virtues of heap leaching. Owen stretched out his legs and listened content-edly, inserting an occasional question and soaking up information.

His mood slightly less bleak, he returned to the penthouse an hour later to hear the phone ringing. It was Tug, calling to wish him a Merry Christmas. The Sheppards would be leaving for Whistler as soon as Liz was ready. He'd called twice before and got the nurse both times. Owen had no recollection of his call the day of the blizzard. "No? Okay, listen up. Liz would be real happy if you'd come to dinner sometime after Christmas. She specifically told me to tell you to bring anything you want. She really misses you. Am I getting through to you on this?"

"Sure. Why are you whispering?" It turned out that Tug wanted to surprise his wife with this news, an explanation that made no sense at all to Owen, so he disregarded it.

"Does this mean you're not going to try and deck me if I happen to bring a gift?"

They had a candid exchange of views on who would deck whom, and then began catching up on each other's news— which lasted until Liz called, and Tug said, "Gotta go," and rang off.

Owen suddenly felt a whole lot better about things, and his mood lightened still more when he took yet another call from Wendy. Iris and Spider were with her and all three were delighted with his gifts. He chatted with each in turn, wishing them a happy Christmas and getting a kick out of their pleasure.

He disconnected with kindlier thoughts of Sara. After all, she had not voluntarily assumed mountains of debt like some banana republic; it had been thrust upon her. Furthermore, he reminded himself, he hadn't wanted her to feel beholden to him. He'd wanted her to forget it. Beholden. "The Adairs aren't beholden to anyone." It was a good rule, but Owen knew he was sometimes dogmatic about it; Tug had made him see that in college. "Quit being so rigid, buddy."

Improvise, he thought suddenly, and phoned Monica. "I want the number of the boy who played the piccolo in that bus rescue," he said without preamble, and waited while she put him on hold. Wendy and Iris had told him one afternoon about the bus rescue and the infant prodigy, Sigmund Smith. The boy's explanation, "I improvised," had struck him forcibly. The word seemed an admirable combination of art and science, reason harnessed in the service of creativity. "I improvised." It resonated, in a way that his mumbled "something I made up" did not. It intrigued him, especially coming from one so tender in years.

Monica came back on the line with the phone number. "I know you'll be a huge hit tomorrow," she added.

"Tell me, Monica. Why the jewelers? Why didn't you use your photo of me at the Newtons?"

A tiny pause, then, "Darling!"

"You were caught between a rock and a hard place, weren't you? You wanted an outdoor ceremony but you were afraid of being accused of recklessly endangering my health."

"Darling, if you've been outside once, presumably you can do it again."

"And of course, if you'd used the Newton pic—"

"I never said there *was* such a pic."

"That might have angered me, which doesn't suit your purposes at all. At least, not at the moment."

She had made exactly that argument to Hoch, warning him that Owen might refuse to appear at all if they'd used the cute picture of Tom and Janey holding hands and facing Owen outside their house.

"Listen carefully, Monica. You people keep your hands off the Newtons from now on. Is that clear? I don't care what you do about me, but stay away from them—that is, if you want any cooperation from me in future."

"Have you reconsidered my suggestion?" she asked. "About making a contribution?"

"Looks like I'm doing that tomorrow."

"No, no, no, you're just giving the drones a thrill. Which is fine, and I have a hunch that you'll come across as fresh and original without being a wing nut. Why don't I call you right after Christmas, and we can get down to specifics?"

He made some noncommittal remark and rang off, then dialled the Smith number, reaching Mrs. Smith.

"Adair? *The* Owen Adair?"

"I don't know," he replied, taken aback. "I guess so—"

"Is this long distance? Who is this?" The voice was mistrustful. "Are you with the network?"

Owen explained why he'd called: Sigmund's story interested him and he wondered if there was any chance the boy and his parents could visit. "I know it's asking a lot, but—"

"Where do you live?"

"I'm at the Pointe. Do you—"

"Oh my God, it is him! Sigmund! *Sigmund!* Mr. Adair? Are you there?"

Owen assured her he was.

"This is a godsend. We'd love to come. So would Sigmund, whether he likes it or not."

On that somewhat ambiguous note, she rang off, and Owen set about tidying the place and ordering a half a dozen eclairs to go with Mary Cavanaugh's fruit cake ("P.S. It'll keep for weeks.").

The Smiths, Mrs. and Sigmund, arrived an hour and a half later. Mr. Smith was doing some shopping and cooking dinner, Owen learned, and Sigmund had brought his flute.

"Everyone always wants me to play," he said complacently, and consumed four eclairs while he surveyed the view, the fig tree and the piano. Owen chatted with Mrs. Smith and studied him covertly. He was a slight boy, with a white face under a shock of black hair, not a child one could readily warm to, but Owen never went by appearances. He himself had been a skinny, pimply kid, all arms and legs and painfully shy. Sigmund was not shy.

"How come you got a grand piano if you can't play?"

"Who said I can't play?" Owen was surprised.

Mrs. Smith interposed, with apologies. The article in yesterday's paper had quoted a schoolmate of Owen's who said he used to play in Sunday school and she'd never forgotten how bad it was.

Owen laughed. "She's right, it was terrible. I never could play for an audience, that's all. Stage fright." He looked at Sigmund. "Doesn't it bother you?"

"Nah. You just forget about the audience. They don't know anything anyway."

Mrs. Smith suggested quickly that perhaps they could play something together, and received a glance from Owen as he rose, a reassuring look that seemed to say he wasn't offended, and she relaxed while they tried one or two tentative songs, then launched into something, surely it was Bach?, delicate and achingly sweet and somehow suited to this beautiful room. It died away finally and she saw them regarding each other with a kindly eye, and knew they were satisfied.

Owen broke the silence. "I'd be fascinated to hear what you did with Joy to the World." Sigmund scowled.

"He doesn't like to play that, Owen. Not while the negotiations are ... up in the air." Owen looked puzzled, and Sigmund explained. One of the networks was negotiating to make a TV movie of the bus rescue. He was holding out for more money and everyone hated him, including his parents.

"That's not true, dear—"

"Mother. Go get my piccolo."

Owen gave her his security card and explained how to use it, then returned to the piano and listened to Sigmund's plans for becoming a millionaire, envying the simplicity of his being. Sigmund's music was the sole purpose of his life. It was his best thing, and Owen was glad for the boy's sake that his best was so good.

"I don't know anything about TV movies," he said at last, "but is there any chance they might write you out of it?"

"How can they do that?" Sigmund's face turned chalky.

Owen stressed that he didn't know, but he'd heard they were sometimes not too fussy about the facts. He thought it best to change the subject then, and asked Sigmund how his creation had come to him.

"Aw, we were stamping our feet, you know? Because it was cold out there. And Carl and Joey switched from Christians Awake—that's so spastic—into Joy without telling me so I thought I'd fix 'em, and I just let go." His face lightened reminiscently. "I just went leapin' up over top of 'em and they tried speeding up to shake me off. I had a lot of runs in there, you know? And they couldn't do it. I'm like all over them." He snickered and Owen watched him, amused, then saw all the light go out of his face.

"What?"

Sigmund scuffed the carpet and said nothing. Owen waited. At last the boy looked at him, and his face was drawn. "I forgot part of it." He halted, then the words gushed out: "I never had that happen before. I don't understand it. I can't see it. It's like I'm turning the page only there's two pages stuck together and I can't unstick them."

"Can't you hear it either?"

Sigmund shook his head miserably. "I wasn't really concentrating at the time, you know?" Owen nodded. "We played it at school a couple days after the rescue, an' I made up a bit, and after, Mr. Eisenmeyer—he's the band teacher, he was in the bus?—he said was I sure that's how it went and—an' I lied and said yes."

"Is that why you're holding out on the TV negotiations?"

"No way!" He was scornful. "They don't know nothin', those guys. They wouldn't know the difference."

Owen began to play idly, studying the boy. "Why lie? What does it matter if you forgot it? There's plenty more where that came from, isn't there?"

Sigmund shrugged. "I guess."

Owen smiled inwardly. The arrogance of youth. "Mind if I give you a tip? Never lie about your music. It isn't necessary and you risk losing a fortune if you do."

"How come?" Sigmund was skeptical.

"Because if you lie about it, you might distort or destroy it. You could kill the goose that lays the golden egg. You wouldn't want that, would you?"

Mrs. Smith returned with the piccolo during O Little Town of Bethlehem and when they were finished Sigmund informed him that the tune was composed by a real estate agent. "An' Joy to the World, that was written by a banker." Seeing Owen's surprise, he elaborated: "Lowell Mason. He was the first American composer to make money. More'n eleven hundred compositions, he had. Wanna hear my latest? I've composed lots. Twenty-nine real songs, so far." He played a short, sprightly tune and Owen complimented him sincerely. The piece was immature but tremendously stylish. "I call it Crack," Sigmund informed him. "See, I thought of it when I was looking at these cracks in the sidewalk, but it's a good name because people'll think it's about drugs."

Mrs. Smith closed her eyes.

The afternoon flew by as they played and played, and finally, when Mrs. Smith said for the third time that they really had to leave, Sigmund said:

"Wanna play Joy to the World?" He took out his piccolo and Owen savored the artless, soaring harmony. Afterward, Sigmund asked: "Did you know where the bit was?" Owen hesitated, then played a short passage, and Sigmund nodded dolefully and scowled at the piano. "Ma? We have to call the network tomorrow. I'm takin' their offer."

"Yes, dear," said his mother, and shortly after, when Sigmund had gone to the bathroom, she thanked Owen fervently for his help. Something made her add, "Would you like to come over one evening, when you're better? My husband would really enjoy meeting you. Maybe you could come for dinner?"

"That would be great," he said, his face lighting up and she realized he was no great age, really no older than herself.

They talked about the symphony until Sigmund returned. The Smiths were going to give him a season ticket next year, if they could find someone he could go with. As they were leaving, Owen said to Sigmund:

"Bet you ten dollars you'll get that bit back. Just forget about it for now."

The black eyes stared up at him. "Ten, huh?"

Owen laughed. "Ten. But take my advice and forget about it, or you'll be paying me."

He watched them into the elevator, and wished them a merry Christmas. "Good luck tomorrow, Owen," said Sigmund's mother as the doors closed.

He returned inside. What great people. He would get them two more season tickets, then they could go as a family, or Sigmund could take two friends, if he had two.

Tomorrow! He had pushed it to the back of his mind, behind thoughts of Sara, Dexter, the office . . . He thrust it aside again, pursuing a train of thought. Was simplicity the exclusive preserve of children? Tug was simple. At least, he was uncomplicated, not quite the same thing. Owen suddenly yearned to see his old friend, and wished fervently that Tug had not chosen today to leave town.

Tomorrow! His stomach churned, and his imagination shifted suddenly into high gear.

*   *   *

Ronnie Hargreaves had not seen her sister-in-law for more than two weeks, and when Sara failed to drop by as promised, she decided to pay her a visit.

"I've come for the sheep picture," she said, walking into the kitchen that evening. Ronnie had short, tightly curled black hair and green eyes, and looked seasonal in fuchsia sweater and dark green pants.

Sara was full of apologies. "I meant to bring it over, Ron, but I had to drive out to Minton." She took Ronnie's coat and hat and went to find the photograph. Ronnie explored the fridge, settling for a glass of sparkling water. The kitchen was filled with good smells and she wondered if Sara's heightened color came from slaving over a hot stove or other causes.

A newspaper clipping lay on the table, and when Sara returned with the manila envelope Ronnie was absorbed in it. "You can't accuse them of sensationalism, at any rate. I've never read anything so boring."

"He happens to be the most wonderful pianist, despite what that Marilyn Biggs says." She bent over a baking tray on the counter. "And he isn't boring. That's one thing he's not."

"Are those Chocolate Crinkles?" Ronnie asked.

Sara nodded, then looked doubtfully at her. "Do you want one?"

"If they're for Christmas Eve I can be strong." Weight was a continual battle for both Bob and Ronnie, and they had been dieting religiously for several weeks, storing up calorie credits for Christmas. Ronnie sipped her sparkling water and aired her new theory. Calories, she told Sara, clustered like barnacles around the stomach and thighs. Sparkling water was beyond a doubt the best aid to weight loss devised by science because the fizz weakened the barnacles' hold, washing them into the bloodstream and thence into the digestive tract.

"Ten glasses a day and I'm flushing calories away. Literally. It's fantastic."

Sara opened the oven door and popped in another batch of cookies, then poured herself a glass of water. She closed the fridge and hesitated, staring at the phone on the counter, then brought her glass to the table. She met her sister-in-law's quizzical look.

"I'm just—I can't decide whether to call him or not. I'm worried about tomorrow, Ronnie."

"What did Marilyn tell you?"

"Oh her," Sara was scornful. "I didn't see her. I visited the Watsons."

Ronnie glanced at the article. "The people who knew his parents?"

Sara nodded. "They live in a condo, they sold their house eight years ago, they're in their eighties and it was as hot as hell."

Tom mooched into the kitchen trailed by Janey, both with long faces. Janey had a bright pink plastic purse slung across her chest by its strap. "I need a loan, mum," said Tom, coming straight to the point.

"Say hello to your aunt," said Sara.

"Hi, Aunt Ronnie," said Tom, and Janey climbed up on Sara's knee, the purse clinking. "'Lo," she said. Relations between Janey and Aunt Ronnie had become somewhat strained during the blizzard on account of Aunt Ronnie always siding with Megan. She regarded her aunt solemnly across the table while Tom explained his problem.

"I spent all my money already. I don't have enough for Owen's present."

"I've got eight dollars and thirty-one cents," Janey announced. "I broke the giraffe," she answered her mother's look.

"The only other thing I could do is take Janey's present back for a refund," Tom suggested, and Ronnie laughed at Janey's wail of protest.

"Why do you want to buy Owen a present?" She reached for her bag.

"Because he's coming for Christmas Eve," said Tom.

"You've spoken to him?" Ronnie glanced from Tom to Sara.

"He came to see us yesterday," said Janey. "He likes us."

Ronnie bent her head. The light in their faces. . . . She rummaged for her wallet. "We forgot to pay you for shoveling the walks—"

"Oh now, stop that," Sara protested, amused.

"It's true. Isn't it," Ronnie looked at Tom. "Didn't your uncle tell you?" Tom shook his head with a grin, and took the ten dollars she handed him.

"Thanks, Aunt Ronnie," he bounded out, "come on, Janey, we got enough now."

Janey clambered down with a clink, and ran after him.

"He paid you a visit, did he?" Ronnie frowned because a laugh might be misinterpreted.

Sara nodded, tracing a pattern on the table. Ronnie studied her, intrigued.

"I invited him for Christmas Eve," Sara said at last, "and I told him not to bring any more gifts."

"More?"

Sara explained. "He just gives and gives, Ron. Not just presents, but in all kinds of ways. I don't think he ever thinks of himself at all." She paused, then went on, "And now I'm afraid we won't see him again."

"You'll see him tomorrow," said Ronnie briskly, to ease the situation. She opened the manila envelope to look at the sheep picture. "And make sure you stay well away from him. Let's not forget this character tried to molest you—"

Sara burst into laughter and regarded her with affection. "You remind me of Randy Casilio."

"Who might he be?" Ronnie slipped the picture back in the envelope.

"A warped ten-year-old who goes around poking bodies to see if they're alive." Their eyes met. "I'm still alive, Ron."

"Good," Ronnie said briefly. She hated sentiment. "Chelsea moved back in with her parents last week, did you hear?" Chelsea was Sara's cousin, and her marriage was going through a rocky patch. They settled down for a gossip about the family and mutual friends, just like old times. Finally, when Ronnie was convinced that indeed Sara was the same as before or better, she reached across the table and took her hand. "So. Tell me what happened in Minton."

Sara sighed. "Oh, you know what boys are like at fifteen. All hormones and arms and legs."

"They're vile. Thank God for girls."

"When Owen was fifteen his dad broke his back and the dentist his mother worked for retired and things were very tough. Agnes, his mother, was a proud woman. Anyway, people began sending things round. Casseroles and preserves and all kinds of things and Martin—Owen's dad—said that was fine, but Agnes wouldn't tolerate it. She made Owen take everything back."

She fell silent then went on, "Small town. You know. They had about eight thousand people then, and twelve churches. Now they've got nearly twenty thousand but only ten churches. In Mrs. Watson's opinion, that, in a nutshell, is what's wrong with society today."

Ronnie rolled her eyes. "Oh right. They have no street crime in Minton. It all takes place behind closed doors."

Sara chose not to be sidetracked. "Back then it was just a small farming community. Martin drove in one day in forty-six and decided to stay. Gord said he was in the war but he never talked about it. Gord doesn't think it did him much good but Mrs. Watson said that's no excuse."

"No excuse for what?" Ronnie looked at her askance.

Sara shook her head and sighed. "He was odd. Anyway, Owen turned up at the Watsons' door to return a casserole and Mrs. Watson felt sorry for him because he was so embarrassed, and angry because the casserole was no big deal, and she got in the car and took it back and lit into Agnes. But Agnes always was stiff-necked, and wouldn't even discuss the matter."

"How long did this go on?"

"Martin was laid up for six months. Agnes was a great saver, according to Mrs. Watson. But the savings ran out and for about six weeks they hadn't got a thing. Owen did odd jobs, and Agnes worked in the cafe, and then she finally got another job as a dental assistant and things improved. But you can see how that might affect a teenager, especially if he's proud to begin with."

She fell silent, thinking back. "You get two different pictures, depending on which Watson you listen to."

"That reporter didn't listen at all, judging by the story. There's nothing about that in here," said Ronnie.

"He didn't know what to ask, that's all."

Sara glanced at the phone again, then sprang up to check on the oven. "They used to have a saying in Minton," she went on, peering at the Chocolate Crinkles. "If a party was really great you'd say it was more fun than spending Sunday at the dump." She closed the oven door and turned to find Ronnie gazing at her.

"It's true. Martin used to go to the dump on Sundays. Everyone did. You found out what was going on in town when you took your trash to the dump. People used to go either before church or after, except for Martin. He skipped church so he could take in both acts." Ronnie cackled and Sara added, "I'm quoting Gord. Mrs. Watson was very sniffy and said poor Agnes had too much to contend with.

"He used to take Owen with him, until Agnes found out. That's when Owen started Sunday school." She returned to the table. "Martin used to repair things. He'd find old appliances and take them home and repair them." A laugh bubbled up and she tried to stop it. "I picture this skinny little kid climbing over tin cans and toaster ovens at the dump, then I see Owen sitting in the lap of luxury in his penthouse, and I don't know—" she laughed helplessly.

Ronnie replenished both their glasses as Sara continued. "Martin used to visit the Watsons every Wednesday night after dinner. He went to the Iselings on Saturday because Jerry Iseling was another of his buddies. Anyway, he'd arrive with a bottle of rye and sit in Mrs. Watson's chair in the den—she'd spend the evening in the living room—and they'd trade stories. Gord never told many, it was mostly Martin telling these stories about people he'd come across. Just ordinary people and simple stories but the way Martin told them there was a twist at the end and you laughed and laughed and slapped your knee and said, 'Ain't that the truth?' or 'You can always trust so-and-so for that.'"

She fell silent.

"You wonder why some people marry," Ronnie observed.

"Agnes figured to find herself a stud."

"Mrs. Watson has a way with words."

Sara gave her a look. "Mrs. Watson said Agnes wanted a child, she was nearly forty, and Martin was clean and reasonably intelligent and the only eligible bachelor in town, so—" Sara spread her hands. "Martin always seemed surprised that he'd actually fathered a child."

She traced another pattern on the table. "Depending on who you listen to, Agnes was ambitious, sour, determined, a good housekeeper, a strict mother. Martin was a good friend, a bum, generous, a crank and a waste of time. They only agreed on one thing, the Watsons. Do you know what that was?" Ronnie shook her head as Sara went to the oven and took out the Chocolate Crinkles, removing them from the baking tray to a wire rack. "Gord was explaining that they didn't tell the *Star* about Martin because he's hard to describe, and Mrs. Watson interrupted and said, 'What Owen did, that's Martin all over.' And Gord agreed."

Sara turned, leaning against the oven door. "Martin's funeral was the biggest one Gord ever went to. They had open house afterward, the Watsons did, and Gord said complete strangers kept turning up all afternoon." She looked at Ronnie. "Owen wasn't there. He left right after the funeral and they haven't seen him since."

12

The sirens suddenly cut out, and the motorcycle escort peeled off to right and left. A broad red carpet lay ahead. The white stretch limousine nosed slowly up the ramp covering the shallow steps to the plaza and inched its way along the carpet.

Inside the car, Franklin Briggs sat on one side waving to the cheering crowd lining both sides of the carpet, restrained by city police. He glanced at his companion. "How about giving them a wave, Owen?"

Owen could barely hear through the ringing in his ears. His vision was blurred, his tongue felt deformed and swollen, and a twitch in his right leg was spreading from calf to thigh. Otherwise, his brain laboriously insisted, he felt fine.

The limousine stopped, and Briggs bounded out on the left. Owen's door was opened by a policeman and he stepped out carefully, so his left leg could take his weight. Mindful of his lungs, he had on a T-shirt, a sweatshirt, a turtleneck sweater and a cable-stitched V-necked pullover, and his overcoat felt tight across his shoulders. He was suddenly fifteen again, sprouting out of his clothes, and he slouched, to make his pants longer.

The distant ground beckoned and he longed to lie down but someone was leading him forward and up some steps to a—oh God!—a platform with people lined along the back. He shuffled toward them and was arrested by a hand on his arm, which turned him to face—. His mind refused to acknowledge the crowd. He focused intently on a lectern ahead and to one side.

A short fat man came to the lectern with a Bible. He opened it and began to read.

*   *   *

Sara sat on the right of the line of dignitaries, next to Wendy. Owen had looked straight at her as he came up the steps and she knew he hadn't seen her. She listened to the Archbishop reading the lesson of the Good Samaritan and looked at Owen, standing between Mayor Briggs and Tom, and she concentrated with all her might, trying to send him her support and confidence. Sitting next to her, Wendy was doing the same.

*   *   *

"Mum looks all funny," said Janey, watching the ceremony with Beth Elwing in the Elwings' den.

"She does, doesn't she?" said Beth. "So does the woman next to her. They look like two broody hens." Janey laughed.

The platform was decorated with bunting and a large banner at the rear read "Owen Adair Day." The announcer had estimated a crowd of about 20,000 and a sea of blue surrounded the platform, everyone waving small pennants with "Owen's Day" in white lettering on a blue background.

The Archbishop wound up the story, closed his Bible and stepped away. The camera zoomed in on Tom. Janey watched, her mouth frozen in an "O" as Tom turned toward the far end and marched over to stand before the Clerk.

"Isn't he sweet!" exclaimed Beth and Janey wailed "I want to be there! It's not fair!" Beth soothed her. "Look at mum, honey!" The camera had zoomed in on Sara and they watched as the woman next to her said something and Sara's face lightened in a smile as she watched Tom with pride.

"Gosh, honey, she looks like a movie star, doesn't she?"

*   *   *

Mac Drummond thought the same, watching his TV at home in his recliner. She was wearing the same outfit he'd seen when she arrived at the Pointe, the russet red coat and hat and the white muffler.

Tom took the scroll in one hand and a leather box in the other, then turned and marched back across the platform. He was wearing his ski jacket over his suit, and the knot of his tie showed at the top. He stopped in front of the Mayor and Owen. There was a momentary hesitation as he tried to remember which came first, then he held out the scroll and the Mayor took it.

Tom smiled up at Owen and stepped back to stand by his side. Owen's gaze remained fixed on the lectern. Mac shook his head worriedly, then the Mayor unrolled the scroll.

*   *   *

"Hear ye, hear ye . . ." Dr. Spence shook his head and left the crowd in front of the TV in the hospital lounge. Celebrities! He wished fervently as he walked along the corridor that he'd never agreed to take the case. Adair deserved to scar his lungs if he was prepared to disregard doctor's orders. Spence hoped there wouldn't be a lawsuit.

*   *   *

". . . Freedom of the City to Owen Adair!" Briggs rolled up the scroll as a cheer echoed round the plaza. He stepped back and turned, taking a ribboned medal from the box in Tom's outstretched hand.

Owen lowered his head mechanically and Briggs draped the ribbon round his neck and put the scroll into his hand. Then he took Owen's arm and led him forward.

"Ladies and gentlemen, boys and girls . . . Owen Adair! Let's show him how we feel!" Amid a sea of blue flags the decibel level rose higher, the cheers echoing off the buildings.

Sara smiled at Wendy as they stood clapping. Another moment or two and he'd be coming back to shake their hands, then it would all be over.

"Speech! Speech!" She disregarded the scattered cries. Briggs had assured her Owen needn't make a speech. The cries grew more organized and louder. "Speech! Speech!"

As flowers open their petals to the sun, so politicians facing a crowd open their mouths. Briggs grinned. "I don't know, Owen, seems a shame not to oblige. What do you say?" He looked enquiringly at Owen, who nodded once. Briggs steered him to stand before the lectern.

"No!" Sara stepped forward. Wendy stopped her.

"Let him. If he wants to, let him." She met Sara's gaze. "Don't undermine him."

*   *   *

Owen hadn't heard Briggs's question. He nodded because he was ready to leave any time. But when Briggs steered him forward instead of off to the rear, he found himself confronted by a million upturned faces, cheering and waving pennants.

His brain was a block of ice. His hands were frozen to the sides of the lectern. The cheering began to die down. He couldn't speak, he knew that for sure. Began to fade. He could not speak. Died. He'd have to speak. Blue sky.

"My dad was a failure." Thick tongue. What? What was that? "He told me so himself."

* * *

The crowd waited attentively. He was going to lay another parable on them, rags to riches or something. Whatever. They were content to listen. In the front row, wearing his Calvin Klein jacket, Spider stared at Owen in consternation, then glanced at Iris. She was looking at the ground. On the platform, Wendy stared down at her hands clasped in her lap. Sara had been right after all, and she felt sick.

* * *

The silence was so complete he could hear the cars passing on the far side of the plaza. He could hear. What had he said? What?

"Impulses," he croaked. "I've been," he struggled to breathe, "thinking a lot about impulses." The ice shifted in his brain. "In fact, I've got one right now I'm thinking about." A ripple of laughter and scattered applause. A voice bellowed, "Good on yer, mate!"

Was that an Aussie? What was an Aussie doing here, at this time of year? They were planning a promo in Australia. A subscriber. *Think of him as a sub.*

"What makes us do," his hands flew up off the lectern as he struggled for breath, "the things that we do?" Sara saw them, trembling violently, and bowed her head. A tear ran down her cheek, then stopped and froze where it lay.

The ice was beginning to break up. He labored on: "Most of the time when you have an impulse, you stop and have second thoughts and then you don't do it." He could see a long trailer parked on one side of the plaza, with "Owen Adair Day" and the *Star* logo draped over it. He could see.

"If it's a bad impulse, like robbing a gas station, then second thoughts are good." He could see steam rising from the drinks being served at the trailer. "I hope they put plenty of rum in those drinks." A bigger laugh and more applause and waving pennants. His entire body was shaking and he gripped the edges of the lectern.

"I had an impulse one night a few weeks ago, and I want to tell you about it. Because when I got to the edge of the river, I had second thoughts." They were silent again.

"I have to tell you, I did not want to go in that water. A lot of things went through my mind, I guess, and what they mostly amounted to was, what's the point? It's dark and deep and wide. What can I do, me alone, except maybe get myself drowned?" So why had he gone in? He shrugged under his coat, remembering. Not an exciting or heroic reason, but he'd come this far, better finish. "It can't hurt. That's what made me go in. I just thought, 'well, it can't hurt', and so what I want to tell you is—" he stopped, hearing the words clear as a bell: *Can't hurt, Ag.*

"—is my dad used to say, 'It can't hurt to lend a hand.' He used to say that all the time and it drove my mother up the wall."

Memories flooded in and pushed the words out of him: "He'd be out helping someone move house or paint the fence when he should have been in the shop." Then times got really bad, all the donations, *We are not taking charity, Martin.* Then Dad, protesting mildly, *It's not charity, Ag, it's payback.*

He forced his mind back to the present. "A lot of people have been very kind to me since that night. It's been amazing to me. . . ." A swell of clapping and cheering and he suddenly remembered Tom and turned. Tom looked back at him gravely and a little uncertainly. Owen held out a hand and he stepped forward and Owen put an arm round his shoulders and hugged him clumsily against his side. He spoke into the mike.

"I wish I could tell you what a fine boy this is." The cheering rose still more. Tom seemed to gain a couple of inches and Owen went on, "Fishing him out of the river was the best thing I ever did in my life." He suddenly knew it was true. The crowd let loose and he raised his head. He could see more clearly and a measure of confidence suddenly lodged itself under his ribs.

"I don't know where impulses come from. Maybe our genes, or maybe our upbringing. But I think they're the essence of humanity, good and evil. I think they're human nature distilled." He stared at the lectern, then went on: "It's easy to kill an impulse. You think about the risk, and you don't do it. But we can't get ahead if we don't take risks. That's true in life as well as business. It's those good impulses, to better yourself or change careers, to apologize or lend a hand—they represent progress. So when you have a good one, give it a chance. Listen to your heart and your instincts—" he grinned suddenly and lifted his arm from Tom's shoulders, "and go for it!"

The crowd roared, and a surge of elation buoyed him, then he felt a tug on his arm. Accompanying Briggs to the rear of the platform, with the cheers ringing around the plaza, he was surprised, looking down, to find that his feet were actually touching the ground. Then he looked up, straight into Sara's eyes, and had the shock of his life. He would remember this look all the rest of his days, because her eyes were shining and in them he saw himself, his self, clear and whole and worthwhile as he had never seen himself before. It was a revelation, and he might have stood there forever except that Briggs was nudging him gently. He dropped Sara's hand as another took its place, and dragged his eyes from hers and moved along the line.

But the knowledge blazed away inside him, filling his mind and heart as he shook the hands of city councilors and the Archbishop and a Rabbi and a Bishop. And once he'd finished with Church and State he got another shock, because there at the end of the line were Sol and Ruby! And Sol, heavier than when he'd last seen him, was thumping his back and hugging him, and Ruby took his hand in both of hers and kissed his cheek, and in her eyes he saw a maternal version of Sara's look. He found his voice.

"Come back—can you come and visit? I mean, now?"

Briggs interposed: he had a small item of business to discuss, so Sol and Ruby promised to come by later. Owen stumbled down the steps at the side of the platform into the waiting limousine and left the plaza as he had come, in great state, but slightly improved in mind.

*   *   *

"Did your dad run the store by himself, Owen?" asked Ruby. They were sitting in the living room.

"It wasn't a store. He had a repair shop in the basement, that's where he worked. The trouble was, he was never there." People would come round to get something fixed and find a note on the door: Over at Gord Watson's if you need me. Or Jerry Iseling's or Skip Griswald's or old Mrs. Bellini's. It was no way to run a business. Owen sighed. "He didn't have much ambition." He looked at Sol. "He used to make things."

"What kind of things?"

"Gadgets. Anything. He called them doohickeys."

"You mean, he was an inventor?" asked Ruby.

"Dad wouldn't say that. But I guess he was, in a way. I wish I'd paid more attention to him." He stood abruptly and walked over to the window.

Made a doohickey for Emmy Rensaeler. Stop the kids throwing stuff down the toilet.

Be sure and charge her for it, Martin.

Just made it up out of scrap. Can't charge her for that.

She'd have to pay if she bought it in the hardware store.

She couldn't do that, Ag. They don't sell 'em.

It was after Agnes's funeral that Martin had said he was a failure. Owen had disagreed conventionally but he'd known all his life that it was so. No one had ever said it, at least not in Owen's hearing, but it lay like a grey shroud over the family. He wondered with sudden insight if his father had lacked confidence. Had he ever seen in Agnes's eyes what Owen had seen in Sara's? Before the thought was fully formed he knew the answer.

He turned back to the living room. "I wish to God I'd never said that. I don't know how it came out."

"People understood, Owen," said Ruby soothingly. "Didn't they, Sol?"

"Sure they did," said Sol and looked appreciatively round the room once more. Owen had shown them around the apartment when they first arrived, including the kitchen. "A half-million dollar loan," mused Sol, shaking his head at Ruby, "remember that? And no collateral." He glanced at Owen. "Except here, I guess, huh?" He tapped his head.

They returned to the living room and he took the drink Owen brought him. "Can't see Betty living here, Owen. They got themselves a farm—but I guess you know that." Owen heard all about the farm and the grandkids, and the chain, and the boys—"Clar said to ask how's your accounting software holding up?"—and Owen remembered what a headache that had been, when new programs were coming out before you'd even broken in the old ones.

"Vern sent his best," said Ruby. "He said you should let him know if your building inspector still gives you trouble."

"That's worth somethin', Owen," Sol interjected. "Vern don't deal with inspectors now. He goes straight to City Hall. Knows someone who knows someone in Planning."

Owen heard all the news with pleasure, how Sol was involved with the golf club expansion and Mike was planning to open four more stores next year—"He's got it down to a franchise now," said Sol.

Then Ruby asked what the Mayor had wanted.

"You know, I was so high, I'm not sure." Briggs had taken him back to City Hall and engaged him in earnest discussion about his political future. At least, Briggs discussed. Owen made inane replies to direct questions, his body slowly calming down, his mind on Sara, the crowd, his speech. . . . "I think he wants me to join the Finance Advisory Committee. They review city expenditures and budgets and make recommendations."

"You could do a lot of good there, Owen," said Sol, interested.

"It's not really my line, but I said I'd think about it." A thought struck him. "Was it Vern who got you seats at the rally? Through his connections?"

"Hell, no. That was Sara."

"Sara? You had a chance to meet her, then?" He was puzzled.

"Meet her? She drove in with us," said Sol. "We talked kitchens all the way. Smart girl."

Ruby told him of Sara's insistence that they be on the platform today. "She said you'd like it if we were there, and she phoned the Mayor and arranged it."

He was touched at her thoughtfulness and his mind went back to the rally, until he heard Ruby say, "She would have come with us to visit but she's got too much to do, getting ready for Christmas." He nodded. Christmas Eve. The presents. . . .

The Jablonskys stayed for a couple of hours, until Owen yawned, then yawned again. He protested that it was nothing, just that he hadn't had much sleep for several nights. But Ruby was mindful of his illness and stirred Sol to his feet, and while he and Owen talked she took the glasses out to the kitchen.

As they waited for the elevator, Sol turned to him. "Don't leave it another seven years, Owen. Come see us anytime. Just don't—" Ruby nudged him, "—don't leave it too long," he finished lamely. Then the elevator arrived and he stepped inside rather abruptly. Owen embraced Ruby.

"We're very proud of you, Owen. I know your parents would be too." She entered the elevator and they were both gone.

Owen returned to the apartment, remembering the warmth and noise of the Jablonsky household. They had been so supportive of him, and so helpful. Why, he wondered, couldn't people accept his gifts in return? Liz seemed to have got the message, finally. Why couldn't Sol? Or Sara? He surveyed all his cards, as if they held the key to making Sara understand. The alpine picture over the fireplace caught his eye and he considered it, suddenly dissatisfied. A word crept into his mind: insipid. He wanted something different in its place, something deeper, more full-bodied. Burgundy, he thought, not sparkling white, and turned away.

As he entered the kitchen, mentally reviewing the contents of the freezer, his eye was caught by a small, battered oblong leather case on the counter. He stared in disbelief, knowing instantly what it was, his mind refusing to accept it. The old brown case with the tiny gold clasp. He fumbled it open and brushed aside a folded note. Hohner. Martin's harmonica, with the worn mother-of-pearl sides. He removed it from the case and gazed at it, feeling the weight, touching the chromatic slide. Had he ever held it before? He couldn't recall.

Now Martin, don't be playing that old thing. Let Owen play us some real music.

Sorry, Ag.

Oh Dad, he thought. Why didn't you speak up for yourself?

He opened the note: "Gord Watson wants you to have this. I was so proud of you today. Sara."

He tried to grapple with this discontinuity—Gord Watson? And Sara?—but it was too much for him and he gave up.

The writing was graceful, like the writer, he thought, and traced her name with his fingertips, stirred by the possessiveness of the second sentence.

He sat in the armchair near the fig tree, looking out at the city lights, and blew tentatively, ranging up and down the scale. Memories washed over him at the thready sound, and feelings: teenaged embarrassment and annoyance that his dad had no regular job like other guys' dads; relief in the evenings when he'd disappear after dinner. . . .

"We'll meet again, don't know where, don't know when . . ." He found himself trying the old Vera Lynn wartime song, a favorite of Martin's. His mind drifted further back, to childhood. He stared out at the dusk lights, lost in the past. In the dump game.

Looka here. Martin held up an electric kettle minus its cord.

Is it okay, daddy? The excitement . . .

Dunno, son. Take it home and see.

And they'd taken the kettle back to the basement workshop, and Martin had hoisted his son up to sit on the bench and inserted a new cord in the kettle, added a little water and plugged it in. Sure enough, it worked just fine, and Owen laughed and banged his heels against the side of the bench.

They threw away the wrong part, didn't they, dad! It was a first principle of dumps: people discarded the appliance, never its cord.

Looks that way. Martin emptied the kettle, brought out some polish and cleaned it up with swift, efficient strokes, while Owen watched and waited for the moment when he would be given the rag so he could add a final polish, and when they'd finished there would be a shiny new kettle, or percolator or electric frying pan, for Martin to sell for a couple of bucks.

"We'll meet again . . ." He tried again and stopped, dissatisfied, recalling the clear, flowing notes of his father's playing. "Isn't as easy as I thought, dad," he said aloud. Had Martin picked up the song during the war? What had he done, what battles had he fought and where? I know so little, Owen grieved, I know so little . . . On into the evening he sat, immersed in memories, his mind ranging over the years of his youth.

He did not know when the knowledge actually revealed itself to him, or precisely how: it stole over him first as a sense of discomfort at the words he'd spoken to the crowd, then broadened to encompass his writings, and he became aware of embarrassment, then shame. He sat immobile, growing colder and colder. He had no right to speak of risk, no right to look down his nose at those who took refuge in regulations. He'd cowered behind his mother's unspoken assumptions and fears all his life. Without a second's thought he'd denied his heritage, consigned his father to the dump, and worse—

He covered his eyes. *I threw away the wrong part, didn't I, dad?*

* * *

Flick Jackson leaned back in his chair, feet up on the desk, reading the late edition of the *Dispatch*. The *Star*'s presses were running with the Christmas Eve issue, and staffers were hurrying to depart for last-minute shopping or parties.

"Have a good Christmas, Jackson," Monica passed briskly on her way to a reception.

"You too," he called, and returned to the editorial page.

Owen Adair tried to explain away his rescue of young Tommy Newton as the product of impulse and upbringing [Jackson read]. While we can't help but respect his modesty, we at this newspaper wish to salute him for a far simpler reason. In this whining, self-absorbed age, when seeking the child within is prized even over saving the child without [Jackson winced], when rabid feminism has pulled up the roots of manhood and left them to wither and dry in the sun ["For Christ's sake," said Jackson] we take our hats off to Mr. Adair. Not for his impulses, not for his upbringing, not for his doubts—but for a decisive act, taken alone and unobserved in the cold and dark. We salute his courage, pure and simple.

For it is this courage, and the acts it inspires—acts painfully infrequent in contemporary urban life—that uplift us all, that hearten and inspire us, that build communities, that bind them. So we say, God bless Owen Adair, with the fervent hope that his first foray into public life will not be his last. Our city and—let us say it—our politics, would be the better for his contribution.

"What's all this? Nowhere to go?" Hoch took the paper and scanned the column, while Jackson watched his reaction. Tomorrow's *Star* would include an editorial extolling the moving sight of a man "getting in touch with his inner self and touching us all in the process." It would go on to praise the felicity of Adair's discovery "of the child within, as we should each find the child that is within us all at this magical time of year."

The editor grunted and tossed the paper on the desk. "Nugent's been hitting the Dr Pepper." Nugent was editor of the *Dispatch,* a scrawny individual with a prominent Adam's apple.

"They're saying at City Hall that Adair's going to join them in the next elections." Jackson studied him. "What'll we do if he does?"

"Crucify him, of course. Have a nice Christmas, Jackson."

The editor walked away. He'd nurtured a good story into a great one, negotiated December's doldrums with increased circulation, and taken a few well-placed whacks at Franklin Briggs into the bargain. He was content.

13

The store was called "For Him." It was divided into sections: for the sporting, the formal, the casual him. On Christmas Eve morning, pink plastic purse slung across her body, Janey stood at a glass display cabinet ("For the Executive Him"), watching steel balls that ran up and down Lucite platforms, and little steel men that swung round and round Lucite poles, next to glass paperweights and travel alarm clocks.

Not far from her, in a section that bridged the Formal Him and the Casual Him, Tom was gazing at a tie.

He'd thought when he woke up that a tie might be good, but not, he explained to Janey at breakfast, one of those ones that glowed in the dark or squirted water, or had pictures of naked ladies on them. He had no particular prejudice against such ties; a lot of kids gave them on Father's Day. He just didn't want that kind of tie for Owen.

They'd come to the mall with no clear idea of what they did want, but Tom knew that this was the right one the moment he saw it.

It was a grey tie, darker than light grey but lighter than charcoal. It hung on a rack in front of him. Down the right side, the structure of a skyscraper could be discerned, not so it screamed at you, but darkly, as it would look at night. You could make out the occasional gleam of a window as your eye traveled down the tie until you came to the wide part at the bottom. Here, silhouetted against a full moon so that his features were shrouded in darkness, one hand thrown up high against the building, Spiderman crouched, his eyes staring out at you.

Cool, thought Tom.

A clinking sound heralded Janey's arrival and he stole a glance. Her face was rapt as she stared at the tie.

"It's elvis," she said at last and Tom knew she liked it too.

It was better than cool, he suddenly realized, because although Owen wasn't Spiderman he'd done a Spiderman kind of thing. So he took the tie down from its hook and carried it to the cash register, deeply satisfied in the way that comes from worrying about the right present for someone who matters and then finding something even better than you'd expected.

A minute or so later the satisfaction was replaced by an infinitely deeper feeling when the salesman, having found the right box for the tie, looked over the counter at them and said:

"There's a matching handkerchief, if you want it." Tom felt Janey go still next to him. He nodded, trying to look casual, and the salesman turned away and rummaged in the drawer.

Spiderman had reached the top of the building on the handkerchief, and the salesman showed them how to fold it so that his eyes would peer over the top of the breast pocket. Then he found a box for it, and after that came the matter of payment: $28.95. Tom handed him two tens and a one, while Janey took off the pink purse. He unzipped it and carefully decanted the contents on the counter: $8.31 in pennies and nickels. Janey got thirty-seven cents back, which was an unexpected bonus.

*   *   *

Sara had been content to listen in silence during the drive home from the rally, while Sol and Ruby and Tom all talked at once, savoring all the moments and their reactions. But she suddenly thought of a gift, and before they left for Owen's she took their photo out in the driveway against the snow. Then she called Mac Drummond and bundled the kids plus Tony Elwing, whose parents and brother had gone shopping, into the car and drove over to Mac's. She left the kids in the car and went inside and took Mac's picture in his living room, reclining in his favorite chair in his shirtsleeves.

Then back home, stopping at Ellis Mall to drop off the film at the one-hour photo place, along with the negative of the *Star* picture of Tom and herself. She didn't even try to find a parking spot in the Christmas crush, but hovered outside an entrance while Tom and Tony ran inside with the film.

Later that day, after the Elwings had returned, Sara went back to the mall and picked up the photos and a four-inch clear plastic cube, the kind that sat on people's desks displaying assorted family photos. It was just a small gift that he could choose to use or not, as he pleased, but his desk was nearly bare and she thought it might please him.

That evening, Tom and Janey sat at the table and watched as she assembled her pictures and began to fit them into the sides of the cube. She put Ruby and Sol in one square, and Mac in another. She selected the best of Janey's school pictures, with Janey's assistance, and put that in a third square, and she put the picture of herself and Tom in the fourth. He didn't have to keep any of them, but it made a more cheerful present than with no pictures at all.

This morning she'd had second thoughts, fearing the photo cube was too inconsequential. So she'd left Tom and Janey in the men's store with strict instructions to come and find her before going anywhere else, and entered the china and gift store two doors down.

She browsed along the shelves until she came to a crystal display at the rear of the store. She picked up an object.

"What's this?" she asked a hovering sales clerk.

"It's Waterford."

"I know, but what is it?"

"A vase." They studied it. "What do you think it is?" asked the clerk.

It was shaped somewhat like a highball glass, perhaps three and a half inches high, six-sided and slightly wider at the base than the top. Its facets sparkled in the light.

"It wouldn't do for long-stemmed roses," said Sara.

The clerk agreed. "Perhaps for buds? We have some nice bud vases over here if you're interested?"

"It's too heavy for a drinking glass." Sara stared at it, puzzled. "You could use it as a pencil holder. For your desk?"

The clerk looked doubtful, then another customer claimed her attention and she turned away.

Sara studied the Waterford thing thoughtfully, wondering if Owen liked crystal. He certainly needed a pencil holder.

No one in their right mind used the pencil tray supplied by the desk manufacturer, set into the middle or top right drawer of the desk. She exempted people like Mike Farraday, who only had a couple of pens. But even Mike had many times asked a caller to hang on while he patted his breast pocket or the blueprints strewn over the desk, and then leaned back so he could open his drawer and take out a pen or pencil.

Pencil trays were inefficient. They were also messy, collecting dust and fragments of lead and smudges of leaked ink, which clung to the implements until it was transferred to your fingers and thereafter to your clothing. And they were inadequate: too small, too narrow, too short to hold everything, leaving the overflow to rattle about in a jumbled mess underneath.

If you were efficient and organized you used a pencil holder, positioned on the far side of your blotter, where you could reach unerringly for the precise item required at any moment. You put all your pens and pencils in it, together with your high liters, Jiffy markers, Exacto knife and sundry felt tips acquired as freebies, all of which you liked but none of which were ever quite the right fineness for the job at hand.

The pencil drawer was then freed for its proper purpose: as a repository for stamps, Exacto blades and tubes of .5mm HB lead, paper clips, an eraser, aspirin, miscellaneous screws, a spare block of post-it notes, two pairs of scissors, make-up and assorted keys. Sara's drawer also held a 6" metal ruler which she loved for its convenience but kept forgetting to use.

Owen, she was interested to note, had just as large a variety of pens and pencils as she herself, all jumbled together in and below the tray in his drawer. He even had a Liquid Paper pen, a novelty to Sara.

He probably used his pencil drawer just because it was there, like Everest, and he felt he ought to. She smiled, looking at the Waterford thing, and came to a decision. If he didn't want to use it for pencils it would look fine on the coffee table.

As she stood in line at the cash desk, she thought about silk pajamas and designer shirts. Owen dressed well, not like

Sam, who'd never cared what he threw on, even for business lunches. Dear Sam. . . .

She moved forward and reached for her wallet. Dark green. Or maybe black. He'd look good in black silk pajamas. She fell into a reverie.

"Hi mum."

She looked down. Tom held a bag, Janey next to him.

"Find something you like, darling?"

"Yeah." He was nonchalant but she caught the look of suppressed excitement between the two of them and it acted like a cold shower on her. Pull yourself together, she told herself as she took her credit card slip. It was pointless to dream of any kind of relationship with a man whose response to every situation was to lavish gifts on all involved. His speech had been a triumph and she'd understood and looked at him seeing the whole man, as he could be if he'd only accept himself. But people didn't change overnight —if indeed they changed at all—and if he turned up at the house this evening loaded with presents, or worse still, if he hurt her children by disregarding their gift—

She walked back to the car with Janey's hand in hers and knew that either way, she was in for heartache. Because Owen Adair was a tangled, obstinate, kind, generous and brilliant blockhead, and she was deeply in love with him.

*   *   *

Owen looked round the second-floor showroom as the salesman moved away. Nothing had changed. He walked over to a Steinway concert grand and sat down. The showroom was almost empty. He ran his fingers over the keys, Lord what a sound, and played a few bars of nothing. He tried a little Chopin and then the manager was coming toward him, impersonal courtesy giving way to a smile as he recognized the customer.

"Mr. Adair! How delightful!" he shook Owen's hand.

"Good to see you, Mr. Isaacs."

"What an honor, yesterday! And such excitement! We all watched in the office," Isaacs laughed. "The entire inventory could have walked, who cared?" His thin face was alight with pleasure and Owen smiled.

"I haven't been so scared since my last piano exam, I can tell you."

Isaacs talked about the ceremony as they strolled round the showroom. Finally: "Now you're a great man you want to trade in the Baldwin, is that it? For a Steinway, perhaps?"

"Not a chance." Owen had spent six months in here, all his free time, trying piano after piano until he was in a position to buy and then after, until he found what he wanted. "It's the best investment I ever made. No, I want to buy a piano for a nine-year-old. He's talented, got a good ear. He had some lessons but now he's got a keyboard—"

Isaacs cast his eyes upward. No further explanation was necessary. "We sell them, Mr. Adair, so I may not say what I think." The entire ground floor of the store was given over to keyboards, guitars, drums, amplifiers and other accoutrements of modern sound. "Does the boy have any technique?"

Owen shook his head. "The thing is, Mr. Isaacs, I don't want to—to push him. Either he'll want to pursue the piano or he won't, but I thought I'd get him a small upright, something to pique his interest, and we'd take it from there."

They walked over to look at a selection of uprights. "We all had to be pushed, Mr. Adair," observed the manager. "Good technique does not just happen, it requires work."

"Yes, I know," said Owen. "But it's not my place to push. I'm just hoping to influence things." They stopped at a Kawai apartment upright.

"Would this boy be the same one—?" Isaacs asked discreetly and when Owen nodded, "Ah! How charming."

"He's a great kid."

They moved from piano to piano, and soon ran up against an unexpected difficulty. Owen was seated at a Yamaha when Isaacs commented:

"Cherry, Mr. Adair. A beautiful finish, isn't it? A fine addition to the living room, or—," he paused as Owen looked startled, "where will the instrument go?"

"I hadn't thought about that." Would Sara want it in the living room? Or the basement? If she chose to put it in the living room, then she really ought to be consulted as to finish and, come to think of it, size.

"May I suggest . . . ?"

Owen looked up at him.

"We're open on Monday. Might it be desirable to come in with the young man, and perhaps his mother—?"

Owen considered. Even if he bought something today, Isaacs couldn't deliver it. His suggestion made more sense; besides, it would mean another meeting with Sara.

"Good idea." He began to apologize for wasting Isaacs' time, and the manager implored him not even to think in such terms, it had been a pleasure, he would look forward to the twenty-sixth. . . .

Owen left the piano store and walked along the street, enjoying the sight of throngs of shoppers and bright packages and lights. He had woken this morning feeling tired and dragged-down. Now that feeling began to dissipate, and he sauntered past the display windows of a department store, studying Santa's workshop and the elves and reindeer, and spotted a superb pink piggybank. Janey had shown him a small and scrawny giraffe, full of coins and not nearly big enough, she'd said.

He found the pig in the toy department, and was recognized by two children and several adults. He took the escalator to the sixth floor, thinking that even if he couldn't buy a piano, a couple of piano books would be good. He found the pianos on the far side of the furniture department and had a pleasant discussion with a salesman over the racks of music books. A small boy saw him and told his mother and they came over to congratulate Owen while he was paying for his purchase, and then the salesman had to congratulate him, too.

He descended to the second floor and lingered pointlessly over the lingerie. You couldn't give a woman morsels of satin or black lace when you hadn't even kissed her. He stifled a sigh and took the escalator to the main floor to buy her a pair of slippers, then made his way over to the cosmetics department to find her perfume.

As is the practice of department stores throughout the free world, cosmetics and perfume occupied a large area inside the main entrance doors. He stopped at the first counter, de la Renta, and tried several samples without success. He drifted from counter to counter. "Exquisitely witty, sensual" said a sign. "Seduces with a harmony of floral and oceanic essences," asserted another. He made the acquaintance of Casmir and White Shoulders, Tendre Poison, Cassini and Flore, and Adrienne Fittadini. He came to the Givenchy display, still unsatisfied.

Across the aisle at the Chanel counter, the salesgirl looked up and said, involuntarily, "It's Owen!" and several people stopped and glanced in the same direction. The Givenchy sales rep suddenly materialized before him.

"Can I help you, Mr. Adair?"

"Hi. I'm trying to find a perfume. It's very—I don't know, it's light. Delicate." She invited him to move along the counter and gave him two more to try. No luck.

"Owen," trilled Chanel, "I've got what you want," and several of the throngs of shoppers entering the store turned to look. Owen crossed to Chanel and tried Number 5 and several alternatives, without success. She was so downcast he felt terrible and nearly bought one anyway.

"Mr. Adair? Could I have your autograph?"

He turned and looked down. A small girl stood there with her mother, holding up a paper package and a pen. The mother said it was a real thrill to meet him and now a small crowd had gathered and he could hear random voices, spreading back to the outer edges:

"What's going on?"

"It's Owen Adair!"

"Owen!"

"Who is it?"

"It's Owen!"

"What's happening?"

"Go round the other way, Mavis. No, the *other* way, for crying out loud, we'll be here all day—"

Owen grinned and stooped to face the small girl, took her pen and wrote his name on the paper package. Her eyes were round and blue and she gave an excited hop.

Someone slapped his shoulder as he rose. "Congratulations, Owen," and "You did great!" came another voice, and "We're proud of you, Owen." A clamor of voices requested autographs. Pens were thrust toward him and he signed shopping bags and an arm and a couple of hands, and some notebooks and the back of a check, and all the while the crowd swelled and murmured and laughed, and the Store Manager, who had heard the rumors as he toured the floors, looked over toward the entrance as he descended the escalator, and hurried along the aisles.

Owen felt a surge of affection for these people and their generosity. He'd been hustled off too quickly to meet anyone yesterday and in any case he'd been in no condition to enjoy it then, but now it seemed right and fitting and he forgot to be shy and signed and smiled and laughed at peoples' jokes and shook hands and was patted and pummeled and jostled and thumped.

He bent down again to sign another child's autograph— Vanessa, about 9, he thought as he smiled at her. She clutched the small notepad to her, thrilled, and Owen asked impulsively:

"What would you like more than anything in the world, Vanessa?"

She glanced up at her dad. "A bike."

Owen saw in her eyes all the magic and excitement of her first bicycle. He rose to his feet, and the man, a fellow of his own age, wrung his hand.

"Dave Ryder, Owen. This is one big thrill. That was a great thing you did."

"It was nothing, really. Listen—"

"The guys at work'll want me to congratulate you. We were gonna send a card and I don't know, we never got around to it—."

"Look, I'd like to get Vanessa a bike. I really would, I saw some upstairs, just perfect, what do you say?" He ignored the retreat in Ryder's eyes and pressed on:

"We could just whip upstairs right now, okay?" *Hold your foot up, son.* He heard his father's voice distinctly but swept on unheeding, glancing over the crowd.

"In fact—" he raised his voice, "I'd like to buy all the kids a gift." The crowd buzzed, heads turning toward each other.

"Mr. Adair! What an honor!" The Store Manager was at his elbow. Owen grinned and turned back to the crowd.

"Listen!" He thrust his packages sideways, into the Manager's hands, and reached for his wallet, thinking rapidly. "For every child, one gift! From me." He saw the back of Ryder's head as the man pushed his way toward the entrance doors, Vanessa in tow—*What have I done?*

All eyes were fixed on him. He waved largely: "To the toy department!"

A second's hush, then the crowd whooped and stampeded along the aisles toward the escalators. Owen thrust his Visa card into Manager's hand.

"Fifty dollar limit per kid—I'll be right back." He set off after Ryder. Outside the main doors he looked along the sidewalk. There they were! He followed after them quickly and noticed for the first time that the man's jacket was thin and worn, although the girl's sneakers—sneakers, at this time of year!— were new. His skin crawled and he loathed himself.

"Excuse me?"

Ryder kept walking, holding his daughter's hand.

"Please wait. Please—I just—" he'd caught them.

"It isn't necessary, okay?" The eyes were hard. "Now just butt out—"

"No, no. I didn't—I came to apologize." He steered the man firmly to one side. "I had to. In fact," he took a deep breath, "I owe you. . . ." He stopped and looked skyward, then said firmly, "I owe you. More than I can ever say."

"Forget it," said Ryder. He nodded slightly and made as if to pass.

"What you said in there, I want to thank you for that. It's a wonderful thing, to be well-regarded."

Ryder's eyes were cynical. "I wouldn't know." He looked down for Vanessa's hand.

Owen studied him. "Yes, you would," he said. "I may be a jackass but some things I know. You know what it's like. That's why I appreciate what you said. It means a lot, coming from someone like you."

Ryder's features relaxed slightly.

"Mr. Adair?"

Owen looked down at Vanessa then back to her father. "You're a lucky man." He crouched down to face her.

"You don't have to worry. About the bike, I mean." She smiled up at her dad. "We're saving up for it."

"You know what, Vanessa? That's the best kind. The kind you save up for." He straightened to find Ryder regarding him curiously. "I'm not used to all this attention," he apologized.

Ryder held out his hand. "You were doing fine, only why'd you have to wreck it? You already gave. Let everyone else have a turn."

He nodded and took Vanessa's hand and they set off down the street. Owen stared after them. Wreck? Everyone else?

You already gave. *You already gave.* Sara had said it, Wendy had said it, others had said it in different ways at different times, but not until this moment of extreme vulnerability, his mind open to hear the words and absorb the meaning, did he at last get it. *You already gave.*

Dizziness engulfed him and he put out a hand blindly to the display window. He, Owen Adair, had risked his life to save another, not because there was a worm in the apple but because—Sara had been right: it was not in his nature to stand by—because he was Martin's son and he could not do otherwise. And hard on the heels of that thought came another: he was his mother's son and so he had survived. Generosity and fierce determination had fused in him in that one act.

He began to walk along the street, watching absently as Ryder and Vanessa crossed at the intersection. He'd told the crowd that saving Tom had been the best thing he'd ever done and now he understood why: because on that one occasion he had been truly himself.

"Know what you want, Owen. You'll be ahead of ninety percent of the population if you know what you want." How often had his mother said that? And "If you're going to do a thing, Owen, do it properly. Don't let yourself get sidetracked." "I'll be okay, ma," he used to tell her, answering her unspoken worry only in his own mind: *I'm not like dad.* But unconsciously he'd absorbed her fears whole, suppressing and distorting all that was Martin in him, afraid of failure. He shook his head at his own stupidity and waste. There had been a worm in the apple all right, and he had put it there: the worm of fear.

He reached the corner and tried to remember where he had parked. The anxiety had left him and he was able to look back at his life with no fear, only regret, and he thought suddenly that he had saved two lives that night. An alien feeling began to push its way upward through his regret, like a green-tipped crocus in winter soil. It was pride.

He lifted his head, smiling. "I already gave," he said, tasting the words, and a passerby gave him a hearty slap on the shoulder.

"That's the spirit!"

He suddenly recalled his Visa card and turned, retracing his steps toward the store entrance. *I already gave.* He hadn't thrown away the wrong part. For good or ill, he was the product of two parents, not one. Maybe he could never be simple but by God, he could at least try to be integrated. He entered the store savoring an unusual sense of well-being.

* * *

Earlier, when Owen had bought Janey's pig, the toy department had worn a tired and rather depleted air, but not now, he saw as he stepped off the escalator at the fifth floor. Its aisles were packed with customers, a seething mass so tightly crammed that it didn't move, it undulated. The noise was appalling, adult yells and childish wails mixed with a myriad of shouted disputes.

Someone had worked fast, he noticed: a large sign was suspended over one of the check-out islands: "Owen Adair Gifts: $50 max. All adults must be accompanied by a child." A long line of customers extended from the cash register out of the toy department, and the cashier was ringing in gift selections, the Store Manager standing near her.

A woman brushed past Owen from behind, yanking at her daughter's arm: "Make up your *mind*, Darlene. Which is it to be? Quickly!" They plunged into the melee past another woman brandishing a boxed Starship Enterprise. "How much is this?" she screamed at a flustered clerk. "How much?"

A burly man fought his way toward the cashier with four stuffed Lion Kings held aloft.

"I'm sorry, sir," Owen heard the Manager speak distinctly under the noise. "You can't get them without your children." He pointed up at the sign.

"I left 'em downstairs so they wouldn't get hurt!"

"Give me the toys, sir. I'll save them for you while you get your kids."

Standing to one side, Owen watched as the man held the Manager's gaze and tossed the toys contemptuously over his shoulders, back into the crowd. His eyes moved to Owen's face and he lowered his head, barged through the checkout line and left.

The Manager turned and his face lightened. "Good to see you," he said sincerely.

Owen's shame knew no bounds. "I'm so sorry," he said.

The Manager waved this away. "You see all kinds in retailing," he said.

Owen was not starry eyed about human nature. He believed people generally held enormous potential for good, but that did not blind him to their common failings. What appalled him now was not so much the transformation of a good-hearted, well-meaning crowd into a scavenging, rapacious mob, as the cause. He had done this, and it sickened him, the more so because some of these people, he knew, would not care to remember their behavior later, and they would blame him for it.

A spate of shouting suddenly erupted at the far end of an aisle as a girl in red velvet and green tights joined them. "You've got to do something, Mr. Fisher! This is destroying our Workshop!" She waved to an adjacent section where Santa sat in solitary splendor in a blue-white grotto, his elves milling about aimlessly.

The shouting worsened, and Owen left them, working his way round the side and down an almost deserted aisle of computer games, most priced at more than fifty dollars. At the far end he found two twelve-year-olds screaming over a remote-controlled racing car. He separated them and dragged them, kicking and cursing, to the edge of the toy department, next to housewares.

"I'm the guy giving the toys away, and you two just lost out. Now get out, or I'll call the guard and have you thrown out."

He turned his back and rejoined Fisher, who had just relieved a boy of his Monopoly set and sent him on his way. "He tried to go through twice, the second time for them." He nodded in the direction of a well-dressed couple threading their way toward the elevators. "No relation," Fisher added and Owen shook his head.

The line-up had lengthened still further, and the Manager had instructed the red and green elves to make sure customers' selections fell within the price limit. The grotto was deserted, its occupant now taking a coffee break. "A demoralized Santa is not a pretty sight," Fisher explained cheerfully. He was enjoying himself.

"What can I do to help?"

"Not a thing." He eyed Owen. "Don't worry, it'll get better in a minute."

The Head Elf joined them again, frowning at him. "Hello, Mr. Adair." She addressed the Manager: "That woman's got a Nintendo Donkey Kong. I told her it was too expensive but she wants to make up the difference herself."

Owen glanced over at a woman near the checkout, watching them anxiously.

Fisher was emphatic. "Absolutely not. We'd have to close off Owen's bill."

"Put it through," said Owen quietly. He forestalled Fisher's objection. "It's okay, just this one."

The girl nodded and Fisher cautioned her, "Don't say anything until she reaches the desk." But the woman had seen the nod. Her eyes dropped, but not before Owen saw a flash of triumph in them, and he knew she knew she wouldn't have to pay, and felt a stab of disgust at himself. Never again. Never again would he do this.

He heard a loud wail and looked along the line up. A small boy was crying, face red with protest, as his mother tried to step out of the line. She gave Owen a harassed smile as he joined them. "I wanted to pay for it but he says it has to come from you." She began to rummage through her bag.

Owen looked down at a pair of solemn eyes—the crying had turned off like a tap at his arrival—in a five-year-old face. He crouched and smiled.

"Hi."

"Show Mr. Adair your gift, Patrick."

Patrick held out an action figure. It looked to Owen like a muscular rodent astride a motorbike.

"What's that called?"

"Biker Mouse from Mars."

"Say thank you to Mr. Adair."

Patrick bent sideways and smiled at Owen. "Thank you."

Owen smiled back, and his soreness eased slightly. "You're welcome, Patrick." Patrick's mother held out a box of raisins. A tiny box, Owen saw, exactly the right size for a five-year-old fist. What will they think of next, he marveled, and smiled up at the woman.

"Low sugar," she said. "You learn to time these things. Why on earth would you want to buy presents?"

"I had a seizure," he said and stood up. "Let's see what we can do to speed things up." Patrick suddenly found himself high in the air. He looked doubtfully at his mother but she seemed unworried, so he relaxed and smiled down at Owen.

Along the line, others saw the small child in Owen's arms, noted the cheap action figure in the boy's hand. Muted consultations began between parents and children. Owen and Patrick discussed the problem of how to open your raisin box and hang on to your Biker Mouse, and Patrick surrendered the mouse to his mother. Then they turned away to find the Manager. Behind them, several children left the line with their toys, returning to the aisles.

At a cash desk on the other side of the department, Owen could see two clerks ringing through purchases for a short line of customers. "Would it help if you opened another register?"

Fisher drew him to one side and explained the problem. Five thousand dollars would buy a hundred fifty-dollar toys. "We're already past the two thousand dollar mark. I told Marsha to take her time in the hope that some people would give up and leave."

"I don't care what it costs," replied Owen impatiently. The damage was done. "Let's just get it over with."

Fisher gave him a sharp glance and visions of megasales danced in his head. He turned and beckoned urgently to a tall, weedy assistant in a nearby aisle. "Simon!"

A woman went by with two empty-handed, protesting children. "You don't need any more toys, stop that crying." Owen had seen her earlier, screaming at a clerk. She glanced at him now in dislike and he couldn't blame her. Patrick watched, uncomprehending, and ate another raisin.

The noise level had dropped, Owen realized as Simon joined them. The line up was noticeably shorter and now more parents stepped out of it with their children, some mutinous, some resigned. Patrick's mother was nearly at the till. "I don't get it," said Simon. "A lot of them are putting stuff back." That wasn't all, Fisher realized. Some of the expensive stuffed toys and games had been exchanged for Barbie, small action figures and Lego bags. He repressed a sigh as the visions began to melt away.

Owen returned Patrick to his mother and wished them well. He turned away and stopped to let a woman pass.

"I don't know what I was thinking of," she said to her daughter, then caught his eye.

"Nor me," replied Owen.

She hesitated, then nodded grudgingly. "Merry Christmas."

"And the same to you." He smiled at the girl, whose sulking gave way to a small smile as she followed her mother.

For whatever reason, the frenzy was soon over. Within a few minutes the crowd had melted away, within half an hour the purchases of those who remained had been processed, and Owen signed a Visa bill for $3993.78 while a clerk climbed on the counter and took down the sign. Simon came to the desk brushing off a battered Lion King and Owen glanced at it and shook his head.

"Stop feeling bad," said Fisher. "There's a little larceny in all of us."

"That guy was gross, Mr. Fisher," said Simon.

The clean up began, and Owen insisted on helping, retrieving toys from the floor and corners, straightening stacks of boxes. From Simon he learned that many of the assistants had been pulled off their lunch breaks to supplement the department's regular personnel. Once mopping up operations had concluded, they gathered at the counter, grinning and nudging each other as Fisher handed Owen three Visa credit slips.

"Returns already?" asked Owen.

"Your purchases." Marsha brought Owen's bags out from behind the counter and passed them over.

Owen took the credit slips, but shook his head at the presents. "I don't want them. Thanks anyway."

"But why not?" Fisher was astonished. "They're yours, compliments of Burns & Blanchard."

"I won't be giving any more presents."

The Manager opened his mouth, then decided not to pursue that one. "I see. I hope—" Marsha passed him a Burns & Blanchard box, "we all hope, you'll accept one?" He presented the box. "With our best wishes."

Owen looked down to hide the stinging in his eyes. All his conventional disclaimers rose to his lips—and died away unspoken. He looked at Fisher and the assistants. He took the box.

"Thank you," he said simply. They'd given him a forest green Ralph Lauren sweater, he discovered, and held it up to clapping and scattered cheers.

"Mr. Adair?" A boy held out a pen, his father behind him. "Could I have your autograph?"

Others had heard the clapping and a small crowd was beginning to gather. Fisher looked amused. "It's a lucky man who gets a second chance," he observed. "All right, people," he turned away to address his clerks, "back to your departments. . . ."

*   *   *

Owen signed many autographs, answered questions and asked them, laughed, joked and was grateful for his second chance that Christmas Eve. But he bought no more presents and felt no urge to do so. Late in the day, he left the store and walked outside feeling as though a lifetime had passed since he'd run after Ryder. He breathed in the cold night air, enjoyed the sight of the Christmas lights and the small blue pennants fluttering below them.

He looked up at the night sky, at the stars, remote and benign. He looked along the street, at the stores and banks, and above them, a few blocks over, the high-rises. This was his city; this was his home. He thought suddenly of Monica and Briggs, of Lowell Mason, the banker-composer, of all the possibilities open to him. There were many ways to give, and gifts were the lowliest and least important.

14

Drummond was kept busy from the moment he came on shift at four p.m. Mrs. Warburton's Christmas luncheon had just broken up (a string quartet, proceeds to charity) and forty-five guests departed, along with the players and their instruments, just as deliveries began arriving for the Alewayos' Christmas Eve party. Drummond buzzed in two youths with a large tree for the Alewayos, followed shortly after by another tree for the Jorgensens, whose children and grandchildren would help decorate it that evening as they did every year.

Huge grocery orders arrived for several suites, most including a turkey or goose, and three separate dry cleaners had to be buzzed in, one of them twice.

At five-fifteen, he enjoyed a temporary lull, after assisting Mrs. Ruiz-Guerra, laden with Christmas shopping, to the elevator. He returned to the lobby and picked up a decoration on the floor under the blue spruce, restoring it to the tree. Then he buzzed in another delivery: a vast poinsettia arrangement for the Alewayos: "sixth floor, apartment number eight." The girl took it upstairs and returned, and he checked her out then perched on the tall stool behind the counter, running his eye over the clipboard. Nothing more until about six-thirty when the Alewayo guests would begin to arrive.

He pulled out a toothpick and sucked on it thoughtfully. This was his last shift for a week. At midnight, when Daly took over, he'd go home for a few hours sleep, then out to the airport to catch an early flight to LA for four days with Dolores and the kids.

A movement caught his peripheral vision and he got rid of the toothpick and turned to find Owen watching him, from the vestibule.

"Evening, sir." Drummond smiled. "Saw your speech yesterday. That was good, what you did. Took guts."

Owen walked over to the counter. "Mac . . ."

"Yes, sir?"

Owen rubbed his fingers along the grain of the marble countertop. Drummond looked down at his clipboard.

"It's better to give than to receive. Ever hear that?"

"Yeah," Drummond admitted, his heart sinking. Not another present. . . .

"It's baloney." Owen clasped his hands on the counter and studied them. "If you want to dress it up there's grace in receiving as well as giving. Putting it plain, you can't have one without the other."

Drummond pulled out his toothpick and chewed on it for a while. "I wouldn't know," he said at last, and added, "People don't all give the same."

Owen nodded slowly. "That's so true. Now, my dad—my dad wasn't much for gifts. But you couldn't find a more generous man." He lifted his head and met Drummond's eyes.

Drummond regarded him silently. "You've come quite a piece, last few weeks." He removed the toothpick. "I'd like to hear more about him sometime, Owen."

"I'd like to tell you, Mac," Owen nodded. He straightened and turned for the elevators.

"Over lunch, maybe."

Owen stopped. Drummond fiddled with the clipboard, setting it flush to the edge of the desk, musing aloud. "Have to be somewhere classy, I'm thinkin'. You being a celebrity and all."

Owen turned. "There's one thing you have to understand, Mac."

"Yeah? What's that?"

"Celebrities don't pick up the tab."

"What, never?" Drummond conveyed outrage.

"I'm afraid not," Owen grinned. "Better be careful where you choose, Mac."

Drummond laughed and came out from the desk, following him to the elevators. "I'm on 'til midnight, same as always. Why don't you come down later? Be like old times."

"I can't, I'm going out—." he stopped. The guard was scrutinizing the elevator button. Owen smiled. "I'm going to Sara's."

"She's a fine woman."

"Yes she is."

"About that lunch, Owen. Maybe next week sometime? When I get back from LA?"

The elevator door opened.

"I'll look forward to it. Say hi to Dolores."

"Will do. And you have a real good Christmas, Owen."

They faced each other. Owen put his arms round the guard. Drummond's eyes misted.

"Well, now. Well, now, Owen." He patted the younger man's back.

"There were a lot of people at his funeral, Mac. A lot of people."

"I reckon he'd have been proud of you. I know I was."

* * *

The doorbell rang just as they started "The First Nowell." Sara shot out of the living room like a scalded cat, and Tom and Janey had to be restrained from following. She stopped before the front door, took a deep breath, said a silent prayer and opened it.

"I'm sorry I'm late," Owen began, but her face was alight with such gladness that he fell silent and stepped inside. She was wearing red, and one part of his mind wanted nothing more than to drink in the sight and scent and sound of her, but he refused to let himself be sidetracked. A chasm yawned between them and he had to cross it. He shoved his hands deep in his pockets. This was much worse than the river.

Sara closed the door and turned to him, and her heart sank at his expression. To give herself time to think, she began to unbutton his coat.

"Here's the position, Sara. No more gifts—"

He felt her arms slip round him inside his coat and bent his head over hers. He spoke into her ear, because it was easier.

"—just me."

He was falling through space and she was his only lifeline.

"That's all I want, Owen."

The singing filled his ears. *And to the earth it gave great light. . . .*

"Can you believe that?" She lifted her head and her gaze was clear and direct. Owen hesitated, wanting to give her an honest answer, and suddenly he did believe it, through to the marrow of his bones, through to his soul. The awareness flooding into his eyes brought tears to her own.

"Sara!" He took her in his arms and she heard the triumph in his voice. Then they were kissing each other and all the strain and longing of recent days was finished, gone in this moment, and for each of them there was no other living person in the world.

The wonder of that night! They stood together in the hall, lost in each other, while in the living room verse succeeded verse, and the voices acquired a dogged note. Only on the last line of the last verse of "The First Nowell" did Sara finally awaken to her duties as hostess.

That evening, Owen met Bill and Martina, Bob and Ronnie, and great-granny Hargreaves, and was welcomed as one of their own. He was introduced to the Elwings and their children, renewed his acquaintance with Mrs. Griff and met her husband. Then great-granny Hargreaves made him sit down next to her on the couch and asked him a number of wicked questions about his past, which made him laugh. Later, Janey climbed on his lap while Tom and the Elwing boys performed a heavy metal "We Three Kings" that brought the house down.

* * *

Three months later, Owen gave the second speech of his life, at a conference hosted by the Bank for International

Settlements in Basel, Switzerland. He was gratified by the audience response, but one reaction in particular gave him intense private pleasure. A banking colleague took him aside and asked, with the neutrality born of years of practice, where he had obtained his tie. Owen smiled a slow, wide smile. "From my kids," he said.

THE END

ABOUT THE AUTHOR

Helen Yeomans was born in England and raised in Canada. She worked in book publishing in Toronto and London, then launched her own firm, providing editing and later writing services to corporate clients worldwide. She began writing fiction more than 20 years ago. *Owen's Day* was her first novel. She is currently working on her seventh.

Other Books
Ang Tak
The Money Tree
Return to Kaitlin
Cruising to Danger

For Children
A Knock at the Door

www.helenyeomans.com.

Printed in Great Britain
by Amazon